Running From Forever:
Book One in the
Blood Resonance series

K. Aten

Mystic Books
by Regal Crest

ISBN 978-1-61929-398-4

First Edition 2018

9 8 7 6 5 4 3 2 1

Cover design by AcornGraphics

Published by:

Regal Crest Enterprises

Find us on the World Wide Web at
http://www.regalcrest.biz

Published in the United States of America

Acknowledgments

I was extremely excited to meet my Regal Crest team at GCLS in 2018. It's one thing to communicate via phone and email, it's another to actually meet someone face to face. Cathy is funny, wise, and full of good advice. Patty is supportive and patient (and probably really glad there were no maps in this one). And my editor, Micheala, is just really good at what she does. Thanks for supporting me so well and helping bring my books into the world. My babies are your babies, or... it takes a village to raise a novel.

Dedication

Running From Forever was the first novel I ever started and consequently the first one I completed. Even if that completion took me 8 years, with 7.5 of that as a hiatus from my stuttered and stalled fledgling interest in writing. My inspiration for the book was an album by Katie Reider called Wonder. Katie was a talented singer and songwriter from Columbus Ohio, and each chapter of my novel coincides with the songs of the record. We would take road trips to see her play at least four times a year. We joked that we were her biggest fans and she would greet us with a huge smile as soon as we walked into her shows. One evening in Chicago, she snatched my winter hat off my head and wore it for the gig. You know the kind, a trapper hat with the crazy furry ear flaps? Then she gave it back a few songs later because she said she couldn't hear anything while singing. She even let us help her write the set list once.

I cried the evening she sang a new song about the mother of her best friend who passed away from breast cancer. I felt Katie's pain when she spoke of her own mother's multiple bouts with cancer, because I too had lost people very close to me from the disease and the subject was particularly hard.

It broke my heart the day I learned that Katie herself had been diagnosed with a rare type of tumor. She fought for 2 years as it ate into her jaw and face and stole her voice. Then as if to taunt her more, it left her blind in one eye and finally killed her in 2008. She was 30 years old and left behind a beautiful wife and two young children. The world lost something with Katie's death, but we will always have her music.

Also...mom? This one is really steamy. Don't say I didn't warn you!

Prologue

TWO WOMEN STOOD next to a freshly-washed RAV4. The older one was about five feet ten and had long dark hair plated back in a French braid. Sarah Colby's green eyes were full of tears as she hugged her younger sister and gave her a watery smile. "I won't be gone forever, Annie. And I'll call all the time." She held up two fingers. "Scout's honor."

Annie wiped her own tears and pushed her sister's hand down. "Oh stop! You were never a scout." Before Sarah could reply, Annie had a hand over her mouth. "Not one word about brownies either!"

They laughed, easing the sense of loss both felt. Still, Sarah swallowed the lump in her throat and looked at the girl she had raised for the last five years. Their parents were killed in a car crash when Annie was only fifteen. Sarah was twenty-five and working at a charter academy as a music instructor at the time. In the blink of an eye, she became Annie's legal guardian and a full time parent. It wasn't easy and she still feels guilty for that time of her life. She was trying to deal with her grief, juggle a career, and raise a hormonal teenager who had also just lost her parents.

The first two years were especially hard. Annie became angry and rebellious and Sarah, never wanting children, resented putting her life on hold to become a parent. But everything turned out fine in the end with the help of some solid therapy and a few good friends. Standing in front of her was a beautiful young woman who was surprisingly well adjusted and happy. Annie was a junior in college working on her business management degree and working part-time as the server/bartender at a local club downtown. Sarah could not be prouder of her. As for herself, at the ripe old age of thirty, she was finally able to pursue one of her dreams. She quit her stifling job at the school and was ready to see the country and sing her own songs. With many friends in the music industry, things went surprisingly smooth. Sarah shrugged free of her memories and picked up her battered guitar case. At her feet, an eight-month-old rescued Husky mix was peering out from between her legs. She smiled at the dog then looked at her sister with fondness. "Looks like we got him trained just in time, huh?"

Annie's gaze switched from the person who was closer to her than anyone else, down to the dog's unique display of peek-a-boo and laughed. "I'd say Duke's probably the best present I've ever gotten you."

At the sight of tears on the younger woman's face, Sarah said, "Annie, please don't cry."

"I can't help it; I'm going to miss you so much!"

"I know, me too." Sarah sniffled.

Annie smiled with her own sad hazel eyes and reached down to pat the timid dog's head. "You take care of each other now, okay?"

They juggled their way into one more hug. "Sure thing." Once in the SUV, Sarah rolled the window down. "I love you, Annie, and I'll call as often as I can."

Annie left the new tears unchecked and leaned into the open window. Quietly, she said, "I hate that you're leaving but I understand."

Sarah kissed her on the cheek and tugged her earlobe, just as she used to do when they were younger. "Thank you."

As the older woman drove away, the younger one walked into the house, lonely already.

Columbus, Ohio
October, Two Years Ago

TWO WOMEN SAT in an office, separated only by a scarred oak desk. Both were wearing business suits, but that is where the similarities ended. The older one had stylishly cut short dark hair that was starting to turn gray at the temples, and the younger one had short blonde hair that was waxed into longish messy spikes. The interview was near completion and both seemed satisfied with the outcome. The older woman leaned forward to rest her forearms on the desk before speaking. "Well Ms. Keller, I don't think I need to look any further. Although my first instinct was that you are too young, you have the education and experience the job requires, and all your references check out." The woman smiled, "As a matter of fact, the mere mention of your name brought nothing but praise."

Noble Keller smiled in return. "Well I'm glad to hear that and please, just call me Keller."

Joanne Markham chuckled and replied, "Keller it is then." She shifted slightly and a more serious look came over her face. "Now that I've made up my mind, I should probably go over a few things one last time. I know you heard all this on your tour, but humor me, okay? As you know, The Merge is two connected bars under one roof. Spin, is our dance club with two full bars, a dance floor, as well as a game area with pool tables and a dart board." She stopped for a second and smiled. "And Voodoo Pony is our music club where we feature local bands and artists. It is a lot more intimate with a single long bar across the back, a few leather couches and chairs on a raised dais along one side, and regular tables and chairs throughout the rest of the room, all of which face a low stage. There is a single outside entrance to each club plus a connecting door between the two. There is also a garage door near the stage that can be opened for equipment and supplies." She looked into intelligent blue eyes, "Still with me?"

Keller smiled, "Sure. Two clubs, three bars, four doors, dance and live music."

The older woman laughed and shook her head, "Of course you are. Anyway, Diamond Enterprises, a firm specializing in business ventures, owns The Merge. We buy, revamp, and sometimes sell again once a solid profit margin has been established. Sometimes, we even hold onto the business and reap the profits for a while." Her brows drew together in consternation. "This is our least profitable venture to date. Even though the bar primarily caters to the LGBTQ community, I think there is a lot of potential here. We just need the right manager running things who can make it happen." Keller nodded and Joanne continued, "We're looking for a fresh approach and we're willing to put money into it to see a return. I know in the first interview you said you were looking for a challenge, does this meet with your expectations?"

A mischievous twinkle appeared in the blue eyes. "Yes, I believe it does. As you know from my resume, revamping is a specialty of mine."

The older woman stood and held out her hand. "Well then, welcome to the family, Keller."

The younger woman shook her hand. "Thank you Ms.

Markham, I can't wait to get started." For a split second, when their eyes met over the joined hands, Joanne saw something that made her breath catch. It lasted only a second but brought with it an instant flash of heat, arousal, and strangely enough, fear. She mentally shook it off and by the time she returned to her office ten minutes away, she had all but forgot about it.

Chapter One

Columbus, Ohio
March, Present Time

THREE STORIES ABOVE the street, a window was open just an inch. Outside, small moans and cries could be heard drifting from under the sill. Fainter yet was the low rhythmic beat of one of the latest dance songs, more sex than music. Inside, two women lay on a bed with sheets and bodies entangled. They were locked in a passionate embrace, bodies sweat-soaked and writhing. The women, one taller with long auburn hair and one shorter one with short blonde hair, were straining against each other. Their cries increased in intensity, matching the music in the background. The short woman with blonde hair was kissing along her neck when suddenly, the redhead's body arched off the bed and she cried out. The other woman rode out the waves of her release and toward the end, caught one of her own. For a few minutes afterward both lay collapsed on the bed. Slowly the blonde rose and got dressed, aware of the half-lidded gaze of her companion. Before leaving, she knelt on the foot of the bed and crawled toward the other woman until the entire length of their bodies was pressed together. She leaned down and slowly trailed her tongue up the side of her neck until her breath caressed a warm pink ear. "Lover, I was never here..." As she left the room, the taller woman drifted into a sated sleep. Forgetting.

Noble Keller walked along the quiet street toward her car, deep in thought. Somewhere a dog barked into the night and down an alley she could hear small animals scurrying away. A cat hissed at her from a doorway and she picked up her pace. Once inside her car she ran her hand through her short blonde hair and growled in frustration. She was sick of her life and tired of the rut she'd allowed herself to fall into. Over the years there had been too many women to count, but no love. Love was something she gave up long ago, but the yearning left her with a constant ache. What good was anything physical in life if your existence is spent guilt-ridden and alone? Unfortunately, she had no choice but to carry on the meaningless motions. Angry at her pathetic thoughts, she jammed the key in the ignition and started the car. With careless speed, she raced the rising sun home.

IN A HOUSE just minutes away from that same apartment at roughly the same time, a phone was ringing. While one hand haphazardly grabbed for the cell on the nightstand, the other pulled the spare pillow over tousled dark hair. "Hlo?"

A familiar, too cheerful, voice sounded over the other end. "Wakey wakey sunshine!"

Suddenly the woman in bed was up and alert. "What the hell—Sarah? What's wrong?" A laugh could be heard on the other end.

"Chill baby sis, nothing's wrong. Can't I call just to talk?"

Annie sighed and blew her messy bangs out of her face. "Jesus, you had me worried there for a minute. I mean, it's like freakin' —" she glanced at the cell face "—five in the morning! What were you thinking? For that matter it's Sunday morning, didn't you have a gig last night?"

"Yeah, but it was an early one so I could get an early start this morning." Sarah waited a minute for the imminent question.

A puzzled look crossed the younger sister's face. "That's not your usual routine, so where are you off to in such a hurry?"

A shaky breath precluded a pause. "I'm coming home, Annie." Sarah sighed, "I'm ready to come home."

Annie yelled in surprise. "Are you freakin' serious? You mean to stay, right?"

"Yeah, I'm coming home to stay. Are you going to let me stay with you for a while when I hit town?"

Annie stood up on her bed and did a happy dance. The loose blanket wrapped around her feet, tripping her up, and she nearly bounced off the bed. "Ooooff!"

Sarah pulled the phone away from her face and looked at it then put it back to her ear. "Uh, Annie? Are you okay?"

"What do you think, you big doofus! I haven't seen you more than a few days in the last year and a half. Why didn't you tell me you were coming home to stay? And when are you going to be here?"

Sarah's heart swelled with love. She missed Annie so much, but the eighteen months of touring and singing were exactly what she had needed to ground herself again and to shake free from the tethers that bound her, but it was always nice to have someone you love welcome you home. "Well, I wanted it to be surprise. I'm still about two states away so probably sometime tomorrow morning. Is that okay?"

"Yeah, that's great! Actually, I have to go in early for a delivery so I'll be working when you hit town. Just give me a call so I can give you a key to the house." Annie thought for a second. "Actually, why don't you just stop by the bar and pick up the key. Just ring the buzzer at the back door and I'll let you in. You still have Duke don't you?"

Sarah looked at the Husky that lay at her feet. When green eyes met blue, she smiled and the dog wagged his tail. "Of course I do! He is the best gift you have ever given me. Besides, he's my road buddy." She scratched the big dog's ruff. "Anyway, that sounds good to me. I should be there sometime between nine and noon but I'll call if I'm going to be any later than that."

Annie laughed. "That's better than the cable guy!"

Sarah laughed with her and smiled affectionately, unseen over the phone. "Okay, sis, see you then."

As they hung up, Annie threw herself backward onto the bed then her eyes popped open and grew wide. "Oh shit, the spare room!" She glanced at the clock then thought about the fact that she'd only had a few hours of sleep since getting home from work. "Later." The house was silent as sleep claimed her once again.

A thousand miles away, woman and dog both shared a sigh. "Come on, Duke, let's go home." As she started the SUV and put it in gear, she thought to herself, "Cowtown, here we come."

SARAH PULLED HER RAV4 into the parking lot and glanced at the clock on the radio. The dim green numbers read 10:26. "Right on time." She looked around the lot that only held a single white car, then at the bar's sign. It was two interlocked stainless steel triangles with "The Merge" written in black lettering across them. Sarah remembered many good and bad times at that bar. She shook her head ruefully and opened the door, calling the dog as she got out. "Come on, Duke, let's go see Annie." Duke, who was already up and wiggling around on the passenger seat, jumped over the gear shifter and the driver's seat in one bound. He sat patiently while she clipped the lead to his collar and engaged the car alarm.

One thing she noticed while walking toward the back door was the landscaping and outside appearance of the bar. From experience, she knew that many places had a run down, dingy appearance on the outside not usually noticed at night by the revelers. This was especially true about many gay bars because they were typically in the seedier parts of town. The Merge, however, was very stylish and modern. When she drove by she saw that the front was finished in stainless steel and black textured blocks, and it had large full-length tinted windows along the street. The landscaping was incredible too, and none of this had been started the last time Sarah was here. She rang the buzzer and was brought out of her musings when the back door opened, revealing a smiling woman with shoulder length brown hair.

"Sarah!" Annie wrapped her older sister in a fierce hug and then reached down to do the same to Duke. Only one gave doggy kisses in return though. Annie opened the door wider and invited them in. "Come on, I'll give you the tour. I'm pretty sure you won't recognize the place with all the remodeling we've done since you've been on the road."

"Yeah, I could tell just from the outside that things have really changed. Everything looks great by the way, that new manager must really be something huh?"

Annie laughed and gushed. "Oh yeah, she's something all right! You would *not* believe the business we are doing since she came on board with all these ideas and changes. We're now the hottest girl bar in town!"

Sarah looked at her well-behaved but still canine companion. "Do we need to lock him in the break room while we walk around?"

"No, we occasionally have benefits for the Humane Society and Paws for a Cause, so we've had animals in here before. We'll just keep him out of the kitchen."

They walked around the bar, Annie pointing out the things that had been changed or added during the renovation. She explained that the dance floor and sound system in Spin was one of the most expensive changes. The system was state of the art and the floor was an original creation by a company in northern Ohio. While it appeared black during the day, it would light up from below when the system was on. Geometric shapes would randomly appear in rainbow colors, and lasers would do the same around the walls and ceiling. It was a sweet setup and the dance club was very popular among the men and women of the gay community. The inside of Spin displayed a modern Goth look with a stainless steel bar and tables. The soft furnishings were finished in black material with a spiral design that was drawn in such a way that it appeared to be spinning. When they moved on to Voodoo Pony, Sarah saw that it was decorated in much the same way. The fabric on the bar stools and chairs was the same black material but with primitive silver ponies instead of spirals. The music bar also had the low-slung leather couches and large black and white framed pictures of famous female musicians. When the tour ended, Sarah whistled appreciatively. "Wow, this place is great! I had no idea you guys were taking on this big of a renovation job."

Annie laughed, "We didn't either. It was all Keller's idea. And let me tell you, that woman knows how to get stuff done! I wish you could have met her today, but of course she won't be in until later." She cocked her head to the side, "You interested in coming out tonight?"

Sarah groaned. "Honestly, no. I'm more interested in a shower and a place to unpack my bags." At her kid sister's pout she added, "Soon though, I promise."

Annie conceded and began walking Sarah to the door. "Okay, now do you want to hear my excellent and phenomenal news?"

Sarah looked at her, curiosity piqued. "What?"

"You know I graduate in a few months right?" At her sister's nod, Annie continued. "Well, Keller told me that she's going to promote me to assistant manager, running the Voodoo Pony!" She beamed after delivering her news.

Sarah let out a whoop and hugged Annie. "Hey, that's great! How did that come about, I thought she had Lynne running Spin and Robbie over the Pony?"

Annie smiled. "Well I actually have you and Robbie's wife to thank for that." When her sister looked confused, Annie added. "It seems Robbie's wife is pregnant and she made him take a day job managing his father-in-law's car lot. And because of you, I have a lot of friends and contacts in the music industry. All those years of nipping at your heels and watching how things were done finally paid off."

Sarah's eyebrows shot up. "Huh, and you've only been lead bartender for what, ten months?"

Annie stuck out her tongue at her sister's doubt. "Well, since my promotion to lead bartender, liquor sales are up and I found out where we were losing money with our stock. Keller is pretty confident that I'll do a good job!" She bumped Sarah's shoulder. "And get this, she's also going to let me start booking acts next week."

Sarah laughed at her sister's dogged sincerity. "I believe you. I was just jerking your chain." She hugged Annie again. "That's really great news kiddo." She whistled for the dog and started toward the door. "Now, how about that shower?"

Annie laughed and walked Sarah to her car before handing her the spare key she had made. "Don't lose it and for God's sake, clean the hair out of the drain when you're done!" She tugged the end of Sarah's braid. "You've got more hair than Chewbacca here."

"I'll keep that in mind. See you later, sis."

Annie was still laughing when she went back to the bar to finish her paperwork.

EARLY THE FOLLOWING Friday afternoon, Sarah was up reading the paper when Annie stumbled out of bed. Coffee and scrambled eggs sat untouched in front of her but she seemed more engrossed by the front page of the paper. Sarah looked at her sister when she sat down with her own cup. "Hey, what's this about a string of hate crimes happening downtown?"

Annie grimaced at the taste of her coffee and added more sugar. She shrugged, "I don't know, they started a few weeks ago. Four people have been attacked or run down within a few blocks of gay establishments." She took another sip of her cooling coffee. "Nobody knows anything yet. The police have no leads, and they don't have a description of the vehicle since the people were usually alone and the attacks happen so fast."

Sarah frowned. "I hope everyone at the bar is being careful. I'd hate to see someone we know get hurt, especially you!"

Annie gave her a serious look. "Don't worry, Keller has us all taking extra precautions when the bar closes each night. And the new bouncer, Teddy, takes a walk outside every so often to look for suspicious vehicles."

"Good!" Sarah pushed the paper away and started eating her cold eggs.

Annie grinned at her protective sibling. "So, are you feeling settled enough to go out with a group of friends tonight?"

Sarah looked at her. "What about work?"

"I've got the night off! So what do you say, do you want to hit Club Diversity for ladies night?" Annie smirked, her tone now teasing. "Unless, of course, the famous Sarah Colby can't handle a few hot women—"

Sarah burst out laughing. "Oh please, I've probably served more hot women than you have, Miss Lead Bartender!"

Annie blushed and threw a wadded up napkin at her. "Whatever! So, are you in?"

Sarah laughed again and threw the napkin in the trash. "Yeah, I'm in."

ANNIE AND SARAH met up with three friends they'd known for years. Though they were more Annie's friends than Sarah's. Kylie, Shell, and Micha were excited to hear that Sarah was back in town for good and agreed to get together for her homecoming. All five women took a vote and it was a unanimous decision to go to Club Diversity for the evening. They had a great time dancing and playing pool. Sarah saw many of her other friends and acquaintances that she hadn't seen in ages. Annie was glad that her sister seemed to be having fun. The last part of the night found Annie and Shell busy running the pool table. Kylie and Micha had left to go to another bar around one a.m. Sarah was out on the packed dance floor by herself moving to the music when something unusual happened. The space was hot and dark and the air was thick from the smoke machine. Sarah had felt vaguely uneasy for the past hour but attributed it to the shots they had drank earlier. The DJ was spinning a popular song and she could barely move so she used the opportunity to watch the other dancers.

Something made her look toward the back wall, through the maze of writhing bodies and flashing lights. Across the darkness her eyes met those of another woman. The woman gave her a slow, dangerously sexy smile. Fear and arousal hit her at the same time and she gasped, unheard in the pounding club. Then like a dream, one minute the woman was there and the next she was gone. Sarah stumbled from the dance floor and into the bathroom, which thankfully happened to be empty. She leaned on the sink, breathing hard and stared at her flushed face. Her heart was racing and she could feel the sweat forming on her upper lip. At first she thought maybe someone had spiked her drink but her pupils appeared normal and she was thinking clearly despite feeling mildly panicked. Desperate to calm herself Sarah splashed cold water on her cheeks from the tap and took a few deep breaths.

While Sarah was having a mini-meltdown in the bathroom, Annie was walking around looking for her. She spotted her boss Keller heading out the door, glued to a gorgeous woman with curly blonde hair. She shook her head and frowned. Keller never went home with the same woman twice, but Annie had also never heard any gossip about her boss either. "Damn, she must be good!" A minute later Annie walked into the bathroom and found Sarah. "Hey, I've been looking for you. Are you about ready to go?"

"Yeah, sure. Just give me a second, okay?"

Annie looked a little closer when Sarah didn't return her gaze, thinking that maybe her big sis was one too many beers in for the night. She walked over and rubbed her back in a comforting gesture. "Hey, are you all right? Are you feeling sick?"

"No, I'm fine. I'm just—" Sarah shook her head to clear the confusion. "I saw someone out on the dance floor that—" She attempted a feeble smile. "I think it's a case of instant lust with a little weirdness thrown in." She stood and dried her face. Feeling a little better, she took a deep breath and poked her tongue out at her sister. "I'm fine now, thanks, Annie."

As both women were leaving, Sarah glanced back at the emptying bar. She saw no one that looked like the mysterious dancer. Maybe she had imagined the whole thing.

NOBLE KELLER DROVE toward Westerville, following the woman she picked up in the bar. Or maybe the woman picked her up, it was hard to tell. Carol said she lived about twenty minutes from downtown so she decided it was worthwhile to follow her back to her home. Keller never brought women to her own condo but she was unwilling to travel far from downtown either. She preferred to wake in her own bed in the morning for more than one reason.

Twenty minutes was a long time to think about things, especially things concerning the woman she caught a glimpse of across the dance floor. She had been scanning the crowd looking for someone suitable when she spied the brunette. Her first instinct after catching the attention of a beautiful woman was always the same. Sex. However, it became immediately apparent that there was something different about that particular woman. Keller was drawn to her in a way that surpassed all others before. Keller could feel the instant tightening in her chest and for a second she stopped breathing. She was the one. That thought scared her beyond reason. When a twirling dancer blocked their immediate line of sight, Keller disappeared into the crowd. It was then that she bumped into Carol. The woman with the shoulder-length curly hair was more than willing to help her forget the mystery dancer and promised an easy night of passion. Still, twenty minutes was a long time to think.

Keller sighed. "Who was that woman?" Her musings were cut short when she spied Carol's black Mercedes turning into the drive of a gated community. She put her blinker on and followed close behind. Carol's house was a gorgeous, multi-story loft style home with her bedroom on the top level. As they climbed the stairs, a cat dodged past, hissing and heading down. By the time they reached the top step, Carol was pulling her toward the center of the room. Then Keller took over and it wasn't long before they were both naked and panting, rolling around on the king-size bed. Suddenly, Keller pinned Carol on her back. She leaned down and aggressively began nipping and licking her lips, then worked her way down to her neck. She whispered in her ear and Carol's eyes darkened with passion. The pinned woman squirmed when Keller tangled one hand in her hair and slid the other across her soaking wet sex. Carol looked into blue eyes gone black and growled. "Do it!" A second later Keller thrust two fingers deep inside her.

They were straining against each other and the woman on the bottom was moaning with each thrust. Keller swallowed Carol's moans with a vicious kiss. That seemed to turn her on more, which also spurred Keller on. She kissed her again and tasted blood that was not her own. The bar manager shuddered in surprised arousal and the other woman used that moment to thrust her own fingers into Keller. She gave a guttural yell and kissed her again. The blood and cries of pleasure were sending them both into sexual overload. When Carol's moaning changed in pitch, Keller knew she was close. She tightened her grip on the curly blond hair, catching Carol's attention.

In a low voice, she said, "Tell me what you want."

Carol struggled against the hand that was inside her not moving. When a thumb grazed her clit, she cried out. "God, just make me come!"

Keller drove into her, thrusting hard as her thumb pressed rhythmically against Carol's clit. At the same time she feasted on the woman's mouth then neck. She rode Carol's fingers and Carol rode hers. When they came, it was loud and within seconds of each other. Shuddering and exhausted they collapsed onto the bed, lying atop tangled, sweaty sheets. A short while later Keller rose and got dressed. Carol drifted in a sexual haze, following her with sleepy eyes. When Keller was fully clothed, she crawled up the bed toward Carol. Halfway up, she bent down to lick a still hard nipple and the somnolent woman gasped. All the way up, she ran her tongue along the length of her neck, taking her time on the side, then continued farther and gently bit her ear. Her soft whisper barely moved the hair that was tangled in Carol's earring. "Lover, I was never here..."

Carol was too sleepy to hear clearly and the words seemed a little blurred. A particularly strong aftershock from her orgasm left her memory a little blurred as well. Keller disappeared as Carol drifted off into sleep.

SUNDAY, TWO DAYS later, Annie was holding tryouts for the alternating Friday night gigs that would run for two months. It was a promotion the Voodoo Pony was beginning that would hopefully showcase some of the local bands, maybe give them a little extra exposure. The two bands selected would receive a gig fee, as well as a percentage of ticket sales for the nights played. She urged Sarah to show up and tryout, since the older woman still didn't know what she wanted to do with herself. She assured Sarah that impartiality would be guaranteed. Annie had two other employees that would be helping select the musicians.

During the tryouts, Sarah was pleased to notice that she was one of the more seasoned and professional artists there. She was chosen along with an alternative rock band comprised of four twenty-something women. She admired the reasoning behind the choices. She was a good performer to bring in the softer, folk crowd and the other band would draw in the younger, alternative hip crowd.

When Annie met up with her afterward to go over the paperwork and details, the younger sister was a little disappointed. "I wish Keller was here so I could introduce you. You guys just keep missing each other."

Sarah smiled at her sister's persistence. "Yeah, well maybe next time." She chuckled. "Jeez, you'd think you were trying to set me up or something."

Annie snorted. "Definitely not!" She shook her head to reinforce the words. "While Keller is a great boss, a good friend, and a freakin' hot, there's no way I'd want you to date her!"

The older sibling looked at her curiously. "Why not?"

Annie frowned. "Sis, Keller doesn't date. She's a major player."

"And? What's the big deal with that?"

"Let's put it this way, I couldn't even begin to count the number of women I've seen her leave the bars with and I've never seen her go home with the same woman twice."

Sarah laughed. "Wow, she's got me beat! Seriously, I am not looking for anyone or anything right now. I just want to settle in and plan for the future."

Annie grinned and shoved a pen across the table. "That's good to know, now sign! I know what a great singer you are and I'm not about to let that go to waste while you decide whatever it is you want to do with the rest of your life."

Sarah sighed and said no more about the subject.

LATER IN THE week, Annie and Sarah went to dinner at Vineyard, a popular restaurant in the gay and lesbian community. Annie had to work that night so she was going to take Sarah home before the start of her shift. Sarah felt a strange sensation after they were seated and given menus. It was the same one she felt in the bar the night they all went out and it caused the hair on the back of her neck to stand on end. When she looked toward the darkened corner of the room, she sucked in a surprised breath. Her mystery woman was drinking a glass of red wine and looking right at her. The sexy smile she received from the short-haired blonde left her a little breathless and aching for more.

Annie noticed her sister's preoccupation. "What?"

Sarah nodded her head toward the woman who was now walking toward their table. She whispered, "That's her, the woman I saw at Diversity right before you found me in the bathroom!"

The younger woman glanced behind her and laughed aloud, causing a few people to look at her. When the mystery woman reached the table, Annie grabbed her hand. "Sarah, I'd like you to meet my boss and friend, Noble Keller. Keller, this is my sister Sarah."

They shook hands and both women tightened their grip at the sudden jolt they felt. "It's nice to meet you Keller. Annie has told me so much about you."

The shorter woman smiled disarmingly. "Nothing bad I hope?"

Annie raised her eyebrows at the unusual familiarity between the two women. Not wanting it to develop into something more, she quickly jumped in. "I would never say anything bad, at least not as long as you're my boss!" Though she felt a little like a third wheel after their display, she still did the polite thing and pulled out a chair. "Care to join us?"

Keller laughed and sat down. "Sure."

Annie didn't like the fact that Keller turned out to be her sister's mystery woman. And she really didn't like the obvious attraction between the two. She shrugged it off however and simply enjoyed the conversation between her two favorite people while they ate their meal. They talked so long that Annie didn't have time to take Sarah home before she went to work. When Keller offered Sarah a ride and her sister immediately agreed, she was more than a bit irritated. There was nothing she could do about it except allow Sarah to walk her to her car.

When she got in, she tried to give a warning. "Sarah, Keller doesn't exactly do relationships and —"

"I don't want to hear it, Annie. I'm a big girl remember?"

"I know that, I just don't want to see you hurt."

"Now who sounds like the older sister? Seriously, It's just a little lust, I'm sure neither one of us is looking for a moving truck or anything."

"All right, just be careful okay? She moves pretty fast, I've seen her in action!"

Sarah gave her a quick hug. "I can do that, now get to work or I'll tell your boss!" She watched Annie drive away before heading back into the restaurant. When she got just inside the door, she stopped and observed Keller from across the room. The woman was relaxed in her chair and slowly swirling her wine around the wine glass. She seemed lost in thought as she stared at the shimmering red liquid. Keller suddenly looked up and Sarah was caught in her gaze. A sexy smile from the bar manager drew her back across the room to her own chair. Sarah squirmed in her seat, accepting that the single look had left her already damp sex throbbing. Sarah thought to herself, "God, it's been a long time!" At Keller's raised eyebrow, she took a deep breath and asked in a low voice, "Are you doing anything later?"

Keller took another sip of her wine, spilling a lone drop down the side of the glass. "That depends."

Sarah cocked her head to the side in an unconsciously similar way to her sister. "On what?"

Keller caught the errant red drop on the tip of her tongue and retraced its path back to the rim. Never breaking eye contact, she licked her lips and replied, "On you."

Sarah sucked in a breath and her hand clenched around the stem of her martini glass. She was grateful that their tab was already settled so there was no need to stay. "Let's get out of here." Keller chuckled as she followed the taller woman out the door.

Keller disengaged the alarm on her midnight blue Audi convertible and Sarah got into the passenger seat. She pulled out of the parking lot and headed toward Annie's house. Catching Sarah's questioning look out of the corner of her eye she shrugged. "Annie told me you're staying with her. She *is* my employee you know, not to mention my friend. I *do* know where she lives."

Sarah laughed, taking in Keller's profile while she maneuvered the city streets. She looked different in the dark of the car than she did in the romantically lit restaurant. Sarah vividly remembered the clear blue eyes that always seemed to be looking at her. And the blonde hair that easily reflected the candlelight at their table was only a light blur against the black leather seats. Feeling the throb of arousal, she sighed and squeezed her legs together. The rest of the trip was made in tense silence. When they finally got to the house, Keller parked on the street and shut the car off. This time the silence only lasted until Keller leaned over to whisper in Sarah's ear. "Do you want me to come in?"

Sarah's hands clenched at her sides as she shivered with arousal. She turned to meet Keller's eyes in the dark. "What do you think?"

Just like that, they were out of the car and heading through the front door. Once inside, Keller pinned Sarah against the wall and started kissing her, ravaging and tasting every square inch of Sarah's mouth. Sarah could feel her legs growing weak and grabbed both Keller's wandering hands before leading them toward the spare bedroom. Halfway down the hall, the women were stopped by a low rumbling growl. Sarah tried to call the dog off. "Duke, go lie down!" Duke kept growling and inching closer to the newcomer.

When Keller got a good look at the large Husky, she dropped to a knee and made eye contact with him. There was a second when the dog looked ready to lunge but then suddenly he whimpered and rolled over baring his belly to her. She gave him a friendly scratch and stood up to look at an astonished Sarah. "What?"

Sarah looked from her to the dog. "He's never done that before! He's very protective but he's never looked like he was going to attack anyone I introduced him to." She gave Keller a curious look. "How did you get him to back down like that?"

Keller shrugged and smirked. "I just needed to show him who was alpha here." Changing the subject, she said, "Now weren't you going to show me something?"

Sarah wet her lips and smiled. "Oh yeah!"

Once in Sarah's bedroom, she gave the door a kick, sending it closed behind them. Both women shed their clothing on the way to the bed. Clad only in underclothes, they frantically caressed every inch of skin they could reach. Mouths explored each other with tongues intermingling. Keller slowly pulled back and worked her way down Sarah's chest. In one quick motion, the bra was undone and flung across the room. Sarah laughed and did the same for the bar manager. Breathing hard, they removed the last of the clothing and slowly slid their bodies together.

Sarah moaned and dug her nails into Keller's back. "Oh God, you feel incredible."

Keller was too busy to reply. While her mouth was nibbling and sucking on Sarah's neck and collarbones, her hands massaged Sarah's breasts and twisted stiff nipples.

Sarah was ready and knew she couldn't wait much longer.

"Keller." That one word came out as more of a plea than anything else.

Keller looked into dark green eyes and slowly ran her hand down Sarah's side. "Look at me and tell me what you want."

Sarah trembled as Keller's fingers found their way through her trim, soaked sex and teased. "Please—"

"Say it!"

Sarah cried out. "Oh God, just do it! Fuck me please!" She shuddered convulsively and dug her nails into the shorter woman's back. Keller sucked a nipple into her mouth as she thrust two fingers into the other woman. She was riding the taller woman's leg, painting it with her pleasure while she worked her mouth up to Sarah's neck. She hesitated there for just a second before moving to the taller woman's lips. When Keller added another finger and started massaging Sarah's clit with her thumb, Sarah yelled into Keller's mouth. Their movements were frantic, almost manic with the need for release. As if by some unspoken agreement, they began to move faster. Sarah could feel it start, the shuddering that signaled the beginning of her orgasm. Just before she went over the edge, Keller called her name.

"Sarah."

Sarah looked into Keller's eyes and saw them change from blue to black. Unable to look away, she was caught by the gaze of a predator. It was in that moment of clarity and fear that she was swept over the edge in a mind-shattering orgasm. She was only dimly aware that Keller gave a hoarse cry at the same time. They collapsed side by side on the bed. Sweaty and exhausted, Sarah could only lay there while aftershocks ran rampant through her body. It had never been like that for her before. It was almost as if everything she felt was echoed, multiplying the effect it had on her. She sighed and drifted in a sexual haze, eyes heavy with sleep. She looked at Keller and that was all it took to start them off again. Hours went by in mere minutes, with each touch and moan fanning the flames higher. Sarah lost count of how many orgasms she had. She was barely aware of her own name and the unfamiliar ache of too much sex. She smiled as they both caught their breath and cooled off.

They lay curled together for a while before Keller reluctantly left the warmth of Sarah's body under the sheet and prepared to leave. Once she was dressed, she knelt on the foot of the bed and crawled toward Sarah until the entire length of their bodies were pressed together. Keller leaned down and gently kissed the side of Sarah's neck, eliciting a shiver. "Lover, I—" She paused and lifted her head to look into the other woman's half-lidded green eyes. Sighing, she kissed her again on the lips. "I have to go." And just like that, she was gone.

Sarah was in too much of a daze to think about what just happened. She reached up and touched the lips that were still tingling from Keller's soft goodbye. With a smile on her face, she rolled over and drifted off to sleep.

Chapter Two

SARAH WOKE THE next morning feeling completely rested. She blushed, remembering the night before in Keller's arms. She stretched in bed, thinking about the best sex she'd ever had with Annie's hot boss. As she was brushing her teeth, she took the opportunity to savor every second of the remembered pleasure. She smiled as she relived a particularly erotic moment, loving most of the after-effects of a marathon of really great sex. However, she could do without the ache between her legs. She looked up into the mirror and was caught in her own green-eyed gaze. A memory surfaced of that split second of fear right before she came the first time. It was in that moment that Keller seemed to waver in her vision, becoming something darker and more sinister. Sarah shivered at the memory of blue eyes turning nearly black. She ran a hand through her long hair and the lingering smell of sex brought her back to the present. She grinned and shook her head at her reflection before washing her face and hands. The soap and water seemed to wash away the dark memory, leaving only the leftover throb of animal attraction. Sarah muttered to herself as she wandered off to find breakfast. "Fuck, I need to get a grip this morning."

When she walked into the kitchen, it became pretty obvious that her sister was mad by the scowl etched on the younger woman face and the fact that she refused to meet Sarah's gaze. She finally looked up when Sarah poured herself a cup of coffee and sat in a chair across from her. Looking directly into angry hazel eyes, she spoke firmly. "Get over it."

Annie frowned even more. "Whatever! I notice she was long gone by the time I got up this morning." She shrugged. "But like you said last night, you're both adults. What do I care what you do? "

Sarah smiled in a pushy older sister way. "Why are you pissed at me then?"

Annie's simmering temper broke free. "For one thing, she's my boss! And in case you haven't noticed, you're my sister!"

Sarah took a sip of her coffee, grimaced, and added more sugar. "Well it's not going to affect your job at all, so don't worry about it. Besides, it was only a one-time thing anyway."

Annie growled. "God! What's the matter with you, how can you be so — so — casual?"

Total confusion washed over Sarah's face. She had no idea what the problem was so she wasn't really sure what to say. "Annie, it's just sex. Casual sex is meant to be *casual.*" She reached for Annie's hand only to have her sister pull away. "What are you really mad about, huh?" She had the thought that maybe Annie had heard them. "Oh, were we too loud? I'm really sorry if we were, I'll try to be more considerate in the future."

"Jesus, Sarah, you don't even know her! How could you go to bed with her so soon?"

The truth came out of nowhere like a truck. Sarah wondered, for the first time since she had been back, if she really knew her sister anymore. They had both been through many changes in the last few years. She took a stab in the dark. "Annie, you work in a bar. How did you end up such a prude?"

"Prude! *Prude!*" She shoved away from the table and stood. "Just because I happen to respect myself enough not to whore around? What happened to a little thing like being in love?"

The whore remark really hurt. Was that really what Annie thought? Sarah had known early on that they shared their sexual orientation but they were far enough apart in age that they never sat down and talked about things like sex and relationships. Hurt and offended, Sarah's voice was quiet. "Just because I haven't had time for something like falling in love doesn't mean I don't believe in it." She sighed and gave her sister a frank look. "I just haven't really considered the idea since Mom and Dad died. I've been busy the last few years. And before that, I wasn't in a place in my life where I would have been very good relationship material."

At Sarah's unwavering gaze, Annie looked at the linoleum floor. She sat down, leaned her elbows on the table, and returned her sister's sad look. "I'm sorry, I didn't know..." She took a deep breath. "It was hard for both of us but I guess I never stopped to consider everything you had to give up for me."

"Why would you? You were a kid, Annie. A hurt kid at that and I didn't want to put any kind of burden on you. I tried my hardest to make sure you didn't have to worry after Mom and Dad died."

Annie sighed, seeing her sister in a whole new light. "But

still, I know I was horrible back then. I was selfish to not consider your feelings too and I'm really sorry."

Sarah stood and walked around the table, holding out her hands for a hug. "It's okay, A. I don't miss or regret anything. I just wanted you to be happy."

Annie stood again and threw herself into her sister's arms, crying. "I can't believe I jumped on you for something so stupid. I must be PMSing or something."

A little nagging thought crept into Sarah's mind. She straightened and gave her sister a serious look. "You don't have to answer but, how much experience do you have?" Annie blushed and ducked her head, mumbling something too quiet to hear. Sarah leaned back in their embrace and caught Annie's eye. "Sorry, I didn't quite hear that."

Annie smiled shyly. "Um, none?" When she saw the shocked look on Sarah's face she added, "I mean, I've kissed and stuff. I wanted to fall in love with someone first. Before—you know."

Sarah gave her a look that was both proud and astonished at the same time. "Wow! That's really awesome, sis, I think it's kind of cool that you're waiting for the right one."

Annie smiled at her sister's acceptance. "Thanks. And—" she hesitated "—I am really sorry about the 'whore' thing. I didn't really mean that." She gave her sister a look that pleaded for her to both understand and be understood. "It's so odd how different we are in some things but that we're exactly the same in others. I'm sorry I wasn't more open and that I just assumed things about you."

"Hey, it's okay, sis. We've both changed a lot over the last few years and we haven't really spent a lot of time together to understand our differences. And listen, I know I kind of barged in here and made myself at home. If you want I can start looking for my own apartment right away."

Annie gasped and grabbed her hands. "No! I don't want you to go!" She wanted to make Sarah feel like this was her home too. After Annie had graduated high school, they sold the house that had so many memories. Sarah suggested buying another right away but Annie wanted to wait until she was a few years older to pick out something. That was how she ended up with her current house at such a young age. It was a great deal and Annie had fallen in love with it at first sight. But she realized that Sarah probably felt a little like an intruder. She smiled at her sister.

"Uh, I don't think I ever told you but this house kind of belongs to you too."

Sarah was confused. "What do you mean?"

"When I signed on the house I had them put your name on the title." She shrugged her shoulders. "You know, in case anything ever happened." A gentle squeeze on her hand made her look up into loving green eyes.

Sarah softly smiled. "Thank you. Just so you know, I don't want to go either. I'm kind of enjoying getting to spend time with you again." She cleared her throat nervously. "Uh, you just tell me if either Duke or I are cramping your style. Okay?"

Annie made a face. "I'm a prude, remember? I don't have a style!"

THE NIGHT OF Sarah's first gig rolled around and she was excited to be back in action again. Between covers of popular songs and her own, she had enough music in her repertoire to fill the four Saturdays she was booked. She was also glad to note that Annie was working behind the bar, as well as one other bartender and two servers. Her younger sister had predicted a good crowd. Sarah could already see the beginning of it while she was setting up. Nearly half the tables were full an hour before her scheduled set. With ten minutes to spare, Annie left the bar to wish her luck and take care of her bar order.

"Hey hot shot, are you all set here?"

Sarah grinned at her sister's teasing. "Yeah, I like the way Bruce set up the lighting earlier, it's perfect." She gazed out at the crowd thoughtfully. "It'll be a little different with all those people swallowing some of the sound but I should be fine."

Annie smiled at her sister's enthusiasm and at her own. It was her first shot at proving Keller's faith in her and she could not have picked a better performer for the night. "You want something from the bar?" She laughed. "Wait, let me guess. You want a large glass and a pitcher of water without ice, right?"

Sarah chuckled. "Of course!"

Annie gave her a quick hug for luck and left to fill her order. When the performance started, Sarah pulled no punches. She began with a song that all the women, young and old, knew. "Dog Days Are Over" by Florence and the Machine was a crowd favorite at every gig she'd ever played and was a great way to warm up the audience. After that, she sang a few of her own and the crowd ate those up as well. Her charisma and natural charm had the packed room eating out of the palm of her hand by the fifth song. It had been a while since Annie had seen her in action and she was very pleased with the performance. Sarah's talent and humor gave her a stage presence that few people could ever attain. She was friendly, funny, and at ease with the large group, and it showed in both her demeanor and her music.

Toward the end of Sarah's set, Annie caught a glimpse of her boss in the back of the room. Keller was watching intently from the shadows with the strangest look on her face. If they hadn't been so busy the past week, she would almost swear that her boss was avoiding her. Odd. Suddenly, she heard Sarah fumble a chord for the first time that night. Annie quickly glanced toward the stage and her sister. Sarah was still singing, but she was staring at the back of the room where Keller was hiding in the shadows. Both women were locked in a visual duel of sorts. Always the professional, Sarah didn't let the small gaffe affect the rest of her song. When Annie looked back at Keller, she was gone. Definitely odd. Her boss almost seemed interested but that was impossible. Keller was never interested in someone more than once. As far as Annie had seen, no woman was ever interested in Keller more than once either. It was very strange in any lesbian community. Being a bartender, Annie was familiar with the drama that circulated like a whirlwind through the girl bars. She thought it was extremely odd that Keller never had any drama. She would have to grill her boss about it later. After all, that's what friends were for.

After Sarah was finished for the night, Annie ran up and gave her another huge hug. "That was totally awesome!"

Sarah laughed. "Thanks, sis. Even though I think you're biased, I'll have to agree with you. This venue is a great little place to play. It has wonderful acoustics and sound." She began packing up her gear. "I think I'm really going to like this gig."

The women were laughing and talking while a dozen feet away Keller was hiding in her office. She started pacing and mumbling to herself. "What am I going to do?" Every few turns around the desk, she ran her hands through her short hair, messing it even further. She was afraid that she had made a mistake sleeping with the singer, and she was even more afraid that she almost did *not* sleep with her. She knew that Sarah had caught a glimpse of her darkest self and feared the other woman finding out her secret. Her voice was a whisper in the small room. "So why did I do it? I just left, letting her remember. What was I thinking?" She stopped and in a sudden rage cleared the top of her desk. Luckily, the laptop was locked away in the safe for the night. She leaned onto the edge of the heavy piece of furniture and squeezed her hands around the stainless steel top. The desk groaned and thumb-size indentions formed in the smooth surface. Keller looked down and noticed what her anger had accomplished. "Fuck!" She stalked across the room and threw herself onto the leather couch sitting against the wall, holding her head in both her hands. "She's inside my head and I can't get her out. Fuck!"

THE BEGINNING OF the next week found Keller and Annie both working early at the bar. Annie was looking over some posters she wanted to hang around town and Keller was helping stock the garnish in the small prep bins. Julie, the newly promoted lead bartender working the afternoon shift, ran out to get more juice leaving the two women alone. Keller was industriously slicing limes when Annie took a break to study her. "Hmm..."

Keller glanced up without stilling the perfect rhythm of her hands. "What?"

Annie cocked her head to the side. "I just noticed that you don't wear earrings. Are your ears even pierced?"

The question caused Keller's perfect slicing to falter and miss the lime. "Shit!" She immediately stuck the cut finger in her mouth and set down the knife. Annie jumped off her bar stool and went to help.

"Let me see." She tried fruitlessly to get Keller's finger out of her mouth. Keller just shrugged her off.

"Ifs owfrite!" She mumbled around the hurt digit.

Annie frowned. "Keller!"

The bar manager pulled the finger out with a pop. "Fine, see? It's okay. I must have nicked it or smacked the nail, or something. Let me go clean it up just in case." She hustled toward the back leaving Annie standing there in astonishment. The unmarked finger was as vivid in her mind's eye as the blood on the stainless steel cutting board. It only took a minute and Keller was back sporting a plastic Band-Aid on the finger in question.

She gave a reassuring smile to her employee. "I found just a tiny little cut, so I cleaned it and opted for a bandage." She grabbed some paper towel and a spray bottle of bleach then went to work on the cutting board. "I'll just clean this up and get out of the way before I hurt myself again."

Annie nodded and played along. "Okay, Julie can finish those later anyway." Inside her head, she was screaming. *What the fuck?*

Keller went into her office and returned a few minutes later wearing her favorite sweatshirt. With hood up and sunglasses on, she headed for the door. "I have a few errands to run, I'll be back tonight to help out a little in case it gets busy, okay?"

She was out the door before Annie could finish replying, "Sure thing, Keller." She thought to herself, once again, "What the hell?"

THE FRIDAY AFTER Sarah's first performance found her back at Voodoo Pony. This time she was there as an observer, watching the band chosen to alternate with her on the gig. The crowd was a lot younger than the previous week and the band, Mary's Angels, appeared to be a local favorite. She studied the setup on stage, taking note of the bass and lead guitars, drums, and a very nice electronic keyboard. Like herself, the band had CD's to sell afterward and she actually enjoyed their stuff enough to buy two of them.

She had seen Keller a few times since their hookup. Each time they flirted shamelessly with each other. But other than the night she was playing, she hadn't gotten any real indications of further interest from her at all. Sarah couldn't help thinking about their night together. She was drawn to the other woman in a way that was completely foreign to her. Sarah had not talked to Annie about it because she was afraid her sister would lecture her again, but she knew that she felt a connection with Keller. That brief stumble while she was playing was a testament to that. Nevertheless, Keller had yet to seek her out again, reaffirming Annie's previous statement that her boss was definitely a once only kind of woman. And Sarah would never chase another woman simply because the sex was good.

Sarah left Voodoo Pony and went to sit at the main bar of Spin, right across from the dance floor. After ordering her drink she hopped up on a vacated stool to observe the milling chaos around her. The band had done a good job drawing a crowd and Spin was packed with people left over from the show. She scanned the large group of mostly twenty-something women and shook her head in disgust. "God, I feel so old!" Sarah sucked in a breath when she noticed a familiar blonde head across the dance floor. She knew Keller was off duty and from what she could see the bar manager would not stay much longer. She had a leggy brunette grinding into her ass and her face was a study of hot pleasure. Suddenly Keller looked up and straight across the packed room. A wave of goose bumps marched over Sarah's skin. The singer was taken aback by the fact that Keller's gaze seemed so remote. Then, just as fast as the two dancers appeared in Sarah's line of sight they were gone again. The music changed to an even faster beat and she caught a glimpse of the Keller and her companion heading out the door.

Sarah felt immediate pain at what she had just witnessed. She was angry with Keller and more than a little hurt by the other woman's actions. More so though, she was angry at Keller's indifference. Not that Sarah expected any sort of loyalty after a one-night stand, however it would be nice if Keller didn't appear to look right through her. Sarah jumped off her stool and headed for the door to go home. She was going to do her best to put Keller out of her head.

THE NEXT NIGHT she went out to dinner by herself and spent a few hours at the bookstore on Gay Street. She was doing her best not to think about Keller. Finally, she gave it up as a lost cause, collected her purchases, and went home. When she arrived, she was greeted at the door by a very anxious Husky who was in need a potty break. She smiled to herself as she walked Duke down to the park and back. It seemed so strange how quickly she got used to another person's presence after being by herself on the road. She had been on her own for the evening because she hadn't completely reconnected with her old friends and didn't really feel like calling any of them. Also, it was Annie's night off and she chose to spend her evening out on a date. Sarah made a face and spoke to the Husky pacing at her side. "Dating, Ick!" It had been a very long time since she had been on a real date with anyone. Her opportunities had been few and far between with raising Annie and later touring.

After they relieved the Husky's needs, both woman and dog returned to the house. Sarah noticed an unfamiliar car parked in the drive as they came up the sidewalk. When she unlocked the door and stepped inside, the lights in the living room were dimmed and music played softly on the stereo. She quickly clapped a hand over her mouth to stifle her imminent laughter when she realized some of the noise coming from the next room was definitely not from the surround sound speakers. She let Duke off his leash and quietly hung it with her jacket on the coat rack in the entryway. Then she comically peeked around the corner with the dog mimicking her movements. Annie sat straddling her date's lap, grinding against the other woman. They were kissing feverishly and moaning softly. Sarah thought to herself, "Aww, she's all grown up. Not looking very prudish now, are we Annie girl!"

Sarah got Duke's attention and motioned toward her sister. The smart dog trotted over to the two women who were so busy making out that neither heard him approach. When he cocked his head giving Sarah a questioning look, she motioned him on toward the women. Mentally counting down, she grinned and waited for the inevitable. Duke did what all dogs do and put his nose somewhere it didn't belong. The dual screams made the dog yip and scramble backward, practically tripping over his own tail. Sarah, for her part, was doubled over in laughter as the other two women hastily straightened their clothes.

Annie jumped off the unknown date's lap. "Sarah!" When Sarah looked at her, she laughed even harder. Annie looked down and hastily fixed the buttons on her shirt so they were aligned properly. She mumbled, "Jesus, I thought you were asleep."

Meanwhile, her date stood and ran a hand through her short dark hair. "Uh, I think I should probably go."

Sarah finally stopped laughing and Annie grabbed her date's hand. "Sarah, this is Jesse." Laughing herself, she added, "Jesse, this is my older sister, Sarah." She pointed at the innocent looking dog laying on the love seat. "My friend over there with the cold nose is her dog, Duke."

Jesse laughed too and shook Sarah's hand. "Nice to meet you, Sarah." Turning back to Annie she added, "Babe, I really do need to go. I have to work at seven tomorrow morning."

Annie pouted for a second. "Damn, that's right. Sorry I kept you so long."

Jesse wiggled her eyebrows. "I'm not!"

The two women were lost in the moment, only moving when Sarah chuckled and walked into the kitchen. She was still in the kitchen when Annie returned from walking Jesse out to her car. Sarah was sitting at the breakfast bar with a glass of milk and a plate of cookies. Annie spied the treats. "Ooh, yum!" She got her own glass of moo juice and sat down on the other stool. She grinned as she dunked her cookie. "Just like old times, huh?"

Sarah smiled at the memories. "Uh huh." The age difference made it hard for them to have the usual sister-sister relationship. Or maybe it was easier because neither ended up hating the other. One thing both women absolutely loved while growing up was cookies. Whenever Sarah came home from college, she would always spend the first few hours with Annie. More often than not they could be found sitting up in one of their bedrooms with milk and a package of the sweet treats. Even better were the times that their mom had batches of homemade for them. That was how they maintained their bond and caught up with each other.

Annie also smiled at the memories. It was the times with just the two of them that she cherished above all else. She practically idolized her older sister when she was younger. All her friends thought her sister was totally cool. The two girls spent as much time as possible together whenever Sarah came home. That was the stuff that held them together after the death of their parents.

Sarah swallowed a bite of her cookie. "Sooo, how was the date?"

Annie blushed. "Good. I really like her."

"Heh, I could tell."

Annie bumped Sarah's shoulder with her own. "No, I'm being serious!" She looked thoughtful. "There's just something about her that drives me crazy. It's like—we just click. You know?"

Sarah thought of her own reaction to Keller. "Yeah, I know." She grabbed another cookie off the plate and dunked it into her milk. "So, is it serious?"

Annie, mouth full of cookie, nodded and swallowed. "Yeah, we've known each other for a while. We started dating a couple months ago." She blushed and giggled. "It sounds silly, but just tonight we decided to be a couple."

"But I thought you said you've been seeing each other for a

while now?"

"Well, we decided to get serious tonight. I mean serious as in monogamy and spending more time together kind of serious. We've been taking things really slow." Annie laughed again. "No moving van yet though."

Sarah snorted. "Good to hear."

Annie smirked at her older sister. "What about you?"

"What about me?"

"Have you met anyone interesting since you've been back?"

Sarah shrugged. "Not really." She did not want to mention her fascination with Keller. Somehow, she didn't think that bit of information would go over too well with her over-protective little sister. "I'll let you know as soon as I find anyone of interest though."

Unfortunately, Annie wasn't fooled. Nonchalantly she said, "I've seen the way she looks at you."

Sarah choked on her cookie in surprise. "What! Who?"

"Oh, come on. I'm not stupid Sarah. I see the way you look at each other." She put a comforting hand on Sarah's arm. "I just wanted you to know that whatever you two may have going on, I've never seen her act this way before."

Sarah wiped her mouth with a napkin. "I, uh, don't really know what's going on. I've never been drawn to anyone like I am to her." She shrugged, "It's not like I don't know the score. The sex we had was great but clearly that's all it was. I'm fine with it."

Not really believing her, Annie nodded anyway. "Just be careful, okay?"

"It's just a little harmless flirting, we'll be fine." She reached over and tugged her Annie's earlobe. "Thanks for worrying about me. It means a lot."

Annie stood and rinsed her glass. "Anytime, sis, but right now I'm off to bed. I've got class in the morning."

They said their goodnights and made their way to bed. Even as Sarah drifted off to sleep, she couldn't help thinking about what her sister had said. It just confirmed what she already felt deep inside her. She and Keller had a connection but only time would tell what it was and if it would lead them anywhere.

WEEKS WENT BY and slowly Sarah began to re-establish her old life. She still hadn't decided what she wanted to do with herself. They had a lot of life insurance money still in savings even after paying for Annie's college education, and Sarah was technically entitled to half. Lately she had been seriously considering two options. The first was one she had been thinking about for a very long time. Sarah had always wanted to be a private music instructor. She truly enjoyed music in all forms and always had a knack for teaching. Being a night owl, she never really cared for the regimentation and the hours that a school required. She hated the politics and being in the closet when she worked for the academy. On the other hand, her other option had a lot of stress and politics involved too. She was considering opening her own recording studio. She had already talked to Annie about both ideas in length. Annie told her that she would completely support her, no matter what she wanted. Therefore, she was taking her time just to be sure she knew what that was.

Things were still heated between her and Keller. Every time Sarah performed, Keller would stand in the back and watch. The feelings that the silent gaze evoked were beyond anything Sarah could explain. Even when they spoke to each other, they were very flirtatious and the sexual tension had begun to wear on her nerves. Unfortunately, the two women had not shared another night together. In fact, Keller left the bar with a different woman every time Sarah had seen her out. If something didn't give soon, she was sure to explode. But one thing she knew for certain, the first move would have to be made by Keller.

KELLER WAS HAVING problems of her own. The rash of violence against the LGBTQ community had escalated. There was another bashing in the alley behind Vineyard. Everyone was getting worried and they were taking extra precautions outside the bar as well. Better lights and new security cameras had been installed around the perimeter. So far, nothing had happened near The Merge but she wasn't going to take any chances. On top of her professional problems, she was having personal problems. She could not get the beautiful singer off her mind. She was having trouble sleeping and wasn't eating enough to sustain her. Her string of sexual conquests had become a meaningless blur. The last two she left the bar with went home disappointed. Keller had lost her need, her lust. All of it had narrowed down to focus on Sarah. Every day that went by since the night of their shared passion only served to convince her that Sarah was the one.

Keller had always believed there was a love meant for everyone. She believed that people had a one-time bond that would last forever and complete their soul. She didn't just believe it, she'd seen it time and time again through the years. Because of her unique circumstances, she gave up finding the other half of her soul. But Sarah was the one, Keller was certain in the depths of her heart. All the signs were there—the instant attraction, the deep magnetism that drew the two women together, and the emotional feedback from their orgasm was beyond comprehension. The bond was partially sealed the night she went home with the singer. Now she was afraid. If she told Sarah the truth, all of it, she would lose her. But if she didn't tell her the truth, she would lose herself. It didn't help that Annie was becoming more and more perceptive every day. Lately she had been asking a lot of strange questions and Keller was afraid her employee might stumble onto the secret on her own. Things were slowly getting out of control and she feared that she would have to leave the life she had been building for herself over the last few years. More importantly than her life though, she would be leaving her heart.

Chapter Three

FOUR WEEKS AFTER her first gig, Sarah found herself back at Voodoo Pony, listening to Mary's Angels. Their sound had grown on her over the past few weeks and now they were quickly becoming one of her favorites. Annie had to stay and clean up so after their set was finished Sarah wandered back into Spin for a little dancing before calling it a night. She set her drink down and promptly lost herself in the bass thump and flashing lights. Around one-thirty she felt a familiar tingle marching its way up her spine and stopped dancing. Opening her eyes, she saw Keller standing barely three feet away. They both froze, staring at each other until someone bumped into Sarah. She would have been knocked to the ground if Keller hadn't caught her with strong hands. Keller steadied the singer. "I've got you."

Sarah gasped at the closeness of her. Keller had one hand on her arm and the other wrapped around Sarah's waist. Sarah's shirt had ridden up and the heat from the other woman's skin was almost hot enough to burn. She was breathing hard and caught in Keller's gaze. It took her nearly a minute to come to her senses. "Hi."

Keller smiled. "Hi."

They started to speak at the same time, and then stopped, laughing. Keller continued, before Sarah could say anything more. "Would you like to come back to my place?"

Time seemed to stop while Sarah made up her mind. She looked into Keller's open gaze, her blue eyes were almost invisibly dark in the flashing lights. Without a second thought, she leaned over and kissed the smaller woman hard and deep. Only after eliciting a moan from Keller did she break the kiss and answer. "Sure." Hand in hand, they wove their way off the dance floor with an ease that almost seemed like magic. Just before they reached the entrance, Sarah pulled Keller to a stop. "Wait!" Keller looked up, afraid that Sarah had changed her mind. Sarah quickly eased her fears. "I need to tell Annie that I won't be home until later so she can take care of Duke." She winked. "And so she won't worry about me." She took off across the bar, back toward Pony's entrance.

Keller walked to the door and leaned against the wall next to Big Teddy, waiting. The large behemoth of a man grinned at her. "Hey boss, how's it hangin'?" He waggled his eyebrows. "Who's the hottie tonight?" Keller looked at the bouncer with cool blue eyes and didn't say a word. Teddy seemed to sense his mistake and held his hands up in apology. "Heh, sorry, just kidding."

Keller sighed. "It's cool Big T, no harm done." Sarah walked up and smiled at the big man. "Hey Teddy. Things were pretty quiet tonight, huh?"

Teddy chuckled. "Oh yeah, the ladies were no trouble at all." He gave the two women a concerned look when he realized they were leaving together. "You two be careful out there, okay?"

"We will. Thanks, Teddy." She turned expectant eyes to the smaller woman. "Ready?" They locked gazes again and all the sexual tension came back in a rush.

Teddy, sensing a private moment, mumbled, "I guess I'll see you two later," and backed off.

Sarah followed the familiar blue convertible through the lit city streets, heading farther downtown. She was surprised when Keller pulled into a parking garage a few minutes later. Sarah left the engine idling while she waited. She rolled down her window so she could find out where to park when Keller came out of the garage. She held the steering wheel in a white-knuckle grip. The short drive had allowed the overwhelming lust she felt for the other woman to cool a bit and she started to have doubts about following the feisty manager. She heard the distinct *chirp chirp* of a car alarm and seconds later Keller reemerged from the doorway with keys in hand. She gave Sarah a smile that was unlike any of her previous ones. It was flirtatious but also more than a little shy. Keller motioned toward the small lot right next to the parking garage. Sarah smiled in chagrin as she read the sign above the entrance. The word "Visitors" was written in large, stylized white letters.

After Sarah locked the SUV, she walked back across the lot. Keller seemed lost in thought, leaning against a street lamp with her hands stuffed into the pockets of her coat. The singer admired her for a second. Keller looked sexy wearing nothing more than jeans, a tight white t-shirt, and her leather coat. When Keller heard her approach, she glanced up. As their eyes met, the lust returned full force and Sarah gave a little whimper. She blew out a shaky breath. "God Keller—" She laughed, "Are you trying to kill me?"

Keller gave her a sexy smirk. "What's the matter rock star, can't handle it?"

Feeling bold, Sarah stepped into Keller's personal space and felt her lower regions start to throb. She touched a finger to the wildly beating pulse in Keller's neck. When she knew she had the other woman's complete attention, she slowly ran her finger down the middle of her chest and stomach, only stopping when she reached the black leather belt. Sarah looked into Keller's intense blue eyes and whispered, "Oh I think I can handle it. The question is can you?" Seconds later, she had her fingers threaded through the smaller woman's hair and was kissing her.

Keller gripped the fabric on the back of Sarah's shirt and long, dark hair cascaded over her hands and arms. Both women moaned as their bodies pressed tightly together. It took all Keller's will power to pull away before things could spiral out of control. She could see Sarah struggling to catch her breath and calm the racing pulse throbbing just below the surface of her neck. Keller licked her lips and gently took her hand. "Coming?"

Sarah smiled, running a hand through her messy hair, and then fanned herself in play. "Soon I hope!" She leaned in a little closer when she saw Keller's amused expression. Sarah wanted to wipe that look off her face so she raked nails blunted from years of guitar playing across Keller's firm stomach. "Come on hot stuff, I'm ready when you are." Keller, for her part, was completely enthralled by the tall singer. It was a level of interest that she had not felt for a very long time, if ever.

As both women went into the large brick building, neither saw the battered pickup that sat two blocks away with its lights off. Not long after they were inside, the engine fired up and the truck squealed off into the night.

The two women shared another heated kiss in the elevator on the way up to the fifth floor. Upon entering Keller's home, Sarah looked around in appreciation. The condo was half the size of the top floor. She took in the loft ceilings with rough-hewn wooden beams then turned to the bar manager. "Wow, this place is amazing. Did you design and decorate it yourself?"

Keller blushed at the compliment and was unsure why. So little actually affected her any more. "Yes I did."

"I thought so. I recognize a similar style to that of The Merge." She smiled at Keller. "You are a truly talented woman."

Keller grinned and raised a single eyebrow. "So I've been told!"

Sarah gave her a playful shove and laughed. "Uh huh. I'm being serious."

With an uncharacteristically shy smile, Keller hung up their coats in the closet by the door. "Thank you." Afterward, she walked into the kitchen, her boots ringing loudly on the hardwood floor. The area gleamed with stainless steel appliances and black granite counter tops. "Would you like something to drink?"

Sarah followed her. "Bottled water would be great, if you have it."

When they both had their water Keller nodded toward the rest of her home. "Do you want the tour?"

Laughter met her question. "Well, duh!"

Keller smiled and walked toward a wall containing a flat touch screen computer monitor. She touched a few buttons and right away the soft sounds of a Native American flute and an acoustic guitar could be heard throughout the condo. Then, the previously dark windows that surrounded two sides of the apartment, cleared. Sarah walked over to get a better look. "Ooh!" She admired the night-lights of the city and the dark serpentine shape a few blocks away that could only be the river. Sarah turned back to Keller. "Great view"

Keller chuckled and touched another button. Two sets of track lights came on. The first set illuminated the living room with its black leather couches and a large flat screen plasma television hanging on the back brick wall. The second set of lights was situated directly above a baby grand piano. It sat in the corner where the two walls of windows met. Sarah immediately walked over to the beautiful instrument and ran her hand across the smooth black finish. She sighed reverently, asking, "Do you play?"

Keller thought for a second. "Sometimes, when the mood strikes. I play mostly when I'm feeling particularly melancholy." Sarah looked beseechingly across the distance that separated them and Keller nodded. "Go ahead."

The singer carefully slid the bench out and sat down. She ran her fingers over the keys gently, not making any sound. By the expression on her face, she was clearly reveling in the simple feel of the cool ivories against her fingertips. She sat for a moment, thinking, or maybe just listening, Keller couldn't really be sure.

Then Sarah shut her eyes and began to play. At first, the quiet piano blended with the background music. Then slowly, the music changed and took the lead. Sarah's off-the-cuff melody wove in and out of the sounds of the pipes and guitar. After a few minutes, she ended it and stilled her fingers. When she opened her eyes again, Keller was staring at her intently. "Beautiful."

Sarah nodded her head shyly. "Thank you, but I think most of it was the piano. It is a remarkable instrument."

The other woman smiled. "I wasn't talking about the music, though that was beautiful too." Keller walked over and sat on the leather couch, then patted the seat next to her. "Will you sit with me?"

Sarah returned the bench to its original position and moved over to the couch to comply with Keller's request. "Your home is gorgeous." She gave a little laugh. "Do all the women get the red carpet treatment when they come over?"

Keller answered quietly. "I've never brought anyone here before tonight."

Sarah gawked at her in disbelief. "No one?" When Keller nodded, Sarah stared her straight in the eye. "Keller, why am I here?"

Keller looked down and took a deep breath then leaned forward on the couch and rested her elbows against her knees. She sat with her hands clasped together, like a child praying. Thinking for a second, she answered honestly. "I don't know." At Sarah's confused look, she straightened up and moved closer to her. Keller reached up and touched Sarah's lower lip with two fingers. She gently rubbed the smooth skin. Sarah closed her eyes at the tingling sensation and her heart rate immediately increased. Keller's other hand was resting against Sarah's stomach just above her jeans. She spoke quietly. "This is why you're here. You can feel it too, can't you?"

Sarah opened her eyes, looking closely at the other woman. As she gazed intently into Keller's deep blue eyes, she opened her mouth and drew the digits into warm wetness. Keller moaned and Sarah's arousal increased at the sound. She pulled away from the fingers and took a ragged breath. "Yes, I feel it too." She then tangled both hands in Keller's hair and kissed her.

This time it was slow, with plenty of opportunity to explore. The heat they felt was a steady burn and they were stoking it with each little touch and taste. Keller wrapped both arms around her and slowly pulled Sarah over to straddle her lap. She cupped the taller woman's ass and Sarah's hips moved to get purchase below her. When the kiss escalated beyond the limits of the couch Keller pulled back. She looked up with honest blue eyes that were full of hope and longing. "Will you stay the night with me?"

Sarah smiled. "I thought you'd never ask."

Keller gave her another one of her strange shy smiles and kissed her again. As if in unspoken agreement, both women went into the bedroom. Keller left Sarah sitting on the bed while she went around the room lighting candles. When she turned back to her guest, Sarah was reclining on the fluffy comforter, wearing nothing but a smile. She patted the space next to her in invitation. Keller grinned and started toward the bed, stripping on the way. "You have no idea how beautiful you are, Sarah." She added, "There are so many things I want to do with you."

Sarah flushed at the compliment and waited in anticipation. When Keller opened a drawer next to the bed, Sarah gasped at what she saw. Keller peered inside her drawer then back at Sarah. "What would you like to do?" She gave the singer a lecherous look and wiggled her eyebrows. How adventurous are you?"

Sarah sat up and looked into the wide, shallow drawer full of sex toys and tools. She was quite amazed at the selection and felt a little like a kid in a candy shop. "Nice!" She looked back at Keller and grinned. "I love adventure, so bring it on."

Keller smiled and grabbed the first thing at hand, which happened to be a blindfold. She left the drawer open and climbed onto the bed. When she moved so she was straddling Sarah's pelvis, the taller woman groaned and thrust her hips upward. Keller just chuckled and clamped her knees tight to Sarah's sides, preventing the needed friction. "I don't think so. Not yet, lover." She leaned down and slid the blindfold over Sarah's eyes. "How is that? Can you see at all?"

Sarah groaned again at Keller's one-track mind. "No, I can't see a thing!"

Keller waited a second longer before stealing a heartbreaking kiss then sliding off the bed until she was once again standing next to the nightstand. When she reached into the drawer again, it was to pull out a soft leather harness. Once it was firmly in place, she attached an eight-inch phallus with a large knob-shaped end. Before she got back onto the bed, she slowly ran her hand from Sarah's hip to just beneath her breast. Sarah gasped at the sudden contact. When Keller leaned over and took the nearest nipple into her mouth Sarah grabbed her head and moaned again. The prone woman could feel her wetness seeping down her thighs to soak the comforter below. "God, Keller!" she panted, "I think if I get any more turned on I'm going to ruin your bedspread."

Keller released the nipple with a pop and laughed. "Don't worry, I've got more." She then crawled back onto the bed toward the opposite end. She positioned herself on her knees, and then she sat back onto her heels. The phallus jutted obscenely out from between her thighs, unnoticed by the blindfolded eyes of the other woman. Gently lifting the leg in front of her, Keller ran a warm tongue along the bottom of Sarah's foot. Sarah giggled and tried to pull out of her iron grip. The blonde then pulled the two middle toes into her mouth and caressed them with her tongue and lips. Sarah moaned again with unexpected arousal. That was one thing she never had done to her and her sex clenched unexpectedly. She was more than game for anything Keller wanted to try but she had never been one for long drawn out foreplay. Sarah was more of an action kind of girl and her impatience was quick to show. "Fuck, just touch me already!"

Keller laughed softly. "You are an impatient woman aren't you?" She set the foot back down and slowly spread Sarah's legs apart. Once they were wide enough, she began to move up Sarah's body, between them. She paved her way along the taller woman's legs with her hands and when questing digits met in the middle, Sarah squirmed on the bed.

Sarah called out a warning. "Keller, you didn't tie my hands. If you don't get this show on the road I'm going to have to do it myself!"

As if that were the cue Keller was looking for, she quickly bent down and ran her tongue along the length of Sarah's sex. Strong hands held Sarah's hips to keep her from bucking. Keller pulled back and taunted, "Is that want you wanted?"

Sarah hissed, "Shit!"

Keller then laid herself out flat, more than comfortable on the king-size bed. She spread the trim folds apart with both hands and began to feast. Sarah writhed and cried out at the onslaught of pleasure. She had both hands holding onto the low headboard behind her head. As Keller kept up her ministrations, Sarah wrapped one leg around the smaller woman's shoulders while the other foot dug into the blanket. It only took a few minutes to get her close and Sarah cried out in frustration when Keller abruptly pulled away. The cry soon turned into a growl when Keller moved and she felt something hard and smooth rub the entire length of her sex. "Fuck yes!"

Keller kept rubbing the toy until she was satisfied it was completely lubricated by Sarah's wetness. Sarah was squirming again as the smaller woman placed the tip at her opening. She tried to force herself onto the phallus but Keller pulled back, eliciting another frustrated cry.

"Keller..." Sarah pleaded.

Holding herself carefully, Keller leaned over and lavished attention on a large, hard nipple. When she pulled away, she reached up to the blindfold and pulled it off. Green eyes met blue and Keller demanded, "Tell me what you want me to do, Sarah!"

Sarah's breath caught in her throat when she saw those familiar blue eyes fade to black but she was too far gone to really care. She let go of the headboard and tangled her right hand in Keller's short hair. Gripping tight, she bucked against the woman on top of her. She growled, "I want you to fuck me hard, and I don't want you to stop until you make me scream!"

Keller gasped and jerked with her own arousal. Between the tight grip on her hair and the other woman's words, she was almost out of her mind. Slowly and smoothly, she eased the phallus inside Sarah. However, Sarah didn't want it slow. In a surprise move, she wrapped her long legs around Keller's waist and pulled the toy all the way in. For different reasons they both gasped when it hit bottom. It provided a little cervix bump that Sarah enjoyed and the opposite end was made to perfectly hit against Keller's clitoris. As if that were the signal to begin, Keller began thrusting in an out. She kept the angle such that the head slid along that spongy place inside that kept Sarah moaning and shuddering. Keller's own arousal was almost at its limit. The harness kept a constant pressure on her clit, and the friction she felt with each thrust was incredibly delicious.

Sarah was nearly delirious with pleasure. She had used toys and even strap-ons many times before, but never with someone as talented as Keller. The blonde knew every spot inside that made her tick. The closer she got, the louder and more frequent her moans became until she was nearly yelling. When her legs began to shake she knew her salvation was near. Both women panted hard and Keller could feel herself tightening with the coming orgasm. She watched the flush move up Sarah's body and knew she was close too. At the exact moment that she could hold on no longer, Keller reached down and ran her thumb over Sarah's clit. The orgasm that crashed through both of them made Keller's hips jerk and her motions ended with a single hard thrust. As a result, Sarah's hips lifted from the bed as she bent to the tension of her release. Before her orgasm rolled her eyes shut, Sarah caught one last glimpse of her lover. Keller's head was thrown back and Sarah nearly drowned in her black depthless eyes. However, the one thing that left her mind reeling was the sharp white canines, gleaming brightly in the candlelight.

They both collapsed back to the bed, and when Keller pulled out, Sarah was hit with another round of aftershocks. Once she caught her breath, she turned wide green eyes toward her lover. Quietly she asked, "What the fuck, Keller? What happened to your teeth? Is this some sort of role play?"

Keller sighed and shut her eyes, hoping to delay the truth but knowing it was not possible. She knew the bond was complete and there was no choice left but the truth. Keller slowly removed the harness and set it on the table on the far side of the bed. When she was finished, she lay back down on her side facing Sarah. Sarah mirrored her position waiting for an explanation, more curious than fearful.

Keller responded quietly. "No Sarah, it's not part of a role play. They are my real teeth."

The singer looked at her, full of questions and with a mind still reeling. "How?" She reached to touch them but Keller's hand was too fast, her grip on Sarah's wrist too strong.

"You don't really want to do that, trust me." Keller released her.

Sarah extended her hand slower and cupped the smaller woman's cheek. Gently she said, "Tell me." Sarah gasped when Keller's canines suddenly receded back into her gums. Keller's body had been steadily cooling and coming down from her orgasmic high so things were returning to normal, as much as that could be. "What..." It was a single word that was filled with a mix of curiosity and awe.

"It's a long story."

Sarah put her hand back in front of her, sensing that Keller was sensitive about whatever had just happened. Then unsatisfied with the distance, she reached over to lay that same hand on top of Keller's forearm. "I'm a good listener. And I watch those medical marvel episodes on YouTube all the time."

Keller shut her eyes at the Sarah's gentle touch. "Believe me, you haven't seen this."

"Ancient aliens?" Sarah's tone indicated she wasn't at all serious.

There was a pause after she spoke, then Keller decided to bite the bullet. "I guess you could say I'm a vampire of sorts." She heard a snort and when she opened her eyes again she saw Sarah's look of disbelief and quickly continued. "From all the research I've read and done myself, it actually appears to be more of a virus or disease."

Skeptical, but willing to humor the smaller woman, Sarah prompted, "Go on."

Keller asked her, "How old do you think I am?"

Sarah took a minute to sweep her gaze over the other woman's youthful nude body. "My guess would be a few years younger than myself, maybe as old as twenty-nine. Why?"

Keller gave a mirthless laugh. "Try two hundred and fifty-six years old." She looked at the other woman who was slowly shaking her head back and forth. "As unlikely as it sounds, it's all too true." She reached out and grasped Sarah's hand. "I'm going to answer all your questions and even provide proof if you want, but I need something from you in return."

Sarah nodded cautiously, completely thrown off kilter at this point and still half thinking it was all a joke. "Okay..."

Keller nodded back, accepting her promise. "First, I ask that you keep what is said between us. Second, I ask that you forgive me for what I'm going to tell you."

Sarah nodded again. "Of course I won't say anything. As to the second —" She paused, trying to size up the other woman. " — I can only try."

Keller sighed. "That's all I can ask then, thank you." They made themselves comfortable and Keller began her story. The power of the memories took her back hundreds of years.

"When I was in my late teens, my parents forced me into marriage with a man nearly twenty years my senior. It wasn't entirely their fault, back then you needed to do whatever you could to survive. There were no other men of my generation available and a two-year drought had left the family wealth dwindled to nearly nothing. My marriage to a wealthy landowner was the key to our survival. I was already older than most brides of the time, the lack of eligible young men had put off marriage for a few years. I was grateful for the delay because even then I knew I was different. I had always felt something for women that I never felt for men. To me, the idea of marriage was a horror. Only after the deed was done and I was sleeping in the same bed did I realize what horror truly was." Keller shuddered, the remembered abuse by her husband still left her full of equal parts rage and shame. Sarah reached for her hand in silent comfort, urging her on. Keller continued. "I didn't have to wait long to see the measure of my new husband. His idea of foreplay on our wedding night was to beat me until I couldn't move. He took me while I lay in our bed crying. I lost my innocence to a monster."

She drew in a shaky breath and continued. "The servants all knew how he was but they didn't dare say anything for fear of losing their place. To make matters worse, he wanted an heir and was determined that I would provide one. Every night was the same thing until eventually I woke each morning wanting to die. He wanted a son to pass on his name but ironically enough it was he that prevented that possibility. I was pregnant a total of four times but his beatings never stopped. Each time, I would miscarry, which would drive him further into his rage. We were married ten miserable years."

Running on instinct alone, Sarah pulled Keller closer to give comfort. "What happened?"

A single tear ran down Keller's cheek. "There was a widow, Lady Catherine Montgomery, who owned the land adjacent to my husband's. It was very uncommon for a woman to hold property but she had ties to the crown and was under special favor. My husband was a greedy bastard and wanted a portion of her land, which she was not willing to part with. You see, they made no secrets of their dislike for each other. Then my husband had the idea to invite her to our manor. Thinking her a feeble-minded woman, he planned to use sweet words and duplicity once she was there to get her to give him the land."

Keller cocked her head to the side, thinking. "She was unlike anyone I'd ever met. Her eyes were the deepest brown and when she looked at me, it was as if she was looking right through. We had a feast on the first night. On the outside, my husband was very polite, but I knew it was all an act. That night he was up very late reveling and as a result, he slept in the next day. I could never stand being in bed with him and near dawn I went out into the garden. There was no one around that time of morning, so when she stepped out of the shadows I practically fell off my bench. Without a sound, she came to me and for the first time in my life I knew what passion really was. I was in such a daze for the rest of the morning. That afternoon they sat down to negotiate. We had a well renowned stable and my husband was making an offer that involved some of the least expensive purebred mares. They talked for hours and in the end, Lady Montgomery said she would need to think it over. Of course, my husband thought he had the woman convinced to trade the very valuable land and decided to celebrate. We had another feast that night and when I retired, Lady Montgomery followed and slipped into my room. Things were quickly escalating when we heard my husband's heavy tread outside the door. Catherine managed to hide in the wardrobe just before he entered."

Despite the improbableness of it all, Sarah had become completely engrossed in the story. The further Keller got into her tale, the more Sarah detected an accent. She still didn't quite know what to think, it seemed so far-fetched. Something inside, a feeling, was telling her to believe though so she didn't want to interrupt. She sat quietly until Keller continued.

"He took one look at my disheveled state and flew into one of his rages. He demanded to know who the man was. I protested of course. I knew what he was like and I refused to give up Catherine to his rage. He started beating me, worse than ever before. He beat me to the stone below our feet and when I was down, began kicking me in the ribs. I felt something give and the pain made me vomit at his feet. He kept calling me a whore and said he was going to kill me. I believed him because I could feel everything slip away. I knew I was dying and I welcomed it as an end to my life of misery. He was so focused on me that he never heard her leave the wardrobe. The look of surprise on his face as she snapped his neck was one I'll never forget."

Sarah looked down at the woman in her arms. "But wait, how did you end up with this—disease?"

Keller saw the curiosity as a good sign of Sarah's acceptance of her truth and tapped the end of her nose. "I knew you were impatient! Despite my grievous state I sensed it as Lady Montgomery bent down to look at me, after she'd killed him. I was indeed dying. He had broken my ribs and one must have punc-

tured a lung so I was slowly drowning in my own blood. At first I
thought it was the pain causing me to hallucinate but I learned
later what I saw was very real. She told me to hush, that she
would take care of me. I looked into those deep brown eyes and
everything started to blur. Her teeth were very sharp so I barely
felt a thing when they pierced my neck. When she was finished,
she pierced her wrist and forced some of her own blood into my
mouth. The coppery tang mixed with what I had been coughing
up. She urged me to swallow and afterward everything went
dark. But it didn't end there. The widow was a very canny
woman. She broke the latch and opened the window, making it
look like we had an intruder. I was unconscious for about half an
hour, but miraculously my body had already re-knit itself. I was
fully healed and feeling very strange. Somehow, I made it
through the whole ordeal. Everyone was convinced that one of
the many people my husband had wronged in the past had killed
him. After all, there was no way a small woman, such as myself,
could ever break that hulking man's neck."

Forgetting her earlier disbelief, Sarah was amazed that Keller
could survive such a terrible ordeal. "Wow! So it was Lady Montgomery that gave it to you? And you — became lovers?"

"We were lovers off and on throughout the years. But that
ended nearly a century ago. And yes, she did it to save my life. In
fact, the only way it can be contracted is if the person is near
death. It has something to do with the body's weakened state. It is
a very rare disease and that is the main reason that not many people have it, simple biology. It takes a lot to meet the biological
requirements to keep functioning. It changes the body's immune
system. It also causes genetic physical alterations. Strong emotions or pain will cause tears in normal people, but with this disease, they will cause other physical changes as well. These
changes are produced at need, such as canine pushing out from
the gums and adrenaline-induced strength. I am an empath,
which means I can read and project emotions. This helps me
cloud memory sometimes, when I need to. Another side effect is
that I'm very sensitive to ultraviolet light."

Sarah interrupted. "Wait, I've seen you out during the day!
Aren't vampires supposed to be killed by the sunlight? I mean,
you have a great tan."

Keller laughed. "Well, that is part of the myth that was
highly exaggerated. I'm very sensitive, but it has a curious effect

on me. It doesn't take much exposure at all to darken my skin. As a matter of fact, the tan I get is from the black lights at the bar. Most of the time I cover up as much as possible if I'm out. It helps that I'm a night owl and have a job that is primarily at night."

"Ah, I get it. I've seen you in that hooded sweatshirt and sunglasses pretty often."

Keller nodded. "Yeah, it is my favorite."

They moved apart a little so Sarah could see her better. "So, is that it? You have a great tan, you're strong as an ox and you get fangs when you're horny?"

Keller gave her lover a little poke in the ribs, eliciting a squeak. "No, that's not it. I actually knew a man years ago who also had the disease. He was a scientist who did a lot of research on the subject. Sadly, it does not make us immortal and he was killed in a terrible car accident. Some injuries are too extreme and happen too fast for us to heal. As near as he could tell, it gives us incredible healing abilities, which also means we are immune to disease and other illness." She tried to explain it in a way that was a little easier to relate. "When you cut your finger, it heals and your fingerprint remains the same. Your body has a genetic blueprint that automatically knows the way things belong. With this disease, the body heals extremely fast and it heals continuously. Because of this continuous healing and cell rejuvenation, it also lengthens the lifespan. However, there is a price to pay. I'm sterile, which is probably for the best anyway. I also have to take in an enormous amount of protein, and the whole biological process is stimulated by massive amounts of endorphins." At Sarah's confused look, she explained. "Sex produces endorphins."

"Ohh, that's where the long list of conquests comes in."

Keller blushed. "Well, mostly." Sarah raised an eyebrow in question. "There is another part of the myth that is based on truth. I do take in human blood on occasion. Sometimes the uh— act itself is not completely satisfying. Or sometimes I have waited too long and the mere act is not enough for the amount of energy I need. You see, my canines are extremely sensitive, and the slightest touch while they are elongated is very pleasurable. Perhaps this is to help facilitate endorphin production and make the taking of blood such a rush."

At her explanation Sarah reach up and lightly touched the side of her own neck. "So have you—"

Keller rushed to explain. "No! I have never done it to you. As long as I do not use excessive amounts of energy, I don't need to take blood. But, while I don't need to do it all the time..." Her voice trailed off.

Sarah finished for her. "You still do."

Keller looked pained. "I still do. I'm incredibly drawn to the blood, it's difficult to explain. For me, adding that extra stimulus is better than putting the cherry on top when I'm having sex. It's not so much about feeding as it is about feeling. But I have never tasted yours."

The singer gave her a piercing look. "You wanted to though, didn't you?"

Keller looked down at her hands and whispered, "Yes."

Sarah gently turned the other woman's face so their eyes met. "Why didn't you? After all, you've done it to others before. From what I understand, it's not like I would have known, right?"

Keller caressed her cheek and tried to explain. "Yes I've done it before and of course I wanted to but−" She sighed. "−you are different from the others."

A very jaded Sarah snorted disbelievingly and mumbled, "I've heard that before."

"No, listen to me. Do you think I would have come to you again? Do you think you would be in my home right now if you weren't inside my head every day?" Keller flinched, not intending to say that last part.

Sarah looked at her intently. "I, um−" She took a deep breath and went on. "I've been having the same problem."

Keller felt braver with Sarah's words. She needed to tell her everything, to make her understand. "Sarah, there is a lot more you need to know."

Sarah, almost at her limit of revelation for the night, needed a break. The discussion was straying dangerously far from a casual encounter she thought Keller was looking for. She got off the bed and stood uncomfortably. "Do you have a robe or something I can use? I think I need a little space if I'm going to hear any more tonight."

A little worried at Sarah's abrupt shift in attitude, Keller got up and went to the walk-in closet to retrieve two robes. She could read the other woman's unease and made an effort to back off on the intensity to get Sarah in a more comfortable emotional place. "Come on, I bet you could use some coffee too, huh?"

After making coffee and shutting off the music, both women

settled into the deep leather cushions of the couch. Once there Keller seemed reluctant to continue and it was making Sarah very nervous. She wondered how much worse it could be. Wanting a little proof to ease her own state of mind and to stall before any more revelations, she asked, "Could you show me something, you know, so I can convince myself later that I'm not a complete nut case for believing you?" Keller gave her a penetrating look before going back into the kitchen. She returned a minute later with a sharp knife and some paper towels. She held the knife against the skin of her forearm and Sarah grabbed her hand to stop her. "Wait, you don't need to do anything so drastic!"

Keller moved her hand away and said quietly, "This is the best way." She gave Sarah a look that pleaded trust. "It's okay."

Sarah nodded then watched in disbelief as Keller cut deeply into her own arm. Blood welled up seconds after her hiss of pain. She dabbed at the cut to prevent the blood from running all over and making a mess, then waited for Sarah's reaction. Sarah watched as the wound began to seal up almost immediately. It was completely healed after only a minute. A thin, quickly darkening, pink line was the only evidence of the injury. Sarah's jaw dropped open. "Holy fuck! That's—I don't even know what to say right now. Give me a sec, please."

Keller waited with the bloody paper towel wrapped around the knife blade and let Sarah think on what she'd just done. "Take all the time you need." Opening one's mind to the possibility of unbelievable things was not the same as staring at the proof.

At one time in her life Sarah could have chalked it up to too many beers or maybe another kind of high but she hadn't been that stupid in years. She shook her head in amazement rather than continue to dwell on something that should have been impossible. "Okay, I'm convinced, please continue."

Keller took care of the knife and bloody paper towel, and then returned to finish their conversation. The smaller woman cleared her throat nervously and began again. "After my husband's death, I inherited his estate. Lady Montgomery explained everything she could to me about my affliction so I could take the necessary precautions to remain safe. But I'm ashamed to say that after ten years of abuse from my late husband, the power was too much to rationally deal with. I appointed an advisor to help run the day-to-day things and an overseer for the stables. I became the perfect widow during the day, staying indoors and grieving for my dead husband. But at night I became something else." She picked up her coffee and took another sip then stared into her mug, searching for the courage to continue. "Sarah—I killed people. I went hunting nearly every night searching for abusers like him." Keller stopped when she heard the other woman's quickly indrawn breath and then went on again. Over the years, I became a bit of a vigilante. Of course I had to move every decade or so to avoid suspicion."

"So, you were playing a hero to prevent the horrible things that happened to you? How is that so bad?"

Keller looked sad. "It was more than that. I've seen so much death. I've killed in fear, anger, and sympathy. Sarah, they were executions, murders of a noble kind but still murders. I did not bring anyone to justice, I served my own." She looked up at Sarah, expecting horror and revulsion in her gaze.

Sarah looked back, but instead of revulsion, her eyes only held understanding. "And how long ago was that, centuries? I'm no history buff, but even I know that the world was a very different place then." Sudden clarity flitted across her face. "Noble killer—that's how you got your name!"

Clear blue eyes blinked in relief. "Yes."

Sarah took Keller's hands into her own. "It's okay, I think I understand. But the world is different now, and you're not that person anymore. You should leave what you've done in the past where it belongs."

Keller shook her head sadly. If only it were that easy. "I'm not so sure you *do* understand because if you did you would be out the door." She swallowed and bravely continued. "What ended my old life, the path I chose to take, and the places I have been are exactly what matters. They have shaped me and made me who I am today."

Sarah gently traced Keller's bottom lip and gazed into her eyes. "It may have shaped you but it hasn't made you who you are. Of course, everyone is the sum of his or her experiences but Keller, we are so much more. We love, we hate, and we live. But in the end we are exactly who we choose to be. And you are a good woman."

Keller was touched by the singer's words. "Thank you."

Sarah thought for a second then asked, "What about now? Do you still avenge those in need?"

Keller had a faraway look in her eyes when she answered. "I

no longer kill anymore, if that's what you're asking."

"Why?"

She returned her focus to the singer. "Because survival is about adaptation. Times have changed and so have I. Besides, killing is no longer honorable, and death has become a privilege."

Sarah moved closer. "Do you really believe that, are you ready to be done with all life has to offer?"

Keller looked seriously at the singer. "No, not anymore." Both women stared at each other in drawn-out silence. She turned Sarah's hand over and softly traced the lifeline. It was straight, running close to the edge of Sarah's palm. When she started on the wavy love line, she spoke again. "There's something else you should know."

"What is it?"

Hesitantly, Keller told her the rest. "I'm afraid that you're not going to like this. You know this — thing we have between us?" When Sarah nodded, she went on. "I believe that we've bonded. I knew the first night I saw you at Club Diversity. Sarah, you are the one."

Sarah looked a little alarmed. "The one what?"

"The other half of my soul."

Sarah pulled away from Keller and stood up from the couch. The night had suddenly gone well beyond casual. Dismay was the dominant emotion on her expressive face. "Why do you say that? There is no such thing as a soul mate, that's nothing more than a story made up by the weak-minded when they want a happy ending!"

Feeling the wave of negative emotion emanating from Sarah, Keller tried for levity to lighten the mood. "Um, just like there are no such thing as vampires? I'm not sure why this is the news that makes you upset, over say, my murdering past and the fangs."

"It's one thing to tell me something about yourself, but it's completely different to try to tell me that I am connected to you somehow. That's just bullshit. Jesus, Keller, you don't have to make up something to get me to keep your secret!" She stomped off to the bedroom to get dressed. Keller followed her and painfully watched from the doorway, realizing that she was treading serious waters. Sarah, for her part, was panicking. "Listen — this is a little bit too much and I don't know what to think right now." She looked at the woman in the doorway. "Think about what you're saying, it's crazy!" At Keller's hurt look, she tried to reassure the woman, at least a little bit. "Insanely enough, I do believe you about the rest but I'm not anyone's chosen one. I'm just me, Keller, and I'm not bonded to anyone."

Keller slowly shook her head back and forth. "Just look inside yourself, and think about what you've been feeling. You know it's true."

Sarah whirled on Keller. "Do you want to know what is true, Keller? I know I have my sister and she has me, and that's all that really matters." She slipped on her shoes and directly addressed the quiet woman in the doorway. "I won't deny we have a connection, but it's just sex. I am very attracted to you and I think you are the hottest fucking thing to ever touch my body but that is it! There are no such things as soul mates and there is no forever. That's just a fairy tale."

Keller stepped toward the other woman. "It's no fairy tale, and whether you like it or not we've bonded. That is forever, Sarah! You can't deny it and you can't change it, we need each other."

Sarah hated being told what to do and refused to be controlled by anyone. She stood absolutely still, rigid with her sudden anger. "I don't *need* anything! You can believe what you want, Keller, but I'm not buying it." She stalked past the stunned bar manager and into the kitchen. Then Sarah grabbed her coat from the closet and opened the front door. Standing in the entryway, she turned back for a few seconds longer. "You don't have to worry, I'll keep both my promises. But Keller, you are expecting more from me than I can give right now. I—I just need to think for a while." She looked away from Keller's emotion-filled gaze. "I'll see you around." Sarah walked out without a backward glance.

The minute the door shut Keller sank to her knees. She held her head in both hands, rocking back and forth. "No, no, no..." In an instant, everything went wrong. She had her, and then she pushed too hard. As the tears began to fall, she stilled her movements and sat back onto the floor. "What am I going to do?"

At the same time, Sarah was racing to her car. Desperate to escape, she furiously wiped stubborn tears away. It was too much, she didn't have room in her life for a complication like Noble Keller. Unconvincingly, she thought "I don't need her—I *don't!*"

Chapter Four

IT WAS TUESDAY afternoon and Noble Keller was not a happy woman. She had tried two other security agencies and was told by both that they didn't have anyone available for the times requested. She suspected it had more to do with the nature of the bar than the time. She finally got a positive result from the third agency. She blew out a breath in relief and answered the voice on the phone. "Yes, I'd like two guards. One will focus on the two streets and the intersection. The second will concentrate on the parking lot and the back alley." She listened for a minute and replied, "Yes of course, that would be great. And you're right, week by week would be the best arrangement for now." Keller nodded to the voice on the phone. "Yes, I hope they catch who-ever it is too." When she hung up, she crossed one item off the long list on her desk and dialed again. "May I speak with Joanne Markham, please?" After a slight pause, "Yes, I'll hold."

Keller studied her planner while she waited, pencil tapping on the desk impatiently. Without warning, the music cut off and her boss came on the line. "Joanne, it's me Keller. I took care of that little matter we discussed yesterday." She cocked her head, listening, and replied. "Yes, anyway I just wanted to thank you for approving the request and the last-minute budget allocation. I wasn't looking forward to staking out the parking lot myself so it was appreciated." Keller's eye landed on a flier Annie had placed on her desk earlier. "By the way, my new assistant manager made some fliers to place around the club and the community. She downloaded a page from the hotline website and printed it off." Keller listened some more while she scratched another item off her list. "You know just the usual, safety precautions for patrons and employees as well as the tip line phone number. As a matter of fact, I think I'm going to fax copies to the other club owners so they can hang them as well."

Keller wrapped up the call and leaned back in her chair. It had been a little over a week since she had last spoken to Sarah. Annie's college graduation was rapidly approaching and so was the end of Sarah's contract with the club. Keller was at her wit's end waiting for the singer to come around. At the knock at the door, she opened her eyes and looked up. "Come in!" The very woman at the forefront of her thoughts opened the door and Keller sat up abruptly. "Sarah!"

The singer walked in and pushed the door nearly shut behind her. "Am I interrupting?"

Keller had a fleeting bitter thought that by not completely shutting the door, Sarah could run away that much faster. She shrugged it off then stood and walked toward her. Right away, she noticed Sarah had gotten her hair cut. It was shoulder length and the ends were flipped up slightly. The singer had never looked better and Keller could barely keep her hands to herself. She wanted to touch her, to hold her, but after their last confrontation she was unsure. "No, not at all."

Sarah began hesitantly. "First I wanted to apologize for the way I ran out last time."

"That's okay, I understand. I threw a lot at you all at once."

Sarah walked forward until she stood in front of the shorter woman. "Keller, I—" She ran a hand through her newly cut hair. "—I can't stay away from you." She reached out to trace Keller's cheekbone then leaned in and kissed her slowly. When they broke apart, Sarah clung to the smaller woman. "What do you want from me, Keller? Ask for something I can give."

Keller was quiet for a moment, soaking up Sarah's touch and smell. She thought about what she wanted and what she was likely to get. "I only want what you're willing to give, Sarah, nothing more." It would have to do until Sarah understood more.

Sarah breathed into Keller's ear. "No strings, that's what I want." Keller pulled away, looking sad but resigned. Sarah added, "I'm sorry, I haven't been back in town very long and I just don't want any complications in my life right now."

The bar manager nodded. "Okay." Making a quick decision she asked, "Will you do one thing for me though?"

"Um—that depends on what it is."

Keller walked to her desk and removed a business card and house key from the top drawer. She handed both to Sarah. "The key is for my condo. My cell phone number and security code are on the back of the card." She paused. "Anytime, Sarah, day or night."

Sarah tucked both into her pocket. She laughed softly. "I don't think I have much of a choice anymore. You are a very addicting woman, Noble Keller." She started to lean in for another kiss when they were abruptly interrupted.

Annie walked through the partially open door, knocking as she entered. "Keller, what do you think about—"

Sarah quickly stepped away from Keller, feeling guilty but unsure why. "Uh, hey, sis."

There was a moment of awkward silence while Annie stared at the other two women in surprise. Taking pity on the uncomfortable looking women in front of her, she asked as nonchalantly as she could, "So, Keller, what do you think of her hair, it looks great doesn't it?"

Keller mumbled, "Oh yeah, definitely."

Sarah needed to leave. She could feel Keller's hot stare and her sister's questioning one. She didn't really want to deal with either. "Well, I'm going to take off. I'll see you both later." She hugged her sister and lightly caressed Keller's arm. She didn't trust herself with more than that.

Annie stood quietly, watching Keller watch her sister leave. There was a lost look on her boss's face that she had never seen before. Curious.

Keller slowly turned her attention back to Annie. "You had something to go over with me?"

Annie began the little persuasive speech she had been rehearsing the entire afternoon. "I've been researching the other clubs to see what types of entertainment they have to offer. Based on what I found, I've come up with—"

Keller held up a hand, forestalling any further explanation. "You know me, I need numbers before anything else. Could you put everything in writing like a proposal or—"

Annie interrupted her boss by placing the folder she was carrying into her hands. "Already done."

Keller smiled. "Uh, okay, thanks. Let me read this over and I'll get back to you tomorrow."

"All right." Annie started to walk out then stopped and turned around. "By the way, the sign-up sheets are full for this Saturday's auditions. I'm going to get Alice and Bruce to sit in with me again unless you want to do it."

"Have you thought about asking Sarah? She may have some good input. She always seems to be in tune with the crowds. And from what I've seen, her knowledge and experience would be a valuable asset when it comes to choosing potential bands."

Annie slowly nodded. "I think you're right, she would be a

good judge to bring in. I'll see if she wants to do it the next time I talk to her."

After Annie walked out, closing the door behind her, Keller went back to her desk and sat down. She leaned her head back and shut her eyes. The events of the past week were catching up with her and she felt drained both physically and emotionally. On one hand, she was thrilled by Sarah's visit. On the other, she wasn't sure how long she could live with just a superficial relationship, subject to Sarah's whims. Time would tell.

KELLER WAS HOPEFUL but Sarah never showed up that night or the ones after. She waited over a week after she had given Sarah her condo key but had not seen or heard from the other woman. She was so hung up on the singer that she couldn't even look at other women now, let along take care of the need coursing through her veins. The drained feeling was only getting worse. Keller helped close the bar on a Thursday night but there was still no sign of Sarah. When she nonchalantly questioned Annie about Sarah's whereabouts, the younger woman looked uncomfortable.

"She's been staying with a—uh— friend, the last two nights. I haven't seen her since Tuesday, in your office."

Keller felt sick. She wasn't sure if it was because of what the singer was doing or if it was because she didn't know when Sarah was coming back. "Wh—what about Duke? Did she take him with her?"

"No, I've got Duke at the house. She said she wouldn't have time to take care of him." Annie's suspicions were confirmed by the look on her Keller's face. Her thoughts raced as she realized that Keller was hung up on Sarah. Trying to reassure her friend, she added, "Hey, her last gig is tomorrow night so I know we'll see her by then." It didn't seem to help. Annie looked at her in concern. "You look tired, Keller, you should go home and get some sleep."

Distractedly, Keller walked away. "Yeah, I think I will."

After closing the bar, Keller drove home in a daze. When she entered her condo, she was surprised to see the light on above the piano. She followed the quiet music only to find the one person she had been looking for. Keller waited quietly, soaking up the beauty of the moment.

When the song ended, Sarah looked up into Keller's impossibly blue eyes. "Hi."

Keller smiled. "You came."

Something undefinable flashed across Sarah's face. "You knew I would."

"No, I hoped. There is a big difference."

It didn't take long for them to end up in the bedroom. Sarah dominated nearly every move. The two women were so insatiable for each other's touch that it was hours before they wore themselves out. Keller never asked where she'd been and Sarah didn't mention her absence. Long after the passion had cooled, Keller watched her sleep. She caressed the dark hair lying across her pillow. Half prayer, half plea to the sleeping woman beside her, she whispered, "Love..." When Keller woke early the next afternoon from an exhausted sleep, Sarah was gone. No note, no strings.

WHEN SARAH GOT home, her dog and her sister greeted her at the door. Duke was happy to see her but Annie seemed upset. "Where have you been?" Sarah, not really up for explaining herself, grabbed Duke's leash. Annie pointed at it. "Don't bother, I just finished walking him." Then she looked into Sarah's intense green eyes. "What's going on with you and Keller, Sarah? Talk to me."

Sarah walked into the living room and sat down. Annie sat next to her, waiting for an answer. "It's just a fling. There's nothing going on."

"Bullshit! You didn't see her face when I had to tell her you had been staying with another woman for the past few nights." Annie slapped the cushion in frustration. Keller was more than her boss she was her friend. "Jesus, Sarah! I warned you about Keller, I never thought I'd have to warn her about you!"

Sarah stood and walked to the window. "I can't believe you told her where I was." She added in a slightly louder voice, "Annie, it's not like that."

"Then what is it? Tell my why she looked like someone kicked her in the stomach earlier?"

Sarah just stared out the window. "It's complicated."

"That's a crock and you know it. Either you like her or you don't, but don't fuck with her, Sarah!"

Sarah looked back at her sister with tears in her eyes. "Annie, you don't understand!"

Annie quickly stood. "You're right, I don't understand but that doesn't really matter." She glared at Sarah. "The problem is that I don't think Keller really understands either. She's my friend, Sarah, don't hurt her." She walked out of the room before Sarah could respond.

After Annie's door shut down the hall Sarah threw herself sideways to lay down on the old couch. "Fucking hell."

SARAH PLAYED HER last set that night. Always the professional, her performance was flawless. Both fun and funny, she was worth the money paid to get in. However, emotionally she wasn't really there. Annie could tell, watching from the bar. The blue eyes watching from the shadows in the back of the room could tell too. Sarah was completely lost.

In a move to make peace with her sister, Sarah agreed to sit in on the auditions the next afternoon. The two bands chosen would replace her and Mary's Angels in their Friday night gigs. Keller was working in her office with the door closed but Sarah could still feel the weight of her presence. After a few hours, everyone took a break and Sarah wandered off to talk to the woman who dominated so many of her waking thoughts. She knocked and let herself in just as Keller was wrapping up a phone call.

The bar manager was surprised but smiled, trying to keep things casual. "What's up?"

Sarah sat on the edge of her desk, idly tracing the oval dent on the steel top. "I probably should have talked to you earlier, but you know Annie graduates next Sunday, right?"

Keller nodded. "Yeah. Actually I wanted to talk to you about that a few days ago. Since I couldn't find you I went ahead with my plans anyway. I hope you won't be angry."

Sarah looked at her curiously. "What are you planning?"

Keller grinned evilly. "I invited all her friends, coworkers, and a few classmates to her open house." Sarah looked confused so she added, "I'm holding it here, at The Merge. We'll stay open to the public but Lynne will come in and supervise hanging the decorations and we'll run drink specials. Best of all, I've got two box dancers coming in from nine until twelve." She wiggled her eyebrows lasciviously. "That should keep little miss innocent entertained."

Sarah blinked in surprise and then grinned. "Wow, that's great! I don't know what to say except thank you."

Keller touched her knee lightly. "It's no problem at all. Annie is a great employee but—" She swallowed. "She's a better friend. It was the least I could do."

Sarah covered Keller's hand with her own. "How about I pay for the food then, as my contribution?"

"That would be great, thank you." She laughed. "Actually, since we're the only people besides Jesse who are attending the ceremony, it's up to us to get her here afterward."

Sarah laughed with her. "Gee, convince her to have a drink after graduating, that's going to be hard!" She stood and gave Keller a kiss on the cheek. "All right, I need to make a quick run to the dry cleaners to pick up my outfit before we start going over the audition results." At the door she paused briefly. "Goodbye, Keller."

Keller could still feel the soft kiss from the mercurial singer long after she was gone.

LATER THAT AFTERNOON, the four judges found themselves sitting at the bar comparing notes. An empty pizza box left over from their lunch sat off to the side and everyone had a beer in hand. The first band was easy to decide, every judge loved Finding Dora. The second was a little more difficult. Annie, Bruce, and Alice all liked the band Shaker Station but Sarah was adamant about Ronnie Williams. Bruce had been a fan of Shaker Station since the band first formed and was very vocal of his support. The look he gave Sarah said she was crazy. "Girlfriend, like—the Station totally rocks!"

Alice and Annie nodded in agreement and Annie added, "Yeah, Ronnie was good but Shaker Station was just a little better. They had great stage presence. I thought the decision was kind of obvious."

Sarah agreed, shocking the other three. "You're absolutely right, they are better" She held up a hand when everyone started to talk at once. "Hold on, hear me out. Let's look at what we're trying to accomplish here." She looked at her sister. "Annie, have you noticed anything significant between the nights I played and the nights that Mary's Angels played?"

Annie scrunched up her eyebrows in thought. "Well, the

crowds you played for were a little older."

"Right! So if you don't want to lose the interest of that demo-graphic, you should stick with picking two different style artists for each gig." Understanding flashed across the other three faces. They were all younger than Sarah and less experienced in the music industry. None of them had thought about things in that much detail. It was about more than just choosing a great band to bring in the crowds. It was about choosing bands that would keep the crowds coming back. They need to appeal to the diversity of their audience. "Now you see why I wanted Ronnie to balance out Finding Dora." She turned her attention solely toward her sister. "However, if I were you I would definitely line up Shaker Station for the next gig. They're too good to let them get away."

Annie smiled "Absolutely." She laughed and stole Sarah's beer. "You really are older and wiser, who knew?" Everyone else joined in the laughter and started cleaning up. When they were finished, Bruce, Annie, and Sarah got ready to leave. Alice had to work that night so she went behind the bar to start stocking her garnish. As the three of them walked out into the parking lot, Annie addressed the other two. "You know, I'm looking at the whole thing from a different perspective now. It's given me an idea." The young woman was excited and it showed in her ani-mated hand movements while she described her plan. "I think I'm going to advertise a little differently. I need to make sure the target audience knows what they're getting. We should come up with a name for the two-month gigs, something that is both fun and descriptive." She stopped walking for a second, looking thoughtful. "What do you think of The Sip and Chug Music Spot-light? We could advertise for bands the same way just to make sure we get diversity at the auditions."

Bruce clapped his hands. "Sweetie, that's a great idea! You know, I could get my hunky boyfriend to make some kick ass fli-ers." He grinned proudly, addressing Sarah. "Rico is an art major."

Annie smiled and rolled her eyes. She knew all about Rico from their many conversations. Bruce and Rico were one of her favorite couples. "Awesome, thanks, Bruce. I will go over the details and let you know what I decide. If we have your honey come up with something, I'll make sure he gets reimbursed."

"Thanks A, I'll let him know. He would probably have done if for free though." They walked him the rest of the way to his

Jeep. "All right girls, I'll see you later. I've got to get going —" He sighed dramatically, "I'm on for dinner tonight. Wish me luck."

The sisters got into Annie's car and Sarah watched the flamboyant man drive away. "He seems pretty cool."

Annie laughed, pulling out of the parking lot. "Oh yeah, he and Rico are a blast to hang out with. They are a very cute couple. Speaking of couples, did you talk to Keller?"

"Annie..." Sarah sighed in frustration. "Look, we're not a couple, okay?"

Annie gave her a serious look as they pulled into the driveway a few minutes later. "I know you. Don't try to tell me you don't like her." She poked Sarah in the ribs. "You two have chemistry that even a blind man could see." They sat for a moment with the car idling. Annie watched as a wide gamut of emotions passed across her sister's face before the older woman answered.

"I do like her, okay?" She gave Annie a sad look. "Is that what you want to hear, are you happy now?"

Annie put a comforting hand on the tense woman's arm. "Hey, take it easy." She rubbed gently back and forth. "What would make me happy is for you to be happy. What's stopping you, Sarah?"

"It's complicated —"

The younger woman pinched her, none too lightly. "Don't start that again!"

"No really, there is a lot more involved than 'who likes who' here. I just need some time to be sure of what I want, and I don't really know if that includes a complication like Noble Keller. Don't worry, Annie, she knows how I feel."

Annie let her go. "All right, I'll back off. But Sarah, I see something when you look at each other. Don't be too quick to throw that away." She smiled tenderly. She had slowly been cluing in to her sister's fear of commitment since Sarah had returned home. "Besides, you need more than just me and Duke in your life."

Annie got out of the car and went into the house, leaving her sister to think in silence. Sarah just sat with her hands on her thighs, staring straight ahead. She could feel the distinct lump in her pocket made by Keller's house key. "No I don't. I don't need anyone else."

FOR THE COLBY sisters, Annie's graduation was one of the happiest and saddest days of their lives. They were happy that even after their parents' death, Annie had finally accomplished one of their greatest wishes. The one dark cloud hovering over the moment was that their parents couldn't be there to see it. "Anne Marie Colby..." When Annie's name was called, Sarah had tears in her eyes. Keller discretely took her hand in a silent offer of comfort and understanding.

Jesse was busy taking pictures but she caught the interaction between the bar manager and her girlfriend's sister. Annie had mentioned something was going on between them but Jesse hadn't seen it until that moment. She smiled to herself as she focused back on Annie.

Many hours later the party was in full swing. Annie was seated in a chair getting a lap dance from one of the box dancers. Jesse, far from jealous, was still manning the camera. Coworkers and friends had been plying the young graduate with shots and she was well on her way to a wicked hangover. A while later, Annie convinced the DJ to play a popular line dance so Jesse sat at the table with Keller and Sarah. She had been getting to know both women very well over the past month and a half, and she really liked them. Her own family had disowned her when she came out, and Keller and Sarah were quickly becoming surrogates. She took a drink of her bottled water, attempting to cool off. "There is no way I'm going to dance to that!" The two older women laughed and agreed with her.

Sarah had been quiet since the ceremony so Keller made small talk over the dance music. "Jesse, Annie tells me you're going to school for computer networking. How long before you graduate?"

Jesse leaned back in her chair watching the antics of her drunken girlfriend. She laughed at something the dancing woman did and then answered. "I still have one more semester to go but I've already gotten offers from two companies here in Columbus. One of the offers is for the place I already work part-time at."

Sarah joined the conversation with Keller and the younger woman. She really liked Jesse. She was smart and had a good head on her shoulders. Her sister could have done a lot worse. "That's great news, so we'll be having a party for you soon too, huh?"

Jesse smiled shyly. "You guys don't have to do anything for

me but thanks for saying that."

The intense and sometimes enigmatic bar manager squeezed her shoulder in a gesture of comfort. "Hey, we're all family here. Anyone that means so much to Annie is part of the family too."

Sarah added, "You're always welcome, Jesse, anytime. If you ever need anything, just ask okay?"

The young woman was touched by their offer of friendship and acceptance. Her reply was almost too quiet to hear. "Thank you." She stood. "I'm going to the bathroom, in case Annie asks. I'll be right back." When she returned, she caught the tail end of Keller and Sarah's conversation.

"Sarah, I would really like you to come home with me tonight."

Sarah looked away from Keller's intense blue eyes. "I can't, not tonight."

"Why not?"

She answered as Jesse pulled out her chair and sat down again. "Well for starters, I have to take Jesse and Annie home." Jesse had met them at the house and the three rode together to the graduation ceremony.

Jesse had witnessed the looks that passed between the two women on numerous occasions. Annie had talked to her a little about the situation, confiding that she thought they would be good together. The young woman decided to help things along. "You know, I could take Annie home."

"I need to be there in case she gets sick. She doesn't handle hangovers well."

Jesse tried again. "You know I'd stay and watch over her too. Go on, have fun, I'll take care of our girl. I've only had two drinks, you can trust me, Sarah."

Keller smiled at the younger woman's assistance. "See, everything's taken care of. Jesse will be there to watch over her." She took Sarah's hand in her own. "Please say you'll come?"

Jesse stayed quiet while they shared a moment. She was practically holding her breath waiting for Sarah to answer.

Sarah took one last look into Keller's eyes and the response slipped out before she could stop it. "Okay."

Jesse mentally patted herself on the back. Yes! She grabbed her water bottle and stood. "I'm going to go let Annie know the change in plans."

There was heat in the gaze shared by the two women remaining at the table. Sarah stood also. "I'm going to go say goodbye to Annie."

Keller stood as well, her breath coming a little faster in anticipation. "Good idea."

By the time the women reached the condo, they could barely keep their hands off one another. Keller had the taller woman pinned against the wall just inside the front door and was feasting on her mouth. When she started working her way toward the side of Sarah's neck, Sarah tensed. "No!"

Keller immediately backed off and looked into her eyes. "What's wrong?"

"No blood, Keller, I'm not going to be your meal tonight."

The shorter woman, hurt, looked at her sincerely. "I would never do that without asking, I thought you knew me better than that."

Sarah relaxed. "I'm sorry; I guess I just—panicked a little. I trust you."

"Good, because I have plans for you tonight that I don't think you will want to miss." Keller gave her a naughty look. She got two bottles of water from the refrigerator and returned. With water in one hand and Sarah's hand with the other, she led the way into the bedroom. Sarah excused herself, heading into the master bathroom while Keller lit candles and turned down the bed. When Sarah returned, Keller was wearing nothing but a silk robe. She gave the singer that dangerously sexy look she remembered so well. "Undress and lay on your stomach please."

Sarah felt her sex clench in anticipation. She did as instructed and waited, enjoying the feel of cool sheets on her over heated skin. She shut her eyes and heard the quiet whisper of Keller's robe slip from her body. The first touch of skin against skin was exquisite. Sarah moaned when she felt Keller's hard nipples rub their way up her back.

Keller started kissing the soft shoulders and neck under her. She used her hands to massage soft skin and beautiful muscles, all the while gently grinding her sex into Sarah's firm ass. Sarah clenched her hands into the sheets, pressing back into the smaller woman. "Keller, you're killing me!"

Keller rose off her lover and sat on the back of the other woman's thighs. With strong hands, she deeply caressed her firm ass cheeks. Keller ran her fingers down toward Sarah's moist center, focusing briefly on her puckered opening. The singer trembled at the onslaught of sensations, begging, "Please...please..."

Keller turned her over and slid along the length of her body, straddling a long, smooth leg. She smiled at the woman below her. "Yes? Did you need something, beautiful?"

Sarah tangled a hand in short blonde hair. She pulled the other woman down and kissed her hard, lips and tongue insistent in her need. They broke away in the search of air. "What I need is for you to fuck me!"

"Oh, I think I can oblige you there." With skilled fingers she slid into Sarah and grazed a thumb over her clit. Sarah arched her back off the bed with a guttural cry. As Keller moved her fingers in and out, she rubbed her own arousal back and forth across the strong thigh trapped between her legs. Sarah was insane with need and when Keller leaned over and started feasting on her breasts, she began to tremble. When Keller saw the green eyes below her darken with desire, she couldn't resist tasting her lips one more time. They kissed hard, never slowing their movements. Sarah abruptly jerked twice when she started to go over the edge. The movements caused sharp teeth to cut into the lip trapped between them. The reaction of that lone drop of blood caused fissions of heat to boil through Keller's veins. "Aahhh!" Her body shuddered, uncontrollably, in rapid succession, each movement causing her thumb to graze the sensitive nub underneath. Time seemed to stop while the pleasure felt by both women echoed and carried back and forth through Keller's empathic connection. When the orgasm finally left them, they collapsed, panting, onto the bed. Trembling and twitching muscles left them both weak. Keller slowly ran her tongue over her lips. She tasted the metallic tang of blood and quickly glanced at Sarah. Her lover had her eyes closed and a smile on her face, clearly enjoying the afterglow. When she saw the small smear of blood on Sarah's lips, she carefully reached over and traced it with her fingers. The sensation caused by her fingers and the tantalizing smell of sex roused the other woman. But when Keller looked into the half-lidded green eyes, her own filled with shame. "I'm so sorry, it was an accident."

Sarah gave her a puzzled look and licked her lips. When she tasted the blood she smiled at her lover reassuringly. "It's okay, I've done as much myself on occasion." She looked into worried blue eyes. "Really, it's all right." Changing the mood she covered her eyes with the back of her hand. Still shaky, she blew out a breath. "God! That was unbelievable, the things you do to me."

Keller wanted desperately to wake next to the singer in the morning. "Will you stay the night with me?"

Sarah removed her hand and slowly looked at the smaller woman lying beside her. She let her heart answer unconditionally. "Yeah."

A look of intense joy flickered across Keller's face before she quickly hid it. She got up to blow out the candles then came back to bed. Sarah was nearly asleep when Keller gently pulled the taller woman to her. The singer fell asleep with her head cradled tenderly on her lover's shoulder.

Chapter Five

LATE THE NEXT morning Sarah woke to find Keller gone. The revelation was followed by the tantalizing smells of coffee and breakfast. She found a single rose on the pillow next to her and a note. "Toiletries are next to the sink. Breakfast is ready when you are." She smiled and slipped on the robe at the end of the bed. When she finished cleaning up, she made her way to the kitchen. Keller had just placed a stack of bacon on a plate and was mixing the ingredients for omelets. Her face lit up when Sarah sat down at the breakfast nook. She walked over and gave her a gentle kiss on the lips. "What would you like in your omelet?" When Sarah didn't answer for a moment, she added worriedly, "You do like omelets, don't you?"

Sarah laughed at the other woman's uncharacteristic nervousness. "Yes I do, I'll have whatever you've got there."

They ate quietly when the food was ready. When Keller took care of the plates, Sarah took her coffee mug over to the large windows and stared toward the river. A few minutes later Keller walked up carrying her own mug. "Any plans today?"

"Not really, no. I need to hunt for some studio rental space. I think I've settled on the idea of giving private music instruction. Why?" When she turned toward Keller, she stared alarmingly at the sunlight streaming across Keller's face. "Doesn't that hurt you?"

"No. For one thing, I can stand being in the sunlight. My body will heal any damage done. It will sap my strength fairly quickly though if I don't take precautions." She laughed, "I could stand on the beach wearing nothing but a smile but it would take an enormous amount of energy. However—" She waved a hand toward the windows. "—these are treated to block UVA and UVB rays, the same as my office at the club, and a lot of vehicles for that matter. I'm safe, don't worry." She finished her coffee and walked over to rinse the mug in the sink. Sarah followed her and did the same.

Sarah gave her a strange look. "Speaking of cars, why do you drive a convertible if the sun is so damaging?"

The shorter woman laughed. "Truthfully? I love convertibles.

Mostly I only put the top down on hot summer nights but occasionally I'll chance it during the day. Call it one of my guilty pleasures."

The singer smirked. "I'm sure you have many others. Do you mind if I take a shower?"

"Of course not, I'll get you some towels. If you'd like, I think I have some oversize sweats and a t-shirt you can wear home."

"Thank you." In a promise that held more than one meaning, she added, "Don't worry, I'll bring them back."

Keller grinned, accepting the statement for what it was. "Sure, maybe we can work out a trade."

"Any time hot stuff, any time."

Keller licked her lips and watched the singer head for the shower. She called out, "I'm going to run down and get the paper. Be right back, okay?"

From the other room, "All right, I'll save you some hot water — then again if you're fast enough we can share!"

Keller ran out the door. When she came back, she threw the paper on the counter then joined Sarah in the shower. They spent nearly an hour under the water. Long enough to get clean then dirty and clean again.

Once they were dressed, they made their way back to the kitchen. Keller fetched a small duffle bag from the closet for Sarah's clothes. Sarah saw the morning paper sitting near the edge of the counter. She flipped it over to read the front page and gasped. "Oh my God!" She covered her mouth with her hand.

Keller turned around and saw Sarah's face pale. She dropped the bag and rushed over. "What is it?"

Sarah pointed at the front page and Keller read the headline aloud. "Club Diversity employee found dead in back alley, the latest attack in a series of hate crimes downtown." Keller sat on the stool next to Sarah, dumbfounded.

"Keller, that's horrible, they've got to do something!"

The bar manager shook her head back and forth, mind already racing about the new precautions The Merge would have to take. "There's nothing they can do without any leads. They don't even have a description of the vehicle that keeps running people down." She stood and started pacing. "I'm going to have to tighten security again at the club. There is no way one of our people is going to be hurt, I'll close first!"

Sarah stood and put a comforting hand on Keller's arm, stopping the agitated woman. "It's going to be all right."

Keller turned and grabbed Sarah's arms in a strong grip. "Promise me—" She shook her a little, focusing on green eyes. "Promise me you'll be safe."

"Of course. What about you?"

"I'll be all right, you don't have to worry about me. I can protect myself."

"You said it yourself, you're not immortal. Don't be foolish, Keller, too many people depend on you and care about you."

"Including you?"

Sarah looked away from those penetrating blue eyes. She took the easy way out once again and chose to run away. "I have to go." She took one last look at the other woman before walking out the door. The scene was already familiar to both women. "I'll see you around Keller. Take care of yourself—" She whispered quietly as the door closed behind her. "—for me."

MORE THAN TWO weeks had passed since the murder. Keller spent every moment from open to close at the bar. Only one more attack had occurred but she worried continuously about her employees' safety. She hired two more security people for outside the bar and had cameras installed that monitored the entire outside perimeter. Many hours were spent in front of the screens in her office. No one was allowed to leave the bar alone and community watches were organized around the downtown area. The manager barely slept, barely ate, and barely saw Sarah. She had spoken to Annie on numerous occasions and from what the younger woman said, her sister was very busy trying to get her instruction studio off the ground. Sarah had only come home with her twice since Annie's graduation. It wasn't nearly enough. Keller was taxing her resources considerably and the few visits from her lover weren't enough to rejuvenate her. She was getting weak and she knew it. Noble Keller had no way of telling how long she could keep up the pace.

It was a Tuesday night when the police finally got a break in the case. The Wednesday papers reported an older model truck had tried to run two twenty-something men off the road near a gay café. A pencil sketch of the vehicle was on the front page but no one had reported seeing it since. Keller was at her desk when Annie walked in.

"Keller, did you see —" She stopped when she saw the open paper on the desk. "Oh, I guess you have." She walked over to the desk and looked closer at her boss. "Keller, when is the last time you ate, or even slept for that matter?"

Keller distractedly traced one of the indentations on her desktop. "Uh, yesterday I think." She waved a hand at her in dismissal. "Thank you for your concern, Annie, but I'm fine. Oh, and will you tell Lynne that I'll take her shift tomorrow if she still wants me to?"

Annie began to protest then changed her mind. "Sure, Keller, I'll let her know." She walked out, leaving the other woman deep in thought. She was worried about her sister and Keller. Keller was spending too much time working, not taking care of herself. And Sarah had withdrawn into herself, spending all her time trying to get her business off the ground. Neither had been making any moves toward having a real relationship. She had talked to Jesse about the situation but neither one of them could come up with a solution. They would just have to wait it out.

SARAH WAS STILL trying to fight the inevitable. She would stay away from Keller as long as possible until the need became too great. What she feared was what she most wanted. The more time she spent with Keller, the more she needed to. Trying to keep her distance was tearing her in two. Another week went by since the write up in the paper with the vehicle description. Unable to take it any longer, Sarah found herself going into Keller's condo one night. Keller wasn't home so she sat down at the piano. She lost herself for a long time, just playing anything that came to mind. She hadn't written any new music for more than a month and suddenly she felt the urge to do something, anything. She retrieved the duffle bag that she had left by the door then sat on the couch. Taking out a tablet and pen, she stared down at the blank paper. Almost as if a switch were thrown, the words began to pour out of her. Like blood from an open wound, each sentence was a catharsis. She emptied everything her body could possibly hold onto the page. All the anger, passion, and pain were there for the world to see. Feeling raw and drained of energy, Sarah finished and lay back on the couch, clutching the notebook tightly. She closed her eyes and drifted off to sleep, knowing the melody would come eventually.

Keller entered later after closing the bar and seeing her employees safely out. She was surprised to see the light on in the living room but instinctively knew who it was. She walked over and gazed down at the sleeping woman. The soft light gave her the face of an angel, or maybe it was the soft expression on her face. Unable to resist, she stroked the dark hair fanned out across the leather. Her actions woke the slumbering woman and green eyes peered up into her own. She smiled tenderly at the gift below her. "Hi."

Sarah smiled in return. "Hi, yourself. Everything go okay tonight?"

"Yeah, everything was fine." She continued the small talk, wanting nothing more than to take the other woman into her arms. "How are things going with your new business?"

"They're good. I'm pretty sure I have a place lined up. I also have fliers up and I have been advertising through word of mouth. I'm hoping to be able to start lessons within the month."

Keller was silent for a moment, and then she walked around the couch and knelt in front of Sarah. She carefully placed the notebook on the coffee table. When Sarah began to speak, Keller placed two fingers over her soft lips. "Shh." In a show of strength belying her small stature, Keller picked her up and carried her to the bedroom. She spent the rest of the night pouring out her own heart. The words spoken by strong hands were silent as the ones on the page but the message was the same. All Sarah had to do was look and she would see the love written in the blue eyes gone black with desire.

Keller woke alone, once again. The silence of her empty home was deafening. She felt like her heart was breaking and there was nothing she could do. The night of passion left her feeling marginally better but it was not enough to keep up with the energy she was expending. She needed Sarah more than anything in her entire life. The singer was the key to her heart and without her, she would die. Keller clutched the pillow used by her lover and inhaled the scent of her. She gave a single hoarse cry then curled around the soft reminder and wept. The tears were nothing less than the blood of her broken heart.

Five stories below in a nearby parking lot, Sarah was pounding her anger out onto the steering wheel of her RAV4. The outlet was different but the tears she cried were exactly the same.

When Sarah returned home, Annie was busy eating her lunch and reading the paper. Sarah stole a chip from her sister's plate and the younger woman half-heartedly protested. "Hey, get your own!" Sarah grabbed a soda from the fridge and the bag of potato chips from the cupboard. Annie looked at her fondly, taking note of the red rimmed eyes. Lightly, she asked, "Where have you been, anyone interesting?"

Using the same light tone, Sarah replied, "Oh, you know, just the usual."

Annie smirked. "So how was Keller?"

"How is Jesse?"

Annie immediately blushed. It had only been a little over a week since Annie and Jesse had taken their relationship to the next level. Since the younger couple had successfully made it past third base, Annie had been insatiable. Sarah had walked in on their passionate displays on more than one occasion.

Annie smacked her on the arm for her teasing. She grinned at her older sister then got serious. "Actually, there is something I've wanted to talk to you about."

Sarah took a drink and grabbed another chip. "Go ahead then, spill it. What did you do now?"

Annie swallowed nervously. "It's not what I did, it's what I want to do." She went on quickly. "You see, Jesse's lease is up in another month and I was thinking about asking her to move in here with us."

Sarah's eyebrows shot up. "Really? Do you think it's too soon for that? What does Jesse say?"

"Well, I haven't actually talked to her about it yet. I wanted to talk to you first to make sure that it's okay." She shrugged her shoulders. "I didn't want to get her hopes up or anything."

Sarah thought for a minute, rolling the idea around in her head. It was only a two-bedroom house but there was plenty of room in the full size basement for storage. Besides, she really did like Jesse. She was coming to think of her as another sister of sorts. She looked at Annie intently. "Is this what you really want, Annie, is it worth the risk?"

Annie didn't need any time at all to answer. "Yes it is. Sarah, I want to wake up with her every single morning, not just the days we have 'sleepovers'. I want to see more of her. I want to be able to watch TV with her, do the dishes together, and fall asleep holding each other every night." She blushed. "That sounds stupid, doesn't it?"

Sarah smiled. "Not at all, it sounds like you're in love."

"Yeah, I guess I am. It's just—it's like the most incredible feeling I've ever had!" She looked sadly at her sister and confidante. "I just wish you could feel the same thing."

"Well, maybe love is something that I'm not meant to find."

"Maybe..." Annie let the comment slide and decided to change the subject instead. "Hey, something has been bothering me."

"What's wrong?"

"Have you noticed anything odd about Keller, anything unexplainably strange?"

Sarah did her best to keep a straight face. Her sister was obviously very perceptive if she was noticing things that Keller had been keeping hidden for years. She hated lying to Annie about anything but it wasn't her secret to tell. "No, nothing. Why do you ask?"

Annie was watching Sarah closely as she answered. Sarah would never make a good poker player, her face gave everything away. The younger Colby sister could easily see that there was something going on with Keller, and Sarah knew about it. Interesting. Annie decided that she still had to voice her concerns. "I don't know if you have noticed but she hasn't been looking very well lately." At Sarah's worried glance she added, "She has been working every day and night for weeks. She's going to burn herself out if she doesn't slow down and get some rest."

Taken off guard, Sarah attempted to speak but no words came out. She was instantly struck with overwhelming guilt for not noticing anything wrong. She had been so focused on her own life that she had not been paying attention to much else. "Wha— um, what's—" She stopped, and then started again. "What can I do? I mean, she's an adult. I can't tell her what to do."

"Could you just talk to her please? Try to get her to take a day off. We'll be fine at the bar without her for a night." Annie gave her a pleading look. "We've been friends for a while and she hasn't been talking to me at all lately. I'm really worried about her, Sarah."

Sarah got up, put the chips away, and tossed her can in the recycling bin. Without making eye contact, she agreed to help. "I'll talk to her and see what I can do."

Annie stood and took care of her own dishes. "Thank you, it

means a lot to me."

IT WAS FRIDAY night and it had been a little over a week since Sarah had made her promise to Annie. She had been putting it off because she was afraid to see if there really was something wrong with Keller. She didn't want to know if she would feel anything, if Keller had made it past the barrier around her heart. She arrived at The Merge around nine p.m. Her reasoning was that it wouldn't be too busy to talk but she could still possibly meet up with some friends later. When she walked through the door, there were a few early birds paying the cover charge and getting their ID's scanned. Teddy waved her through at no charge, one of the benefits of knowing the right people. Sarah wanted to grab a drink then find Keller and get the discussion over with as soon as possible.

When she walked up to the bar, she was pleasantly surprised to see one of her oldest and closest friends, Jill. The two women had lost touch when she went on tour and Sarah missed hanging out with her. Jill was a little taller than she was and had long red hair with a model's face. Sarah slapped the redhead's ass while she was waiting to order. The woman turned around with angry blue eyes flashing. "Hey!" She stopped in surprise and threw her arms around Sarah. "Oh my God, look at you!" They hugged for a full minute, and then Jill pulled back and looked at the singer. Licking her lips, she gave Sarah a naughty smile. "Lover, you get sexier every time I see you." Boldly, she caressed Sarah's bottom lip before leaning in and kissing her passionately. Tongues dueled until the need for air broke the two women apart. Unseen by both, another set of angry blue eyes watched from across the bar. After witnessing the heated display of affection, Keller stalked back to her office and slammed the door. Jill wrapped an arm around Sarah's waist affectionately. "Whew, girl, I think I need a drink after that!" The both laughed and leaned shoulder to shoulder at the bar. Sarah was glad of the unexpected interruption to her plans. It had been a frustrating week of soul searching and she was still feeling a little emotionally raw. She wasn't ready to face Noble Keller and her heartbreaking stare. When the two women got their drinks, they sat in a booth as far from the dance floor as possible so they could talk. Jill gave her another heated look from across the table. "Look at you! I haven't seen you in—" She wrinkled her eyebrows in thought and Sarah answered for her.

"A little over a year."

Jill laughed. "Oh yeah, you rolled into town for a night then rolled right back out again."

Sarah smirked. "But it was a good night though, wasn't it?"

Jill blushed. "Uh huh, no complaints here!" She shook off the arousing memories. "I heard you were back in town playing at the Pony, but I haven't been out in forever. So when are you heading out again?" The redhead worked as a veterinarian at an emergency clinic just outside of the city, so her hours were sometimes random and unpredictable. This meant it was often hard for her to meet up with friends.

"Actually, I'm back for good. I'm living with Annie for the time being. You know me, just trying to stay out of trouble." When Jill raised an eyebrow in disbelief, she took a swig of her beer and chuckled. "Well, mostly anyways." Both women laughed, remembering Sarah's uncanny knack for getting herself into romantic entanglements. Jill had to save the singer on more than one occasion from over amorous fans and one-night stands.

They spent nearly an hour catching up and exchanging stories. By the end, they were laughing so hard tears were running down both their cheeks. Jill reached over and took Sarah's hand. She said seriously, "I'm so glad we ran into each other tonight. I always have a good time with you."

Sarah smiled sadly. "I know and I'm sorry we lost touch too. I didn't keep in contact with anyone but Annie while I was on the road. I'm afraid it has cost me a lot of my old friends."

Jill gave her hand a squeeze. "No worries there, not this friend." She tilted her head to the side and added, "Why is it that we broke up all those years ago?"

Sarah shoved the other woman's hand away playfully. "Someone, who shall remain nameless, had a serious aversion to monogamy."

In a flash, Jill slid over to Sarah's side of the booth and tickled her. When she was done, she grabbed Sarah's beer and drank it in three swallows. "Whatever! As I recall, Ms. Colby, you weren't ready to settle down either!"

Sarah looked down, blushing and idly scratching her ear. "Heh, oh yeah, I forgot about that." When she looked up again, Jill kissed her. This time the redhead did not stop until she elicited a moan from Sarah. "What are your plans for the night?"

"Not much really. Why, what did you have in mind?" Sarah played along as she had done many times before with the other woman.

Jill gave her a sexy smirk. "What do you say we cut out early and go back to my place? We can do a little more *catching up*. It will be just like old times."

Sarah let the proposition sink in. It didn't take a lot of internal debate. She was desperate to get Keller out of her head and she knew Jill wasn't looking for anything serious. "Sounds good to me. I just have to pass along a message first."

Jill stood and offered a hand to Sarah. "I'm going to grab another beer and hit the dance floor while you do your thing then. Just come and get me when you're ready, okay?"

Sarah gave her a pinch, eliciting a squeak. "I never could keep you off the dance floor. Don't worry, I shouldn't be too long." Jill made her way over to the bar and Sarah headed for Keller's office. Nervously, she knocked on the door just below the manager sign.

Keller's voice was nearly a growl. "Enter." When Sarah walked in, Keller gave her a look that managed to be both angry and hurt at the same time. "Yes?"

"Can we talk for a minute?"

Keller waved a hand toward the leather chair sitting adjacent to the couch. "Have a seat."

Sarah took note of Keller's tired blue eyes and the dark circles underneath. Signs of the manager's exhaustion were clearly evident. She decided to just say what she had come to say and get out as soon as possible. "Annie is worried about you. She tells me that you're working fourteen hours a day, every day of the week."

Keller leaned forward, with her hands interlaced on her desktop. "Why doesn't she tell me herself?"

"She says you won't talk to her." Sarah blew out a frustrated breath. "She practically begged me to try and talk some sense into you."

Keller stood abruptly, sending her chair rolling backward. As Keller stalked toward her, Sarah came to the alarming realization that the other woman was pissed. And she knew without a doubt that Noble Keller could be a very dangerous woman. "Keller, you can't keep working like this. You will wear yourself out. Trust your employees, they can handle it."

Keller leaned forward and pinned Sarah's arms to the chair. Her voice was quiet but the anger could be heard quite clearly. "I don't think either my job or my welfare is any of your concern." She lashed out, her words cutting deep. "You've made it abundantly clear that there is nothing between us but sex. That you have plenty of other—*friends* to keep you occupied. Unless—you've changed your mind?"

Sarah slowly shook her head and whispered, "No." She was a little afraid of the angry woman in front of her. She was also turned on by the sheer dominance on display in front of her. They were so close that she was engulfed by Keller's scent. Ignoring her racing heart and shallow breathing, she tipped her chin up defiantly. "Fine, I'll leave you alone then."

Keller didn't move for a few seconds. Finally, she released Sarah's arms and put her hands on the back of the chair on either side of Sarah's head. She leaned in slowly, giving Sarah plenty of time to pull back. When the singer didn't, she kissed her. The kiss was as aggressive as the woman doing the kissing. With tongues gliding together, she dominated the mouth of the woman in the chair. Sarah felt like her entire body was on fire and she pulled Keller even closer. Keller suddenly jerked away and stood up. Her blue eyes had gone nearly black with desire. Sarah was breathing hard but she didn't miss the trickle of blood running down the other woman's lip. Keller saw Sarah's look and wiped her mouth with the back of her hand, blood smearing across tan skin. Sarah continued to stare, something nagging at the back of her mind. Then realization dawned. "Keller, your lip—" She pointed. "—why is your lip bleeding?"

Keller's eyes widened for a second then she walked to the bookshelf by the door and grabbed a tissue. She cleaned the back of her hand then dabbed at the small cut caused by Sarah's teeth. Keller ran her tongue over the cut and tasted blood. She looked at Sarah with panic on her face then stared at the floor. "You need to leave."

Sarah jumped up and hurried over to the other woman. "Let me see it. Are you okay? You shouldn't be bleeding!"

With dark eyes flashing, Keller pinned her to the office door. "I said you need to leave. Now!" She abruptly released Sarah and strode to the opposite side of the small office.

Sarah gave her one last look then fled the room. It wasn't the words that sent her away, it was the look in Keller's eyes. She looked hungry. After a few calming breaths, she walked back out into the main bar. In her preoccupation, she almost ran into Jill who was coming off the dance floor. "Are you ready?"

The redhead laughed. "Ready, willing and able!" The look on Sarah's face as she turned toward the front door made her stop and take the singer's hand. "Hey —" Sarah turned around with a questioning look on her face and Jill gave her a compassionate one in return. "Do you want to talk about it?"

Sarah still had a multitude of emotions running rampant through her. Fear, anger, and arousal were the top three. She gave Jill an intense look. "Talking is the last thing I want to do right now!" She practically pulled the other woman out of the bar. "Let's go already."

SARAH ARRIVED HOME Sunday afternoon after spending two nights with Jill getting *reacquainted* and immediately plugged her dead phone in to charge. She could have used the one in her RAV4 over the weekend, but she didn't want to face any potential calls or texts from Keller. She had forgotten how much she missed her friendship with Jill and all the good times they spent together. But deep inside, she couldn't help wishing that it was Keller's hands on her body. In the guiltiest part of Sarah's mind, it was Keller and not Jill that drove her over the edge into oblivion.

Her sister and Duke were gone so she assumed they were at the park down the street. It was Annie's favorite place to go with the rambunctious Husky. She made her way to the bedroom to change out of the clothes she had borrowed from Jill. Her mind was a million miles away as she folded the jeans and t-shirt carefully, placing them on her dresser. Within ten minutes of walking in the door, she was munching cold leftover pizza and drinking a beer. She heard the front door open and seconds later Duke pushed his way into the kitchen. He greeted Sarah enthusiastically so she tossed him a piece of her crust. Annie came into the room a few minutes later and grabbed her own slice of pizza. "It's about time you got home!"

Sarah mumbled, "Why?" around a mouthful of pepperoni and cheese.

Annie launched into the story that had been eating at her for two days. "I tried calling and texting you, but your phone was off!"

Sarah pointed at the phone in question. "It was dead and I didn't feel like using the charger in my RAV4. Why, what's the big deal? I sent a text to let you know where I would be staying."

Annie shot her an annoyed look. "Julie said you were there Friday, but you left too early. You missed all the commotion."

"Commotion? What commotion?"

Annie continued. "Well I was at the Pony when it first started. From what Julie told me, two guys came in and tried to start some trouble. Julie refused to serve them because they were already drunk and harassing the other customers. Big Teddy tried to get them to leave when they started knocking over tables but he was out numbered. By the time Keller got involved, Teddy had the first drunk in a chokehold, trying to restrain him. She ran out just as the second drunk nailed Teddy over the head with a chair. That was when I came over from the other bar. He managed to keep his hold even though the chair cut his head."

Sarah nearly choked on her pizza so she took another healthy swig of beer. "Oh my God! What happened after that?"

"Well Julie had already called the police and they told her it would be about five minutes. But Keller didn't even hesitate. It was—" Annie shook her head in amazement. "—you wouldn't believe it unless you saw it. Before anyone could even blink, she had grabbed one of the tall chairs and was using it to pin the other guy against the wall. It was so tight against his throat he could hardly breathe. Suddenly, he let go of the chair with one hand and grabbed a beer bottle." She made a slashing motion with her hand. "He smashed the bottle on a table and cut her arm open." Annie stopped when she saw her sister's face pale. She walked over and put a comforting hand on the older woman's arm. "She's okay, really."

Sarah just nodded numbly. "So what happened then?"

"Well it was incredible. She threw down the chair and punched him across the jaw with her good fist, knocking his drunken ass out. She did it so fast he didn't even have time to defend himself."

Sarah sighed with relief. "That's crazy! Everyone else was okay though?"

Annie nodded. "Yeah, the cops showed up and arrested the two men. They took statements from witnesses, we got the mess cleaned up, and then it was business as usual." Annie had been having suspicions about Keller for a while. She wanted to talk to

Sarah about them but was nervous. After what she saw at the bar after the fight, she didn't think she should put it off any longer. "Sarah, after the fight I saw something really strange."

Sarah looked up at Annie, noting the serious tone in her voice. "What is it?"

The younger woman was scratching the back of her neck, unsure how to begin. When she did start, her speech was halting and a little disturbed. "Well, um, after everything went down, Keller disappeared into the office to take care of her arm. I stayed to clean the blood off the floor in the main bar but when the police arrived, I went to get her. Sarah, what I saw was—" She paused, searching for words. "Her cut was pretty bad. I saw it before she went to the office. But when I went to get her, she was getting ready to bandage it." She swallowed nervously. "In the office it wasn't even half the original size. It was more than half healed! I mean, it still should have had stitches but—" Annie returned her gaze to her older sister, the woman she trusted more than anyone else. "How? I've noticed strange things going on with her for a while and now I'm more curious than ever to know what's going on." She paused, seeing the strange look on her sister's face. "You think I'm crazy, right?"

Sarah sighed and ran a hand through her hair. "No, I don't think you're crazy." There was no way she could lie to Annie so she did the only thing she could to help Keller preserve her secret. She knew Annie would keep a promise so she swore the younger woman to secrecy and told her everything. She included all the things that had been on her mind for the last few months. Keller's disease and her insistence that they were soul mates were first. She also told of her fears of commitment to Keller, or any woman.

Annie sat in shock for a few seconds, just trying to take it all in. "Jesus! That is so, so—incredible." She looked at Sarah. "You really believe this?"

Sarah nodded. "I've seen it, I can't help but believe. You've seen some of her stuff first hand."

"Wow!"

"Yeah, that's what I said too."

Annie looked at her sister in concern. "So what are you going to do?"

Sarah looked back at her with sadness. "I don't know, Annie, I just don't know."

Their conversation was interrupted when Annie's cell rang. Annie answered it and spent the next few minutes on the phone. Sarah could tell something was wrong just from the tone of her sister's voice and from the worried words from her side of the conversation. After a brief flurry of words, Annie finished the call with reassurance to whoever was on the other end. "Don't worry, I'll find someone to check on her and I'll be there in about fifteen minutes to open up."

Sarah looked at Annie in concern. "What's the matter?"

"Keller never arrived to open the bar this afternoon."

"Was she supposed too?"

Annie started pacing. "I didn't finish my story. She called yesterday and said she wouldn't be in, that she wanted to give her arm a little more time to heal. She has never missed work before and I was worried but she insisted she was fine. And now, she failed to show up for work without calling anyone or answering her own phone." She grabbed her keys off the counter, clearly upset. "I can't even check on her because I need to open the bar for Julie!" She gave Sarah a pleading look. "Could you go over to her place and make sure she's okay?"

Sarah slowly shook her head, remembering Keller's harsh words on Friday. "I don't think that would be a very good idea. We had an argument and she pretty much kicked me out of her office the last time I saw her."

Annie looked thoughtful for a second and mumbled, "Well that would explain her mood." Then louder, "You're the only one that can do it, besides, what if it has something to do with her condition? We can't just let anyone find her."

Pulling herself off the stool, Sarah sighed in defeat. "Fine, I'll go see what's up." She got halfway to the kitchen door and turned around. "For what it's worth, I'm worried too."

Chapter Six

THE CONDO WAS dark when Sarah entered, the windows tinted completely. The only sound came from the steady hum of the refrigerator. The place seemed empty as she quietly made her way toward the bedroom. She hesitated before walking around the corner and precious seconds ticked by. Sarah was afraid of what she might find, but she was more afraid of what she might feel. Finally relenting to the worry that was twisting her stomach, she walked into the bedroom. The sight of Keller's body lying sweat-soaked sent her rushing across the room. Hollow-eyed and still, she looked like a child lying in the king-size bed. Sarah took in the bloody bandage on Keller's arm and the shallow rise and fall of her breathing. She sat on the edge of the bed and took Keller's chilled hand into her own. Guilt and sorrow fought for control as she spoke into the silence of the room. Her words came out as more a sob than a whisper. "This is all my fault—I did this to you."

Keller's eyes fluttered open. "Sarah?"

Sarah scooted closer and rested her palm against Keller's cheek. "Shhh, you don't have to speak, I'm here." Tears filled her eyes as the smaller woman leaned into the caress. "I'm so sorry, Keller, I never meant to hurt you."

Keller weakly lifted her hand to press it against Sarah's, holding it in place. She turned her head to kiss Sarah's palm to reassure her. "It's not your fault, I just overextended myself and when I got hurt I couldn't heal." She shut her eyes for a moment then continued. "Anyway, it's too late now and maybe this is for the best. I can't help but feel as if I've caused more turmoil than good in your life."

Sarah snatched her hand away in shock, suddenly realizing the seriousness of Keller's condition. "Don't say that! There has to be something we can do." She looked at her lover's frail, weak body, completely at a loss. "How can I help you, what can I do? You're just so weak..." She trailed off.

Keller shook her head. "There is nothing you can do, Sarah, just go home."

Sarah could see something in Keller's eyes, an untruth was

ringing in her words. Not sure how she knew that Keller was lying, she confronted her on it. "No, you're lying. There is something I can do, isn't there?"

Keller sighed and closed her eyes. She was very tired and didn't want to answer the question. "I made a promise. I can't and won't ask this of you."

"Tell me!"

Keller smiled sadly. "It's blood, Sarah. This is one of those times that the only thing that will bring me back is fresh blood."

Sarah frowned. "I don't understand. Why didn't you just find some — ?"

"No! You know why." She looked into the singer's eyes and in almost a whisper said, "We've bonded — it can only be you. Being so weak, I couldn't cloud someone to take blood from them and I can't afford to reveal my secret."

Sarah abruptly sat up and ran a shaky hand through her hair. She let out a sigh and glanced at Keller out of the corner of her eye. She saw a mixture of fear, longing, and weariness. In a split second, she made up her mind. "How?"

"No, I won't do it."

Sarah could see Keller's canines, they were extended with hunger. "You don't have a choice. Now what can I do?"

Keller looked into her eyes and saw — something unidentifiable. It was determination, concern, and — something more. For the first time, since meeting the mercurial singer, she had hope. "I'm too weak for empathy and without the pleasure of sex, it will hurt at first."

Sarah climbed onto the bed and lay down next to her. "That's okay, I'll be fine. Now, what should I do?"

Keller looked longingly at the other woman. "First I'd like you to kiss me."

Sarah smiled gently. "No problem." She kissed her slowly, languidly. Their soft lips moved together at a pace set to the rhythm of their beating hearts. Forgetting about the fangs, she slipped her tongue into Keller's mouth. The smaller woman hissed with pleasure as the wet organ slid between ultra-sensitive teeth. Sarah pulled back immediately in alarm. "Sorry."

Keller raised a shaky hand and pulled her back. "Don't apologize, it felt wonderful. More please."

The next kiss started where the first left off, only this time Sarah grew bold with her new knowledge. She stroked her tongue along the lengths of the fangs, careful of the needle sharp points. When she pulled away again, both women were breathing hard with excitement. Sarah's was caused by the knowledge that such a small action from her could thoroughly arouse the other woman. Kissing again, the singer began exploring Keller's body with her hands. Starting at her stomach and working her way up to achingly hard nipples. When Keller arched her back off the bed, Sarah leaned down and sucked one of the nubs into her mouth. She used her tongue in much the same way as she did with the fangs.

Keller moaned weakly at the pleasurable contact. "Sarah, please—I need more!"

Sarah stopped her ministrations and looked into blue eyes gone dark with desire. She slowly lifted her wrist toward Keller's mouth. "Is this what you want?"

Keller's nostrils flared as she stared at the pale blue vein on the inside of Sarah's wrist. Her response was a whisper. "That will do well enough." She lifted her hands to cradle Sarah's arm and made eye contact with her as she slowly moved the precious pulse toward her mouth. Keller was watching for any signs that her lover had changed her mind. When the wrist was close enough, she ran her tongue along the length of it. Sarah sucked in a breath, startled at how aroused the one action made her. Seeing no signs of rejection, Keller gently pierced the skin. Between the combination of needle sharp teeth and slow movements, Sarah didn't really feel anything until Keller began sucking at the flowing blood. The minute the precious thick fluid hit Keller's tongue, there was a flash that seemed to sizzle against their skin. Like static electricity in a lightning storm. Sarah was hit with a massive wave of arousal and the occasional glimpse of Keller's emotions. But the only thing that scared her during the entire experience was that buried within their emotional connection, she found a steady core of love coming from Keller. In that instant, Sarah became completely aware of the depth of Keller's emotion for her. She feared that Keller read hers in return and would know the depth of her own emotions for the bar manager.

After only a few minutes, the singer began to whimper from the combination of emotional overload and arousal and Keller pulled away. She licked the two tiny puncture wounds gently and they closed almost immediately. Her breath caught in her throat as she watched Sarah's eyes flutter open.

"Are you okay?"

Sarah looked into Keller's eyes. It was impossible to make out the blue irises in the darkness of the room. She could only see the eerily light ring around the other woman's pupils. Licking her lips, she answered. "That was—" Sarah sighed with a euphoric expression on her face. "—I have no words for it."

Keller smiled faintly. "It was amazing." Keller sat up, feeling immediately rejuvenated. She was tired of the sickness that clung to her in the form of dried sweat and soiled bandages so she unwound the wrap from her healed arm and took it to the trash in the bathroom. While she was there, she lit a few candles and began filling the extra-large Jacuzzi tub. When she returned, Sarah was still lying in the bed with a languid smile on her face. Seeing Keller's activity, Sarah forced herself to get up from the bed. The two women stared at each other for a few seconds, connecting in some primal level before Keller spoke. "Would you care to share a bath with me?"

A look of raw lust flickered across Sarah's face as she watched Keller peeling off her sweaty clothing revealing nothing but gloriously healthy flesh. She worked a suddenly dry tongue around the inside of her mouth and began taking off her own clothing. She kept her eyes focused on Keller the entire time. "It's funny you should ask. I'm feeling kind of—hmm, dirty all the sudden." She preceded Keller into the bathroom wearing nothing but lavender toenail polish and a smile.

Keller could feel the emotional connection between them stronger than ever and she was desperately drawn in Sarah's direction. The arousal from her feeding was still pulsing wildly within her and only the demanding need to be clean kept her from ravaging the other woman the instant she was healed.

Inside the bathroom, there were vanilla candles placed all around and the golden light reflected in the mirror as well as the water. Keller walked in and saw her lover already surrounded by swirling water. Sarah looked radiant, the candles just bright enough to make out the green of her eyes. She stopped with a sudden indrawn breath. "You are so beautiful." Her eyes fixed on Sarah as the singer massaged her own breasts as they floated in the water. She took special care of her nipples, moaning at her self-exploration. Keller quickly entered the tub and pushed Sarah's hands out of the way. Both women groaned at the feel of skin sliding against skin. With her hands busy palming Sarah's breasts, Keller feverishly devoured her lips and mouth. Sarah raised her leg and firmly planted a knee at the apex of the shorter woman's legs and Keller wasted no time sliding along it to build pleasure. The overwhelming passion both women felt while Keller drank from Sarah's wrist returned full force, sending water over the edge of the large tub with their movements. Keller slid one of her hands lower. In a move that was surprising but not uninvited, she entered her lover with two fingers. It wasn't until her thumb grazed Sarah's clit that the taller woman began moaning in earnest.

"Keller, ugh — baby, I'm going to come!"

Hearing those words caused Keller to thrust harder and faster on Sarah's long thigh. She knew that if one of them went over the edge, their bond would pull the other along as well. All she could do in reply was pant into Sarah's ear. "It's okay, let yourself go. I'll be right behind you."

As if she said the magic words, Keller could feel tremors beginning in both of them. Every bit of her concentration was focused on the way the warm walls felt as they started convulsing on her thrusting fingers. Sarah felt the molten heat begin as a tiny spark deep inside her, and then grow until it consumed them both. When her orgasm hit, she hoarsely screamed as she fell over the edge into oblivion. A split second later, Keller tumbled after her. The two women collapsed in relief into the still sloshing water, letting the Jacuzzi sooth their bodies and the afterglow ease their souls. In a moment of clarity, Sarah realized she would never be able to run from Keller again. She was both disturbed and relieved to feel the bond between them growing stronger with each intimate touch.

The two women spent a little while longer in the tub, touching and exploring each other. The object was not to arouse, merely to physically connect. When they were out and dry again, Sarah put on a pair of her own sweats that she had left at Keller's condo and called her sister. While she reassured Annie on the phone, Keller grabbed a bottle of water from the refrigerator and turned the lights up over the baby grand. Sarah watched her every move intently as she spoke into the phone. "Listen, Annie, I promise that Keller's fine. She'll talk to you tomorrow." She wet her lips as Keller took a seat and started to play a hauntingly familiar melody. "Uh — do you think you can take care of Duke for me tonight? I'll be staying here with Keller." She listened to her sister's affirmative reply then ended the call. Sarah shut the phone off and placed it carefully on the counter then slowly made her way over to the woman playing the piano. Unsure and a little afraid she asked, "How do you know this song? I only just finished it this past week."

Keller slowly stilled her fingers against the keys and captured the musician in a piercing blue gaze. "I heard it when you wrote it."

Knowing she was alone at the time, Sarah pushed. "How is that possible?"

Keller took Sarah's hand and brought it toward her heart, holding it close. "I heard it here, my love." Keller knew she was taking a chance by pushing Sarah so soon after such an emotional upheaval. But she couldn't stay silent about her feelings any longer, not after the connection they shared while she drank from the beautiful singer.

Sarah gasped at Keller's words but she didn't pull her hand away. Instead, she moved closer and sat on the bench next to Keller. She positioned her hands on the keys and looked at her lover expectantly. "Play with me?"

With great concentration and skill, they played the song together. Sarah's left hand and Keller's right, playing the song as it had been written. The music was sad and a little dark but when Sarah's right hand reached out to play a descant in the higher keys it left both women with goose bumps. The melody was both haunting and lost. When the song came to an end, Keller carefully put the cover back over the keys. She picked up Sarah's left hand, idly tracing the talented fingertips, and spoke softly. "I'm tired and I want to hold you, will you come to bed with me?"

Clear green eyes met those of the weary bar manager. "Any time you need me, Keller. I won't avoid you anymore. I promise."

WHEN SARAH GOT home the next afternoon, her rambunctious Husky greeted her at the door. She spent a few minutes giving him love and a few scratches. She laughed aloud as his leg started to kick when she reached a good spot. At the sound of her laughter, Annie and Jesse emerged from the kitchen. Annie was on her sister immediately. "How's Keller?"

Sarah spared a quick glance at Jesse. "Oh, she's fine. She wasn't feeling well and turned her phone off. She forgot that she was going to open on Sunday, you know how it is. She'll be in tonight though." The look she gave her sister indicated there was more that she would tell later, so Annie let the explanation slide.

"Oh, all right. I'm glad she's feeling better."

Sarah was still a little mentally unsteady after the previous day and she was looking for a way to burn off some excess energy. Looking at the young couple, she asked, "So what do you two lovebirds have planned for this fine Monday?"

Both women blushed but Jesse answered. "Neither of us have work and my class was canceled so we were going to pick up some take-out and see if there's anything on cable. Why, you want to come with?"

Annie snickered and mumbled, "She probably already did, earlier."

Sarah shot her a look. "No, I thought that if none of us were busy we could tackle the basement. It shouldn't take long for the three of us to do a little rearranging and organizing to make room for Jesse's stuff."

Jesse turned red and Sarah shot a quick glance at her girl-friend before answering her sister. "Well — Jesse hasn't actually said yes yet." She sighed. "She said she didn't want to impose."

Sarah walked over to the young woman who was fast becoming like another sister to her. She put an arm around Jesse's shoulders. "And how do you think you'd be imposing, Jess? You're practically part of the family already!"

Jesse looked up at her with a smile on her face and tears in her eyes. "Thanks, Sarah, you don't know how much that means knowing that I still have people who care about me, you know?"

"No problem, kiddo. So is that a yes?"

Annie waited in silence for the answer, her face hopeful. Jesse grinned and nodded. In a way, she had been waiting to be asked by both sisters. That way she could be absolutely certain that she was welcome into the Colby home. "There is no place I'd rather be!"

At the affirmative answer, Annie gave a whoop and jumped into her girlfriend's arms, wrapping her legs around her waist. The kiss she gave Jesse had Sarah shaking her head and heading toward the basement door, calling over her shoulder. "Come find me when you're done, and be prepared to work!"

After a few hours, the basement was finished and the three women had each crashed on an old, overstuffed couch. Sarah said, "I'm up for pizza."

Jesse sighed and nodded her head in agreement. "And bread-sticks!"

Annie wiped the back of a dirty hand across her equally dirty forehead. "And beer, I am so thirsty!"

Sarah guffawed. "Listen to you, big drinker!" She and Jesse both burst out into rowdy laughter then proceeded to beat the younger woman with musty pillows. They were still laughing when they chased Annie up the stairs and into the bathroom where she shut and locked the door. When they heard the shower start, they looked at each other simultaneously and said, "Oh shit!"

Sarah shook her head and made a beeline for the kitchen. "I'll call in the pizza order. See if you can get her to hurry." The musician chuckled to herself when she heard Jesse pleading with Annie to let her in. After she made the phone call, she walked back out of the kitchen in time to see Jesse slipping through the bathroom door with a smirk on her face. She groaned and planted herself on the couch with the TV remote. Duke jumped up next to her and put his head on her lap while she flipped through the channels. Petting the canine's head absently, she remarked, "So much for them hurrying, huh?" Duke just whined and nudged her hand for more attention.

Thirty-five minutes later, the doorbell rang just as the bath-room opened to a cloud of steam and giggling girls. Sarah called out, "I don't suppose one of the clean girls would like to get the door?"

Annie came back around the corner heading for the front door, wearing nothing but a towel. Sarah yelled, "Annie!" just as Jesse yelled, "Hey!"

Annie turned back to them with an impish look on her face. "What?"

Jesse covered her face with her hand and went down the hall toward the bedroom. Sarah groaned and started digging in her wallet for some cash as the impetuous younger woman opened the door. "Here, you're going to need this."

"No she's not."

Sarah's head jerked up at the sound of Keller's voice. She had to swallow down the nervous butterflies that threatened to find their way out of her stomach. The bar manager was standing on the front porch, wearing her favorite hooded sweatshirt and a pair of sunglasses, and holding two boxes from the pizza place. Annie immediately relieved the shorter woman of the boxes and scolded her. "Get in here you shit, did you pay for those?"

Keller grinned and came in but kept her eyes on Sarah. "Yeah, but don't worry about it. You can get me next time."

Annie gave her the evil eye but capitulated. "All right, but you have to at least have dinner with us." Giving the two older women their space, she made her way into the kitchen to drop off the pizzas, then back into her bedroom to dress.

Keller stood just inside the door, unsure of her reception. Sarah noticed and immediately stepped forward to give her a long hug as she whispered in her ear. "I missed you."

Keller sighed, truly happy for the first time in months. "I missed you too. I just thought I'd stop on my way to the bar, I hope that's okay."

Sarah pulled back to look at the woman that had come to mean so much to her. "First of all, I know for a fact that this house is not on your way to the bar —" Keller gave her a slightly guilty look and she continued. "— and second, you're welcome anytime. I meant it when I said no more running." They stared at each other in wonder at the direction their relationship was taking, and then gave in to the need for deeper connection. The kiss lasted long enough for the two younger women to emerge from the bedroom, spy them, and retreat into the kitchen with the promise of food. When the kiss slowly came to an end, they pulled back but continued to hold each other. The mood was broken for Sarah when she caught a whiff of something and realized it was her own sweat. She pulled out of Keller's embrace and blushed. "Ew, sorry about—" She gestured to her dirty, sweaty clothes. "We were cleaning the basement and the kids stole the shower before I could get in there."

Keller looked into the verdant eyes of the woman she loved and grinned. "I didn't even notice."

Sarah snorted. "Bullshit but thanks anyway. Listen, if you go save me some pizza, I can be in and out of the shower in five minutes."

Keller gave her a lecherous look. "Better yet, we could take a long shower together and hope for the best on the pizza."

The musician laughed and swatted her on the shoulder. "Nice try but I don't think so. I'm pretty sure they used most of the hot water." She winked at the other woman. "Later though for sure."

Blue eyes twinkled at the promise implied. "I'm counting on it." Keller turned before her libido could get the better of her and set a quick pace into the kitchen. Sarah watched the shorter woman's tight ass walk through the door then went off to take the quickest shower in history.

In the kitchen, Annie and Jesse were busy making silly faces at each other and happily munching away. Keller grabbed a paper plate and a slice of her own then hopped up on a barstool. Annie swallowed her bite and leveled a cool eye at her boss. "Just for the record, Miss Keller, I should so kick your ass for scaring us like that!" Keller kept chewing and pointed at her own chest with a look on her face that said "who, me?" Jesse wisely kept silent. Annie continued. "Yeah, you!" A few minutes of silence went by while they ate then Annie cocked her head to the side. "Well at least you look better than you did a few days ago." She didn't mention the bandage that was neatly wrapped around Keller's arm. She knew without a doubt that there would be nothing underneath but healthy healed skin.

Keller shrugged. "Sorry about that and yeah I feel a lot better. I think I was just tired and sore from the fight at the bar the other night."

Annie grumbled only partially under her breath. "Not to mention pissed at a certain wishy-washy brunette we all know and love."

Jesse, who had noticed Sarah and Duke's entrance into the kitchen, slapped her on the arm and hissed. "Annie!"

The younger sibling turned to the door with a sweet smile on her face. "Heh, hi, sis. We saved you some pizza!"

Sarah growled. "Whatever, brat! We'll talk later about what's appropriate to say to someone's significant other. Unless you'd rather I spill my guts to Jesse now..." She left the threat hanging in the air.

"Don't even think about it! If you tell her anything about me as a kid, I'll kill you."

Sarah laughed and tugged Annie's ear lobe then grabbed her own pizza. "Yeah, you and what army, kiddo?" Despite the friendly squabbling, the look the two sisters shared was full of love.

Keller looked at Jesse. "Have they always been like this?"

Jesse shrugged her shoulders. "Beats me." Then she took another bite.

Sarah pointedly changed the subject. "So when is your lease up, Jesse? We need to come up with a day when all of us are free so we can help move you."

Keller gave the three women a surprised look. "Jesse's moving? Where?"

Annie smiled broadly. "Here with us! Isn't that awesome, Keller?"

Keller smiled fondly at the younger women while an interesting thought concerning Sarah's living situation popped into her head. "Sure is, A."

Sarah smirked. "Be sure to keep your calendar open, Keller, we're going to need some help with the heavy lifting."

Annie looked at her diminutive boss and snorted. She then remembered the bar fight and nodded seriously. "Oh yeah, good thinking, sis." She leered at her lover. "You two can carry all the regular furniture. We'll get the bed, won't we hot stuff?"

A pretty red blush worked its way up Jesse's neck until her face was a vivid scarlet. Her mouth gaped open and she turned to look at Sarah. "Has she always been like this?"

The older sister burst out laughing. "Only since you got into her pants!" She looked at Keller. "Little Miss Innocent has hit the road for good." Everyone laughed at that, even the little miss in question. Keller regretfully broke up the little party when she finished her last breadstick and looked at her watch.

"Sorry to be a downer, ladies, but I have to get to the bar."

Annie grimaced. "Ooh, work, I forgot about that. Sorry, Keller, but I wouldn't want to be you!"

"Oh, I'm sure!"

Sarah set her unfinished piece of pizza back on her plate. "I'll walk you out."

Dusk was falling outside. A fine mist drifted down from the clouds that had been hanging low all day. Keller wasn't looking forward to going in to work. She wanted nothing more than to sit on her leather couch with Sarah and bask in the warmth of her fireplace. She wanted to explore the newfound closeness that had developed between them. As they walked to the car she voiced her fears. "I hate that I have to leave. I'm still a little afraid that you'll change your mind. I'm afraid that you'll start denying how you feel again."

Sarah took her hand before she could get into the convertible and gazed at Keller sadly. "I'm really sorry for that. I wish the things that I've done these past few months didn't make it so hard to convince you now." A look of regret flashed across her face. "I never meant to hurt you, Keller. I was just so scared." She laughed mirthlessly and ran her free hand through her dampening hair. "Hell, I'm still scared shitless but I'm ready to try."

Keller gave her an unreadable look. "That's all I can ask then." She knew without a doubt what Sarah had not quite been convinced of, there was no *try* for them. They were together whether they wanted to be or not. "Will I see you tonight?"

Sarah smiled and leaned in for one last kiss. "Of course, I'll be there when you get home."

Keller nodded once then got into her car and drove away.

Chapter Seven

THE NEXT FEW weeks moved by rapidly. The community had settled down quite a bit with the apparent absence of the mysterious basher. Sarah spent about half her evenings at Keller's condo and the other half in her and Annie's home. The Sunday morning of Jesse's move dawned clear and warm. An hour before noon, Sarah and Annie sat in their kitchen drinking cooling cups of coffee. Per the usual, both women added enough sugar that they didn't need the caffeine jolt. Sarah gave her sister a soft smile. "So today's the big day, huh? Are you excited?"

The younger woman was practically giddy, not needing the coffee or the extra sugar to get her going. To her sister's inquisitive eyes, she almost seemed to glow. "Oh my God, Sarah, you have no idea!"

"So what is the plan for the day, how much stuff does she actually have?"

Annie cocked her head to the side to think. "Her apartment was furnished, so surprisingly little." She slowly ticked items off on the fingers of her left hand. "Let's see...bed, dresser, TV, nightstand, computer and desk, and boxes containing her clothing and assorted odds and ends."

Sarah nodded. "That shouldn't be too bad then. Keller said she would meet us here at noon, so I know we have at least the four of us. Do you guys have any more of your friends coming to help?"

"No, with so few things, the four of us should be able to do it all in no time. She rented a small moving truck so we could get everything in one trip. You know the kind with one of those dolly things?" She looked at her sister expectantly and when the older woman nodded, she continued. "Anyway, when I talked to her this morning, she was on her way to pick it up. I figured when Keller got here we could ride over to Jesse's apartment together."

Sarah stood to rinse out her coffee cup. "That sounds perfect." She glanced down at her pajama pants and tee shirt. "I'm going to go put some clothes on that I don't mind getting dirty and then run to the store for donuts before Keller gets here. Can you think of anything else that we may need?"

Annie shut her eyes and pursed her lips in consideration. "Hmm, how about ice? Then we can put some drinks in a cooler and have them handy while we're loading the truck."

Sarah laughed. "Good thinking, Annie-girl!" She grinned devilishly and swatted the younger woman on the arm as she walked by. Calling over her shoulder, she said, "Just think, someday you'll be as smart as me!"

Annie chuckled and finished her own coffee. "Yeah, yeah, whatever!"

After Sarah left the donut shop, she stopped at the convenience store near the house so she could get some ice for the cooler. Something heavy had been weighing on her mind since shortly after Keller drank of her blood. Not wanting to upset the fragile relationship they were beginning, Sarah had not brought the subject up with her lover. Despite their initial conversation about Keller's vampirism, Sarah wasn't exactly clear on how Keller's disease was transmitted. Because of that ignorance, she panicked a little more each day thinking that maybe letting her lover do what she did wasn't completely safe. Sarah wasn't just against being infected with Keller's disease, she was terrified. She knew Keller could tell something was bothering her but Sarah had yet to confide her fears.

LATER THAT EVENING, the four women finished eating the Thai Guys take-out they had picked up after unloading the last of Jesse's furniture. Tired but content, Annie and Jesse were in the love seat snuggled together watching TV and Keller was in the kitchen helping Sarah with the dishes. Duke sat patiently next to the counter, awaiting any scraps that might fall. Keller voiced an idea she had earlier in the day. "Hey, since this is the girls' first night living together, what do you think about staying the night with me?"

Sarah rinsed the last plate and carefully placed it into the dishwasher. She gave her lover a curious look. "They've been dating for months. It's not like one or the other staying the night is a novelty."

Keller gave her a little grin. She thought to herself in a little singsong voice, *she's missing the point.* "Well, it is a lot different when you're actually taking the big step of moving in with someone." At Sarah's continued uncomprehending stare, she continued, "Not to mention they'll probably be twice as loud tonight as they normally are."

Sarah made a face. "Ahh—I see your point." She thought for a second, scratching at her ear before slowly shaking her head. "I don't think that would be a good idea. Duke has a vet appointment first thing tomorrow morning so I would have to drive all the way over here, then drive all the way back past your condo." She gave her lover a sad smile. "I would love to stay the night with you otherwise."

Keller gave her a smile that was both shy and proud. "Well, I think I have a solution for you then."

"What's that?"

The bar manager watched the other woman's face to gauge her reaction while she spoke. "I made a trip to the pet store the other day and picked up all the things Duke would need to stay the night." She continued before Sarah could think of forming an objection. "There's even a great park that runs between the condo and the river. Many people walk their dogs down there. It's very open and clean."

Sarah was touched by the gesture but almost giggled at Keller's demeanor. She walked over to her lover and slid her arms around the shorter woman's waist. Standing in the close embrace, Sarah leaned down and gently kissed her on the lips. "You didn't have to do that but thank you very much." Looking into the beautiful blue eyes of the woman who was quickly claiming her heart, Sarah didn't feel her usual fear at their deepening intimacy. It felt nice, it felt right. After another slightly longer kiss, Sarah pulled away. With a wink and a grin at Keller, she addressed the dog. "Come on, Duke, let's go pack your pajamas."

On her way through the living room, Sarah informed her sister of her plans. Annie raised her eyebrow. "What about Duke's vet appointment tomorrow morning? Do you need me to take him?" The look on both her and Jesse's face indicated their feelings on that particular idea.

Sarah smiled at the two women on the couch. "No, Duke is coming with me to Keller's tonight." Annie gave her an incredulous look and she added, "Apparently she has made her condo pooch friendly with all the comforts of home. He should be fine."

"Oh, okay then." The last was said distractedly as Jesse began to run her fingers across Annie's neck seductively. Sarah shook her head and went to pack an overnight bag for her and Duke.

She was suddenly very glad of Keller's invitation and was touched by the extent to which the bar manager had gone to make her feel welcome. She also thought that being alone with Keller later might be a good time to talk and voice some of the concerns she had running through her head. Her voice was a quiet murmur in the stillness of her bedroom. "We'll have to see..."

Duke was excited to go for a ride. Sarah laughed at the fidgety dog's actions. Usually he would whine at the door when she would leave to stay the night with Keller. She felt bad for him but she didn't know what else she could do. She smiled to herself during the short drive to Keller's condo. Her lover had come up with a perfect and touching solution. After parking in the visitor's lot, Keller walked up and took Sarah's duffle bag while she clipped the lead to Duke. The three of them went inside the big building but the elevator proved to be too much for the friendly dog. He balked at the opening. Sarah apologized as she tried to lift the reticent dog and carry him through the doors. "I'm sorry, Keller, I don't think I've ever tried to get him in an elevator before."

Even though Sarah was embarrassed for her pooch's behavior, Keller took it all in stride. She laughed. "Well I could carry him through the door with no problem but I don't want to freak him out. So we'll just go with plan B and take the stairs up."

When they walked through the door to the condo, Duke immediately took off to explore his new surroundings. Keller laughed at his antics while Sarah yelled, "You better be good, buddy, and stay out of the toilet bowl!"

Sarah took her overnight bag into the bedroom just as Duke was making his way back to the kitchen where Keller was busy looking for a nice bottle of wine. When the curious dog stuck his head into the wine cooler with her, she laughed and pushed him back out of the way. She sat her selection on top of the counter and opened another cupboard nearby. "Hey, buddy, you want a treat?" The Husky immediately sat on his haunches with his big duster tail sweeping a path on the hardwood floor. Sarah came back and stood near the island, watching her pooch shamelessly perform tricks for the expected reward. Once he had his snack, Keller showed him where his new food and water dishes were, as well as a large fleece dog bed and a few assorted toys. Sarah laughed as she watched the Husky settle into his new bed with a hard rubber chew toy, knowing he was in doggy heaven.

"Now that he's taken care of, what ever shall we do, hmm?"

Keller laughed at the seductive look in her lover's green eyes. She popped the cork on the wine bottle and grabbed a couple of glasses from the rack then walked into the living room. She set the items on the low coffee table then went over to turn on the fireplace. "I think I've got it covered." Even though it was July, the evening turned rainy and cool after they got the last of the stuff moved. The flickering light from the flames provided a nice ambiance and helped take some of the wet chill from the air.

Flushed with interest, Sarah nodded and walked toward Keller, who was already reclining on the butter-soft leather couch. "Oh yes, that will work for starters." Once they were both seated with the wine poured, Sarah raised her glass in a toast. "To Annie and Jesse, I hope they don't wear out the bed on the first night!"

Keller laughed. "Here, here!"

They sat in silence for a few minutes, shoulder to shoulder. Both women were reveling in the simple act of being near each other. Their height difference was even more obvious on the couch yet they seemed to fit together somehow. Keller knew something had been bothering her lover. She could feel Sarah's unease through their growing bond but she knew the hazards of pushing things too soon with the emotionally reticent singer. She had a feeling that some quiet time alone might just make Sarah open up and discuss what the problem was. She didn't have to wait long.

"Keller..." Sarah began tentatively.

Keller was gently caressing Sarah's fingertips with her own. She looked up at Sarah's inquiry. "Yes?"

Nervously, Sarah raked her free hand through her hair and thought of how to continue. She looked at Keller, reassured by the blue eyes gazing back at her. "I—um, I was wondering if you could tell me a little more about how your disease is transmitted."

Suddenly Keller knew what had been bothering the other woman. She put a comforting hand on Sarah's arm. "It's okay. There is no possible way you could *catch* my disease just from letting me drink your blood. You have to be near death to get it and even then there has to be an exchange of fluids for you to be infected." She gave her lover tender smile. "You're safe, I promise."

Sarah blushed at having her fears so easily read. Embarrassed, she pulled her hand free and stood to walk across the room. She looked out the windows into the city. Her fears went so much deeper than merely becoming infected. "I'm sorry, I'd like to explain I—I just—" She stopped, unable to fully verbalize the many emotions she had running through her head.

Keller stood and joined her at the windows. "It's fine, you don't have to explain if you don't want."

Sarah looked away from the window and down at her lover. She sighed and reached out to take Keller's hand. "I know I have a lot of issues, and I know you've been very patient with me."

Keller pointed toward her own teeth. "Hello, you have issues?"

Sarah laughed and jiggled the shorter woman's hand. "Yeah, I guess you're right. But still..." She took a deep breath. "Can we go sit down again? I would like to try to explain this a little better." After the women were seated back on the couch, Sarah began to talk about herself, something she had been reluctant to do in all their previous times together. Keller knew some of Sarah and Annie's history from the younger sister but she really wanted to hear things from Sarah's point of view. Sarah told her what life was like with two loving parents and what it was like having a much younger sibling. It didn't take a psychiatrist to know that the singer's fear of loss and subsequently, her fear of commitment, began with the death of her parents. Keller suspected that that another reason her lover didn't want to be tied down was due to the fact that she was forced into a responsibility that she neither wanted nor was ready for—raising her younger sister.

They talked for hours, starting with Sarah's fears and later progressing to what each woman wanted from a relationship. At the end, Sarah looked seriously into Keller's eyes. "Keller, as much as I care for you, Annie is the most important person in my life. I don't want to watch her grow old while I stay young. In addition, I don't want to watch her die while I'm still alive and healthy. I'm sorry, but I would rather stop seeing you right now if there were any chance of me catching what you have."

Keller thought for a second, digesting her lover's words. She knew they were soul mates but she was also frustratingly aware that there was nothing she could say that would convince Sarah. Keller's survival depended on the other woman now that they were bonded. She could only hope that in time the singer would change her mind. "Believe me when I say that I do understand. I promise that you can't get what I have unintentionally."

Sarah looked at her but she had to drive the point home and make something clear. "It's not just on accident that I'm worried about." She looked deep into Keller's eyes. "You have to promise me that you'll never infect me, no matter what happens."

Keller returned the gaze and gave her solemn vow. "I promise that I'll never infect you – unless asked." She added caveat for her own piece of mind.

Sarah grinned at the other woman's persistence but she felt safe as long as she had her word. "Good enough – " she kissed her lightly on the lips " – and thanks for understanding."

"No problem, anytime." Keller stood from the couch. "Would you care for some music?"

Sensing Keller's need for intimacy after their emotional talk, and wishing for the connection herself, Sarah nodded. With hooded eyes she watched the smaller woman walk over to the computer screen on the wall and delicately tapped out her commands. A mellow voice and smooth acoustic guitar emanated from the speakers in the bedroom. With a few more keystrokes, the lights lowered and she made her way back to the wine cooler. She squatted down and opened the door, raising an eyebrow in question. "Any preferences?"

Sarah stood and brought the glasses and empty bottle back to the kitchen island. They had finished it sometime during their long talk. "Anything sounds good to me. Are you interested in a Jacuzzi bath?"

Keller looked up from her rummaging and smirked at the other woman. "Are you feeling a little dirty tonight?"

Green eyes twinkled back at her. "Maybe. I'll go run some water just in case."

Their time in the tub started out innocently enough, it was both relaxing and comfortable. The wine, candles, and music added a sensuality that soon escalated their physical interaction. Wanting to show trust in her lover, Sarah let Keller take the lead. They were nearly horizontal with Keller facing Sarah in the tub, nestled between the taller woman's legs. The kissing was slow and languid at first, with gentle touches and teasing thrusts of the tongue. A moan escaped Sarah when Keller's knowing fingers grazed her nipple. Both women were nearly overwhelmed by the feel of skin sliding together in the water. After only a few minutes of caresses and kissing, their arousal began to simmer over. Keller eased back and slid to the side of the woman below her in the tub. Sarah whimpered at the lack of contact when Keller pulled away but was curious as well.

"Keller, what are you—" Her question was cut off as Keller silenced her with a single finger to the lips.

"Shhh, just close your eyes and let me lead for a while."

Sarah bestowed a look of trust onto her lover as she relaxed into her arms. Keller began placing tiny kisses along her neck and face as her right hand continued to wander. The left was under the singer caressing the firm globes close at hand. Sarah whimpered when fingertips strayed too near a taut nipple. And she hissed in pleasure when Keller followed the finger with moist lips.

"Let me love you." And Sarah did.

JESSE HAD LONG since left for work and Sarah was on her second cup of coffee when Annie stumbled into the kitchen.

Sarah looked up from the paper with a smile on her face. "Hey you! Guess whose name is in the paper, in the entertainment section?"

Excitedly, Annie dropped the box of cereal she considered opening and ran over to the paper that was on the table. "Hot damn! They've got a write up about our Sip & Chug Music Spotlight!" Beyond ecstatic, she did a little happy dance in the middle of the checker-tiled floor. Sarah laughed at her sister's antics, simply happy that her sibling was happy. Annie began reading the article out loud.

"There is an out of the way nightclub downtown that has been soaring in popularity in recent years. This place is called The Merge. Named for its combination of two bars, it features a state of the art dance club and a live music venue all under one roof. And let me tell you, the combination is nothing less than sweet harmony. Two years ago, the nightclub had an influx of fresh blood with the addition of Noble Keller, the manager and mastermind behind The Merge. She started with the stable guidance of long term Assistant Manager of the dance club, Lynne Jackson. Then she successfully renovated and rebranded the business in a way that few ever get to see. Spin, the dance club side, became one of the hottest spots in town. Finally, with the promotion of Annie Colby as the Assistant Manager of the music side of the business, Voodoo Pony has definitely cast a spell over the Columbus live music scene. Their fingers are clearly on the pulse of what is now and happening in the music world today. One example is the addition of the Sip & Chug music spotlight. These are limited series bi-monthly engagements featuring local bands of differing styles, playing opposite Fridays from each other. Nearly five months into the new series and locals are still thirsty for more. Catering to a diverse crowd of music fans inside an already diverse city, The Merge seems to be living up to its name and it's certainly doing everything right."

Annie was practically glowing with excitement when she stopped reading. "This is insane!" She paused for a second and then exclaimed "I need to tell Keller!"

Sarah could only shake her head as she watched her younger sister dash out of the kitchen in search of her phone. Sarah was rinsing her mug when Annie returned a short while later.

"Hey, I just spoke with Keller, and Jesse. Keller suggested we have a celebratory dinner tomorrow, can you make it? I wasn't sure if you had any lessons on your schedule but the rest of us are all free."

Sarah laughed at her enthusiasm. "Well it just so happens that I'm free as well. But I'd reschedule even if it was the mayor of Columbus, just to celebrate with you!"

Annie burst out laughing and then hip checked her sister away from the coffee pot. "Give me a break, you hate the overly-conservative mayor! Some compliment that is."

Green eyes twinkled. "Okay, you got me. But still, I would have worked out something if my schedule had been full." Giving her sibling a serious look, she said, "I'm really proud of you, Annie, and I think Mom and Dad would have been proud too."

With watery eyes, Annie replied, "Thanks — for everything." The hug that followed was full of love.

When they released each other, Sarah subtly pulled herself back together. "All right, I've got to get out of here. I have a one o'clock with a seventy-year-old that wants to learn the drums."

Annie gave her a look of disbelief. "Isn't he a little old? What happens if he has a heart attack?"

Sarah smirked and corrected the other woman. "She. And she turns off her hearing aids when she plays." She walked out of the kitchen with the sound of laughter following her.

SATURDAY NIGHT WAS heavy with the lingering heat that had been building all week. The dog days of summer settled over the city of Columbus and the three women living in the Colby household dressed accordingly for the sweltering evening ahead. Dinner was fairly informal. They planned to meet Keller at a popular tapas restaurant downtown. There was no agenda beyond dinner, they'd decide what to do while they ate. Pitchers of sangria preceded the small dishes of various foods. Keller remarked on the latest news in the bar scene as small plates passed around the table. "Have you guys heard of the new club that opened on Division and Fountain?"

Sarah cocked her head curiously. "I don't remember a club there, just that creepy old gothic church. Or did they finally tear it down?"

The bar manager smiled and shook her head. "No, actually that creepy old church *is* the new club. They've done minimal renovation, mostly removing the bulk of the pews, adding drink bars on every floor, and turning the altar and nave of the main cathedral area into a stage and dance floor."

Sarah raised an eyebrow. "Wow. That just seems so—"

Jesse chuckled, tickled by the idea. "Sacrilegious!" She shook her head and took another bite, then added. "That's great though, I can't wait to see it."

The younger Colby sister giggled as well. "I've heard about the place, it's called Temple du Loup. I also heard it's pretty pricy to get in. But supposedly every Saturday night they have steampunk themed circus performers wandering around and up on a wire above the dance floor. And somehow they scored the hottest DJ in the state, Jon Kaydell! That place is definitely on my radar, if only for professional reasons. I seriously want to check it out—right after my boss gives me a pay raise because the fee to get in is ridiculous."

Keller looked around the table at her dinner companions, then reached into her back pocket. As she pulled out four paper passes, she asked "Well, your boss isn't giving you a raise but you can still satisfy your curiosity. How do you all feel about checking out the place tonight?" She smiled enigmatically. "An old friend of mine is the new manager there. I've got VIP passes if you're interested."

Annie leaned across the table so fast she nearly knocked over her drink. "Oh my God, shut up! Seriously, Keller, how did you score these?"

Sarah grabbed for the glass at the same time Jessie pulled her girlfriend back into a seated position by the waistband of her shorts. Keller just snickered at her employee's enthusiasm. "So is that a yes?"

Jessie shrugged. "I'm down with it, sounds like fun." She glanced over at her girlfriend, who was wiggling in her seat while she stared at the tickets she'd snatched out of Keller's hand. "I think we already know how you feel, babe."

Sarah just laughed at her sister's antics and nodded. "Yeah, sounds good. I've got nothing going on tomorrow so I can stay out late as I want."

After spending a leisurely amount of time over their tapas, the group decided it was time to make their way to the new club. They didn't want to take two vehicles there though and since Annie's house was closest, they had Keller follow them back to drop off her car before they all piled into Sarah's RAV4. With Jesse's back seat full of computer parts and Annie's a legitimate disaster zone of fast food wrappers and assorted crap, there wasn't much of a decision to make. Sarah's vehicle was dirty and road worn so she wasn't concerned about parking on the street. Sometimes nice cars invited vandalism, especially in the less affluent neighborhoods. Jesse volunteered to drive them all home so Sarah gave her the keys once the doors were locked.

As they approached the club from a few blocks away, Jessie gave a whistle. "Holy shit guys, look at the line!"

Keller gave her a little chuck to the right shoulder. "No worries, the VIP tickets will let us jump that."

Annie, who was holding her girlfriend's left hand, grinned. "You're the best boss ever!"

Sarah took in the architecture of the massive building. There was a well-lit stained glass widow that took up two-thirds of the main street side face. The building itself was an amazing bit of beauty with its classic lines and architecture that were found on so many of the churches across Europe. It was a glory of stone and wood construction, featuring high vaulted ceilings and spires.

They followed Keller around to the main entrance on the side of the building. The long line actually snaked around to the front, and many people weren't happy when she bypassed it and walked up to one of the two bouncers stationed at the door. She held up her four tickets and pointed a thumb at the rest of the small group. The noise from the crowd echoed between the buildings on the side street, so they stood there silently. He held up a finger said something into the headset he wore, listened, then looked back and waved them through. "Louve will meet you on the other side."

Once inside, the noise took on a whole new quality. Sarah could hear the music and feel the bass through the soles of her shoes, but it was muted. She stared at the massive revolving wood door. It was like nothing she'd ever seen. Each panel face was carved with the relief of a different wolf's head. There were windows on either side of it, so the inner sanctum could clearly be seen. And there was something else, an energy that pulsed around them. Annie and Jesse didn't appear to notice it so she glanced at Keller. Sarah raised an eyebrow when she caught Keller's eye and the shorter woman grinned. Just when Sarah was about to ask questions about the atmosphere, someone pushed through from the other side. The motion of the revolving door let a bit of music seep through as it spun around. The woman that approached them was short and androgynous with slicked-back black hair. She wore an outfit that could only be described as ringmaster steampunk, consisting of black pants tucked into high black riding boots, a cream shirt with ruffles and a black bowtie, a charcoal gray vest with pre-requisite pocket watch, all minimally covered by a short red coat. The entire outfit was finished off with a black felt top hat wrapped with a set of copper-rimmed goggles, and a curious looking cane. It looked like a graduated length of copper tubing, featuring a handle decorated with swirls and a single brass button.

Annie, sometimes lacking a filter, said exactly what was on her mind. "Well fuck me. That is the sweetest outfit I've ever seen!"

The woman gave her a broad grin and tipped her hat with a little bow. "*Merci!*" When she turned her smile and gaze toward Keller, Sarah noticed her eyes were so dark they appeared black.

The bar manager walked right up to the woman and greeted her with a strong hug and a kiss on each cheek. "*Bonjour ma petite* Louve. *Comment avez-vous* été"

The woman that the other three were assuming was the same Louve the bouncer mentioned responded back to Keller in French. "Keller! *Je suis bon, je vous remercie. Qui sont tes amis?*"

Annie snorted and remarked, "I knew I should have taken French instead of Spanish!"

Jesse swatted her arm. "Shh!"

Keller did the polite thing in mixed company and answered in English. Pointing to Annie first, she continued around the group. "This is my Voodoo Pony manager Annie, her girlfriend Jesse, and Annie's sister, Sarah." Turning back to her little group she added, "Ladies, say hello to Louve, the manager and part owner of Temple du Loup."

Louve smiled at them all and shook their hands, but held Sarah's a little longer. She kissed the back of the singer's hand, and in moderately accented English she said, "It is truly my pleasure." When Keller took a small step forward at their prolonged contact, the French woman abruptly dropped the appendage. With a curious smile she looked back at Keller. "Oh, *est que la façon dont il est?*" When Keller gave her the slightest of nods, she added "Âmes-soeurs?" Keller hesitated, and then gave another nod. The French woman's grin got even wider. "Interesting."

Sarah's curiosity was piqued. "So how do you know Keller?" Louve laughed, and the sound flitted down Sarah's spine like a melody of rain. Sarah looked at her sister and Jesse and became slightly unnerved that they didn't appear to be affected in the least. When she dared a glance at her lover, Keller's face only held a slight smirk.

The French woman grabbed Keller's hand and shook it slightly before releasing it again. "Oh, this one and I — we go way back. Don't we, Keller? My late wife introduced us many, many years ago. *Je l'espère, elle a trouvé la paix dans la mort*" A frown graced her lips for but a second before sliding back into her easy grin.

Keller frowned as well. "I will always be sorry for the loss of Catherine." Sarah's gaze narrowed at her, wondering if this was the same Catherine from centuries ago. And if so, who was Louve?

Louve waved her off. "*Non.* It is your fault *mon ange de sang,* but it is forgivable, no? Let us not speak of this again."

Keller's tousled blond head gave a nod before she seemed to shake free from her memories. "Very well. Instead, why don't you tell us about your club? I like the revolving door, it's a nice touch."

Cane tapping occasionally on the floor, the petite ringmaster led them to the large, carved revolving doors. "Oh yes, it was a grand idea! It allows for a steady stream of people in and out, while keeping the noise and temperature from leaking into the foyer here. Our fire-breathing twins actually did the carving. It is beautiful, no?"

Their little group stared at the carved work of art. Jesse's whispered comment was barely heard. "It's amazing!"

Before they could say any more, a lithe costumed man pushed through the door. "Louve!"

Their hostess looked at him and quickly pulled out her pocket watch. "*Merde*!" She turned to the four VIPs. "Forgive me, but I must go. I am the ringmaster after all but please look around and enjoy the show!" Then as abruptly as she appeared, she was gone.

Sarah leaned over and whispered in Keller's ear. "Catherine? Is that?" Keller's blue eyes looked dark in the low light as she nodded her head. The singer glanced at her sister and Jesse and kept her voice at a whisper. "Will you tell me the story later?"

"Yes."

They were interrupted by Annie. The younger women were heading for the revolving door. "Come on you two, I want to see this place!"

Sarah laughed at her sibling's enthusiasm. "We're coming, don't get your panties in a bunch!"

As the foursome exited the revolving doors and stepped to the side, they could only stand in awe. The peak of the vaulted ceiling stood nearly four stories above them. There were high wires crisscrossing one story above the dance floor, and at the opposite end of the cathedral stood a great stage with Louve under a spotlight. The music had been lowered to a throbbing growl, and the French woman's voice cut through like a knife. "Hello, my new friends! I see you have all braved the teeth of the wolf to come worship in our temple. And we, myself and all my antiquated brothers and sisters, give you the warmest of greetings. We have all been so hungry to have you! So, enjoy the music from the famous DJ Jon Kaydell. Let him fuel the beast inside. Enjoy the finest liquors we have to offer, dance like there will be no tomorrow, and welcome to Cirque du Loup! The Wolf's Circus!" She gave a broad sweeping gesture behind her as the aerial silk acrobats unfurled on either side of the stage. Another spotlight hit high above the dance floor, showing a man and a woman walking the tightropes with no safety net in sight. Laser lights came on to create an intricate floor made of light below the tightrope walkers, and the music cranked back up to a level that shook the temple.

The crowd moved on a dance floor that was made of glass blocks and lit from below by even more shining lights. A low fog rolled around at their feet to creating an eerie glow. Closer to where the little group of four stood, lines snaked from each bar on the first floor and most of the tables in the back appeared to be full as well. Keller glanced around and grinned at the layout. Pool tables, bathrooms, and the main entrance were all near the back of the church. Because of the noise, she merely gestured to the stairs leading up, hoping it would be easier to get a drink once they were off the main floor. She was surprised when Sarah reached down and took her hand, and she paused while Annie and Jesse continued their way up the stairs. When she gave the taller woman a curious look, Sarah leaned close to be heard.

"I feel—" She paused to search for the words. "—strange here. It's like there is pressure pushing on me from all sides."

Keller was having the same problem and knew what it was but wasn't sure how to explain it without talking about the metaphysical stuff that Sarah insisted on ignoring. She started, hesitantly. "It is their—energy. Louve and her Cirque du Loup are—more than they appear."

Sarah cocked her head in confusion. "How do you mean?"

A hand raked through blond hair as Keller sighed and tried again. "There are things in this world, people like me, who are—different. They are legends, stories, and myths, but all very real. Louve is—" She paused unsure if she should continue.

The singer whispered. "She wolf." Her brows rose with surprise and a slight amount of alarm. "They are wolves? Werewolves?" When Keller flashed a surprised look in return, Sarah gave a little smile. "I did take French in college. But come on, they don't really turn into wolves, right? It's probably just more stories and fancy scientific explanations, all bullshit."

Keller raised an eyebrow and took a chance. She could feel every single one of Louve's people around them. They broadcast energy like antennas. It would be intoxicating if she didn't have herself well shielded. Still, there was some leakage, which Sarah had picked up through their bond. Keller relaxed her shield just a little and something like heated lust hammered her from all sides. Her pupils narrowed when she heard Sarah gasp. Keller looked up into those green eyes gone dark and spoke. "Am I bullshitting you, Sarah? Does that feel like a story?" Things tightened low on her body, and she felt her teeth begin to prick her bottom lip at the look on the taller woman's face.

Sarah felt sweat break out all over and she licked her lips. Mouth suddenly dry, her voice was a growl over the music. "No." Turning abruptly, she headed up the stairs and called out to her lover. "I need a drink." The sound of Keller's laughter followed her up the steps before the other woman quickly caught up.

The second level was more like an over-sized balcony, wrapping around the building on three sides, leaving the center completely open from floor to ceiling. There was another large bar at the top of the stairs, and red and black leather booths lined the sides closest to the bar. They had a good view of the tightrope walkers from the second floor, though they were still quite a ways out of reach. After getting their drinks, Sarah and Keller went to stand next to the two younger women that had come up earlier. Farther along the balcony and overlooking the crowd below, there were cages on each side of the dance floor. An identical twin stood in each cage, taking turns breathing fire out over the high wire act. Clearly these were the two Louve spoke of. They were the ones who had carved the massive revolving door. Annie shook her head slowly, still in awe. "Seriously you guys, this place is sick!" She turned to her boss. "Why aren't we this cool?"

Jesse slapped her arm. "Annie!"

Keller just laughed. "Well for one, we don't have a giant gothic church, nor do we have a circus troupe. I guess we'll just have to be boring—you know, as the hottest gay club in Columbus."

Annie rolled her eyes in response and was quickly distracted by her girlfriend's kisses.

Seeing the younger women occupied, Sarah pointed to the curtained alcoves along both sides. "Let's see what's over there." Still feeling out of sorts, she held tightly to Keller's hand. The first alcove had a sign above it that read Tarot, but the curtain was closed. The second was titled Palm Reader and was open.

An older woman smiled at them from inside the opening. She had graying dark hair gathered under a colorful wrap, and her eyes were black as coal. The lines on her face told a story better than any visiting palms she would see. "Come, come! You wish to have reading?" Her words carried a heavy accent, something other than French.

Sarah looked at Keller and the got a shrug in response. "Sure, why not." She took a twenty dollar bill from her wallet to pay for both of them. Once the money was paid, the palm reader came around the table to close the curtains. Curtains shut, the sound was immediately muffled. Sarah raised her eyebrow, wondering just what the material was made of. When the older woman was seated again, she leaned forward with elbows on the table. "Privacy is much important when I read lines. Now, please to give minute for me to clear aura." The woman shut her eyes and Keller's brow furrowed, wondering just how authentic the reader was. Sarah, for her part, remained politely curious. After less than a minute, the woman seemed to shake herself and opened her eyes again. "My name is Sylvie, I have been fortune-teller many years." She squinted and leaned across the table, then poked a gnarled finger toward Keller. "You — you are like hole, like sponge." She pulled her finger back and paused. "You are — *bautor de sânge!*" The look she leveled at Keller carried caution, but no judgment. Then she turned toward Sarah. "And you — there is connection. You are — *bautor de sange de sufletul pereche.* Give me minute!" She stood and shuffled over to a cabinet against the wall.

Sarah looked at Keller and whispered. "What is she saying?"

Keller whispered back. "I don't know. I think she's speaking Romanian, but I don't speak Romanian."

The brunette snorted. "You seem to speak fluent French..."

"I've had a lot of years to practice."

They both shut their mouths when Sylvie turned back around holding two polished milky apple-green stones. She set a stone on the table in front of each woman. "Is Chrysoprase, will bring you much luck! Now, let me to see hands. Who goes first?"

Keller glanced at Sarah and gave her a slight nod. Sarah sighed. "I guess I will. She held out her hands toward the mysterious dark-eyed woman. Weathered hands firmly held the singer's. The old woman's skin was rough from many years of life.

"Hmm, much loss I see. Look — look to your lines." She traced the one running under the base of Sarah's fingers. "This is heart line. You have many lovers, but nothing true." She traced small spidery lines crossing the heart line. "You have suffered loss that is very strong. Perhaps someone close, like family." She looked up at the singer. "Your parents — you have lost both your parents, no? Is many years now since they have gone." Sarah swallowed, and nodded yes. Sylvie continued by tracing another line just below the heart line. "And this is line for head. You have much creativity, you are artist or musician. See the way your line curves and slopes across palm. Again, you have many little spidery lines meaning your loss affects all parts of your life."

Keller was impressed at how accurate the old woman's reading was. She looked at Sarah, who sat very still. "She's very good, isn't she?" Sarah merely nodded and waited for the fortune-teller to continue.

Moving on to trace the longest line on her hand, she spoke again. "This is lifeline. See how straight it is, running across your palm close to the edge. You are very cautious when it comes to relationships. Your past has made you afraid of loss. And no wonder, look here!" She moved her finger to trace a deep line running vertical on Sarah's palm. "Your fate line is one of the deepest I've seen, you are much controlled by the fates. But there will be great change for you. There is point where your interests will be surrendered to others." Moving back to the singer's lifeline, she pointed to an area where the line formed a little circle before continuing on. "Have you been gravely injured, maybe in hospital?"

Sarah gave her a curious look, surprised that Sylvie's words were unexpectedly off track. "No, never. I've been healthy my entire life with no major injuries or sickness. Why?"

The old woman looked up at her, and then moved her gaze to Keller. Her voice took on a rougher, darker quality. "*Veţi pierde aceasta femeie în curând, şi vor fi obligaţi sa schimbe aceasta femeie.*"

Sarah looked at her. "Wait, what does that mean?"

Sylvie turned darkened eyes toward the taller of the two women. "You will face great change. Your soul will die and be reborn. When that time comes, you will know what it means. But until then do not be afraid." She closed Sarah's palm gently. "Do not be afraid." Palm still closed, Sarah slowly pulled her hand back, mind awash with confusion.

Sylvie looked up at Keller. "Now you. You still wish a telling, yes? There is much you know already." Keller slowly slid her hand forward, and the old woman grasped it in a firm grip. "You are very much like your *suflet pereche*. You too have had many lovers, but I think not out of fear. You are clear and have much focus—your head is on ground. But you have many big decisions in life. And look here." She pointed. "Your lifeline has a break here meaning something changed you a long time ago. You know what this change was, *primul deces*. Longer than I can see. But after that break, you have additional lifelines start. You have much strength and vitality, *inima de sânge*. But beware, you are as much controlled by fate as she." She aimed a wrinkled finger back at Sarah. She released Keller's hand and sat back with a sigh. "I am thinking you are done. There is much you already know, your future is past, and past is future. This—" she waved her hand to encompass the small curtained alcove "—it is naught but a swallow from your cup."

As if sensing that was their cue, both women stood. Keller smiled at Sylvie. "You are right and thank you for your time. You have given me much to think about—" She glanced at Sarah. "You have given us much to think about." Keller left another twenty dollar bill on the table as a tip on their way out of the alcove. The dark-eyed palm reader didn't say anything, she simply tucked the money into a fold of the sash around her waist.

Sarah was the first to speak when they exited the curtains into the wash of energy and throbbing bass music. "Well that was—weird. I wish I knew what she said though."

Keller merely whispered while Sarah's head was turned. "You probably don't." Then louder, she asked, "Would you like another drink?"

The singer turned her head away from the stage act and smiled. "Yes please! I'm going to go down this way a little farther so I can see the stage better."

Keller nodded, then noticed the upstairs bar now had a line. She grimaced. "It may be a few minutes."

Sarah glanced around the second floor and didn't see Annie or Jesse anywhere so she assumed they either went up to the third floor or back downstairs. She noticed the balcony area was darker the closer to the front of the church she got. When she reached the end, she found herself staring down into a mass of writhing bodies. The high wire act was gone but the stage now featured jugglers and a knife thrower. She was so engrossed in the action below that she was startled by the voice coming out of the shadows next to her. "So how are you enjoying our show, Sarah?"

Sarah jumped at the voice. "You scared me!" Then she laughed self-consciously and answered. "I love it! The work you've done here is really amazing." She cocked her head at the attractively androgynous French woman. "So how long have you been friends with Keller?"

Louve laughed. It was a beautiful and broken sound that caused goose bumps to race up Sarah's arms. "Oh, we have been friends many years now." She squinted at Sarah, sensing more than just curiosity or the questions of a jealous lover. "Our people are much drawn to her kind you know, we have so much to give. Our energy will fill you up and those like Keller can take it all. It is relationship much like plug and socket. Our peoples seem to fit together." She reached a finger out and traced Sarah's jawline and graced her with a secret smile. "You can feel it too can't you? You can feel us?"

Sarah gasped as a wave of that same energy pushed inside her. Her eyes fluttered closed and she hissed, "Yes." She felt things down low tighten with arousal as whatever the force was caressed her deepest spaces. The energy was intoxicating and it made her dizzy. Because of this, Sarah was completely unprepared when Louve stepped near and pulled the singer down into an aggressively dominant kiss. Before Sarah could respond, they were interrupted by Keller.

"*Salope!*"

Louve abruptly pulled back, leaving Sarah dazed like she was waking from a dream. "K—Keller?" Then she looked down at the little ringmaster and realized what had happened. "You! What the hell?"

Their combined anger only made the French woman smile all the more. "My apologies *buveur de sang*, but she is so delicious! I could not resist."

Sarah was still uncomfortably aroused but refused to let the small woman bate her. Instead she turned it around. "I *am* delicious but there is only one whose mouth is allowed on me—" She pulled Keller into an embrace as her words trailed off. Their mouths made a connection while their bodies were forced to wait.

When they finally pulled apart, they found Louve standing mere inches away. Her hand rose as if she would touch them, red lips parted and breathing rapidly. "Mon dieu! *Vous brûlez ensemble comme les flammes d'un grand feu!*"

Sarah snarled. "*Va te faire foutre!*"

Louve pulled her hand away and smirked. "You have certainly warmed me enough, perhaps I will." With one last look her guests, she gave a little wave and walked away. "Adieu, mes belles."

When she left, Sarah sagged with relief. Keller looked at her in amusement. "I can't believe you told her that."

The taller woman laughed. "Yeah, well, I didn't appreciate whatever that shit was that she pulled on me."

Keller frowned. "Sarah, I'm really sorry. I had no idea she would do that. It's been many years since I've seen her, she seems more — predatory than I remember. And you would be a draw for her."

"Why?"

The bar manager leveled a serious gaze at her. "You know why. We are connected, Sarah. She feels the drag of my power through you just as you feel the push of theirs through me. This — " She once again opened herself to the energy that swirled around them and pushed it through to Sarah.

The taller woman gasped and staggered for a second before turning her hot gaze to Keller. She licked her lips and when she spoke her voice was low, barely audible over the music. "Keller, you can't do this to me in public."

Noticing an empty curtained alcove at the end of the balcony, she grabbed Sarah's hand and pulled her toward it. Once inside she quickly tied the curtains shut to block out curious eyes and pressing sound. "So let's make this a little more private." Sarah had time to suck in a surprised breath before Keller was pushing her against the brick wall at the back of the curtained area. Keller's mouth feasted on her neck while knowing hands wandered up the front of her shirt and under her bra. When the shorter woman got to her ear, she hotly whispered. "Sarah, please..."

Fueled by the pulsing lust from Keller, Sarah threaded her fingers through blonde hair and pulled the smaller woman's head back enough to devour her mouth. While their lips remained unseparated, Sarah's hand made a straight line down the front of the bar manager's loose fitting jeans. She sucked in a breath at the wet heat that enveloped her fingers. Keller moaned at the contact and that was enough to send Sarah's arousal into overload.

Keller moved her own hands to unbutton her jeans and simply said, "More." Sarah pulled her over to a couch, bringing the smaller woman down to straddle her right leg. Then, before Keller could think another thought, the long talented fingers of the guitar player entered her fully. A low moan, punctuated by whimpering cries, was muffled by the heavy curtains around them.

Sarah continued to thrust into her lover while roughly kneading her breasts through the thin t-shirt with her free hand. To return the favor, Keller's strong thigh was pressing firmly into Sarah's over-heated crotch. "Keller—open for me!"

With those words Keller dropped her guard. All the heat, emotion, and lust from the crowd that was amplified by the wolf troupe washed over both of them. It beat them down, like hammered bronze, searing their skin and filling them. The coming orgasm, already hot, suddenly raged out of control as Keller and Sarah drank it all in. As one they cried out and the power finally slipped the bounds of their bodies. Exhausted, Sarah found herself collapsed backward on the couch with her sex throbbing, and Keller was draped across her. The fatigue though was short lived and was quickly replaced by a buzzing vitality. She looked into the darkened eyes of her lover. "Holy shit, Keller!" And then she began to laugh, a response that was quickly joined by the woman on top. Once they were able to get control of themselves, they stood and straightened their clothing, only to be startled by a slow clapping just inside the curtained doorway. Neither woman had seen Louve standing there.

"Magnifique! *Vous êtes belle ensemble.*" She approached the pair and stopped well within their personal space. The French woman took in their swollen lips and flushed faces, then gave a small sniff. She placed a hand on each of their cheeks. "Amazing! I could smell and feel your arousal from downstairs. Speaking of downstairs—" She paused before withdrawing her hands. "If you want to continue this with a third, the priest's house was converted to an apartment." She turned her hot gaze to Sarah. "I promise not to bite." Her teeth clicked together with the last word and she let another rolling wave of energy flow across the women in front of her.

Keller glanced at her lover and watched as Sarah closed her eyes and bit her bottom lip. The arousal they thought quenched mere minutes before was now fanned back to flame by Louve's push of power. She tried to speak and then had to clear her throat to be heard. "Perhaps — perhaps another time." She started to pull her and Sarah away only to be stopped by the French woman's hands clasping around their joined ones. There was a not-unpleasant tingle that ran up both their arms. Louve's voice trembled ever so slightly when she spoke.

"Please — it has been so long since I've felt that. Not since Catherine..."

Sarah looked into the dark eyes of the French woman. The attraction was there, curling around her stomach to places lower. Then she looked at Keller and saw indecision warring in her lover's eyes. Was this something they wanted to do? Was this something they could do? She now understood the connection she had to the bar manager, and also understood the connection her lover had to the long-dead Catherine. Perhaps they all needed this in one way or another. "Keller." When she had her lover's attention she continued. "What would you like to do?"

Louve caressed their joined hands, her eyes holding both hope and sadness. "*S'il vous plaît, mon féroce un.*"

Keller glanced at her, then back at Sarah. Her emotions were torn between her new lover and old memories. "Are you sure?"

Sarah looked into Keller's eyes and let her see the arousal still pulsing below the surface. Her anger at the French woman's earlier actions was replaced by lust and a small amount of pity. Loss is always hard. "Let me text Annie and let her know we'll take a cab home."

Chapter Eight

THE THREE OF them stood in the curtained alcove unsure what to do next. After an excruciating minute of indecision, Louve gave one of her frequent grins and opened fully to them. Keller gasped. "So much power!" Then she opened herself as well and let the energy flow to Sarah. She whimpered as Louve let out a low growl. In a flash, the small French woman was in front of Keller pulling her into a hot and hard kiss. They were nearly the same size, though Louve appeared taller in her fancy top hat and boots. Their struggle for dominance was very real and obvious. Sarah was torn between jealousy and lust but before she could say or do anything, the little ringmaster drew back from Keller and pulled Sarah into a kiss that was just as fierce. Their mouths fought for control and Keller made a sound in the back of her throat, her libido suddenly going into overdrive.

Louve once again pulled away with a strangled groan escaping her red and swollen lips. "Come, I cannot control myself here with you two. We must go somewhere private away from all these pulsing people!"

She led them to a shadowed door nearby that turned out to be a hidden elevator. She produced a key card from the pocket of her vest and with a swipe and press of a button they were rumbling along to the basement level of the club. The trio exited into a hall with roughhewn stone walls and walked along until they came to a steel door. With another swipe of the key card they entered into the promised apartment. It featured a reasonable sized living room with a fireplace and an attached kitchenette. Louve merely laughed at the look on their faces. "There is more, come see." She led them through a doorway into the bathroom. Marble tile and stainless steel fixtures were everywhere. Through another doorway they found the bathing chamber. It bore more resemblance to a small swimming pool than any sort of tub. Sarah noticed that the tub was full of steaming water. However, she pushed that to the back of her mind as the French woman led them away until they came to another door. Behind was a giant size bedroom. A massive canopy bed sprawled along one end. There was also a small seating area with dressers and a carved wood armoire along another wall. Louve opened the doors to the armoire and then pulled out the drawers. Sarah raised an eyebrow at the assorted implements inside. Keller sensed her lover's curiosity and leveled a smirk in her direction.

Louve stopped and twirled around in place. "Well, will this suffice?"

Keller smiled and Sarah answered. "Oh yes."

The little ringmaster laughed and clapped her hands together once. "Bon! Now, I don't know about you, but I have found tonight to be very — hot, and I would like very much to bathe." She stripped out of her costume as she walked back toward the bathroom. "Feel free to join me."

Keller chuckled as Sarah watched the brunette's nude backside sway out the door. The bar manager called to her. "Hey." When she had Sarah's attention, she continued. "Are you sure you're okay with this? We can always leave if you want."

Sarah returned her serious look. "Are you okay with this? What is she, your ex-lover's ex-lover? Have you done this before with her?"

Keller nodded. "I have. Catherine and I spent many years together before Louve came along. They fell in love over time and I eventually lost Catherine to her, but before that we had many fun nights together."

Sarah took her lover's hand. "What happened to Catherine?"

Keller's eyes turned dark with the memory. "I lost track of them for a few decades until Louve contacted me. She was frightened and desperate. Sometime in the years since I'd seen them, things just went wrong. For whatever reason, Catherine decided she wanted a child. Neither of them could have one for obvious reasons so Catherine had planned to infect a small child, to stay with her forever."

Sarah gasped. "That's — that's horrible!"

"More than you can imagine. Rather than waiting until a child was near death and bringing them over, she grew impatient. She stole a young child and Louve caught her strangling the little girl in the middle of their London apartment. Anyway, they fought and the girl died. After that something inside Catherine broke. Louve caught her two more times with children draining their life away and not making any attempt to infect them at all. She would just let them die. When Louve couldn't stand any more she tried to leave, only to be beaten and threatened by Catherine.

She called me because she wasn't powerful enough to stand up to her and didn't know what else to do."

"You killed her."

Keller nodded, swallowing the lump in her throat. "Yes. She had become sick and twisted inside and needed to be stopped. I've seen Louve a few times over the years but we never resumed any type of physical relationship."

Sarah laid a hand on Keller's cheek, caressing the smooth skin. "And you're okay with this now?" As an answer, Keller leaned up and gave her a scorching kiss while her hands quickly worked to undress the musician.

"Come on—I feel sticky and I need some extra hands to wash my back."

THE BATHING CHAMBER was warm as the two women strolled in hand in hand. They didn't see Louve at first and then the French woman broke the surface of the bathing pool. Water cascaded off her shoulders and down her pert breasts. The small woman pushed the soaked strands of short dark hair away from her face and smiled broadly. She was lithe, with a smallish chest and a perfectly smooth pubic region. She was not particularly curvy but still very attractive. The ringmaster beckoned from the pool. In a matter of seconds both women found themselves sinking into the warm water. Sarah dropped down to wet her hair and when she broke the surface again, Keller and Louve were locked in an embrace, mouths feasting on each other. With the passionate display and their slicked back dark and light hair, Sarah found the scene highly erotic. Before she was aware of her own actions, the singer pressed the full length of her nude body against Louve's back. She then reached her hands around to cup her breasts and tugged at the woman's sensitive nipples. This elicited a cry from Louve and she squirmed against the front of Sarah's body with arousal. Unable to ignore the new sensations any longer, Louve pulled away from Keller's questing tongue and turned her face toward Sarah. While they kissed, Keller pressed her own nude body against Louve's front. Now sandwiched between the two of them, the small brunette gasped and pulled back from Sarah's mouth.

"Mon Dieu! You will kill me with a thousand little deaths before the night is out!" Sarah let her mouth trail along Louve's neck, tasting that fine curve of skin as she moved down her shoulder. She continued caressing sensitive breasts, feeling the French woman's breathing increase. Keller pressed even closer and Louve tensed for just a second before moaning in pleasure. Knowing the bar manager was intimately working between the moaning woman's legs, Sarah cast her lover a heated gaze. With her free hand, Keller grabbed the back of Sarah's head and pulled her into a kiss that was nothing but clashing teeth and tongues. They were both careful of the sharp points. When they broke free from each other, Sarah rubbed her sensitive breasts against Louve's back. She could feel Louve tense between them, her nipples rock hard. The small woman keened the same words over and over. "*Ça vient, ça vient!*"

When Sarah looked at Keller, the other woman's eyes had gone black as her mouth parted slightly and the sharp teeth became very noticeable. Sarah gave her a feral smile, her lust driving all other thought away. She nodded toward the woman between them. "Do it!" As soon as Keller's teeth broke the delicate skin of Louve's neck, the singer felt it deep inside. The French woman cried out, bucking between them, and Sarah's sex clenched with the strength of Keller's own orgasm. They rode the high for a long time, long after Keller had released Louve's neck and licked along her bite mark. The threesome fell back in the water, finding benches along the edges just below the surface. While riding high with the other two, Sarah had not climaxed with them. She fought to keep Keller out because she was afraid to see any thoughts or feelings her lover may have for Louve and also afraid that Louve would pick up on her own thoughts or feelings. So because Sarah had held back, she sat in the water with face flushed, panting and trying to ignore the throbbing between her legs. She briefly considered taking care of her own needs but Keller was suddenly in front of her lifting her out of the water. She gently placed Sarah on the floor around the sunken tub and immediately began feasting on her sex. Sarah was very close and her cries rang through the chamber. Before a turned on Louve could even begin to join them, Sarah tumbled over the edge into ecstasy.

Louve's laughter cut through Sarah's panting whimpers. "Oh, but that was much too fast, mon amour!" Sarah watched the alluring woman walk up the steps and out of the pool. The French woman called out to them. "Come along. Let us take this someplace a little more comfortable. I do not want to drown when I finally get to taste the beautiful Sarah." The singer blushed at Louve's blatant promise.

By the time Keller and Sarah made their way back into the bedroom, Louve was standing near the bed. The small brunette was wearing nothing but a silk robe and a black leather harness at her hips. The large dildo jutting outward seemed incongruous on such a petite frame. She walked up to Keller with the member swinging distractedly. She looked deeply into the blue eyes of her long-time friend. "I want to feel your lover's nails down my back while I fuck her, for this you can drink from me as much as you like."

Keller smirked. "It's not my consent you need, Louve, you need to ask the lady first." Both the women with *other* blood looked toward Sarah, whose gaze had yet to leave the large strap-on between Louve's legs.

Sarah's mouth was slightly parted and her eyes were glazed with the arousal that choked the room. She gave herself a little shake before tearing her gaze away. "I want—I want you both to fuck me before dawn!"

"*Bon, ce serait la perfection!*"

Keller swallowed and felt her teeth prick with the rising heat. "Why are we still standing here?"

Louve gave a tittering laugh and waved toward the armoire. "By all means, mon ami, help yourself!"

By the time Keller was wearing her own harness, Sarah was slick and ready for more. Louve hovered over the singer in missionary position and started working the large phallus into Sarah's moist opening. The taller brunette cried out when the entire length of the large shaft was fully buried in her depths. Keller began kissing her while Louve set up a good rhythm, the stimulation overload only taking her higher. When Keller pulled back to work on the singer's sensitized nipples, Sarah pulled Louve down into a rough kiss. During the kiss, Sarah fisted the short dark hair. "Fuck me!" The French woman growled in return and let a bit of her wolf come toward the surface. She snarled then picked up the pace and strength of her thrusting, smiling as Sarah moaned with each inward stroke. Strong calloused fingers clenched and blunt nails raked their way down the smaller woman's back. Keller was panting with arousal, feeling Sarah's approach to climax. She slipped her hand between the two women and lightly caressed the singer's clit, fingers dancing in time with their rhythm. That was enough to send Sarah screaming over the edge, back bowed and blunt fingernails breaking the slickness of Louve's skin. She moaned and twitched for a few minutes while Louve collapsed on top of her. The smaller woman had not finished but she was being courteous to leave the toy in place while Sarah's sex recovered.

When the singer still hadn't moved for a few minutes the French woman turned an unrepentant grin toward Keller. "I'm sorry, mon ami, I seem to have broken her. I do not think you will get your turn after all—"

Keller laughed. "Oh, she's not done yet!"

Louve thought of the powerful orgasm that had only a few minutes before caused the woman below her to pass out. "Truly?"

"Oh yes, truly. Watch." With both sets of eyes on her, Sarah's eyes finally fluttered open. Her lips curled into a satisfied grin and she only slightly shuddered when Louve withdrew the toy and lay next to her on the bed. Before any of them could say a word, Keller had positioned herself between Sarah's legs and began cleaning the wetness from her thighs, working her way up. By the time she had her tongue buried as deep as it would go, Sarah had her by the hair and was writhing against the smaller woman's mouth.

"Keller, please! I need more!" Then abruptly, she pulled Keller's head away. "Wait, I want to taste her when I go again."

Louve had removed the harness and was reclining on the bed next to her. As soon as Keller sat up, Sarah rolled over and buried her face between the French woman's legs. This still left plenty of room on the massive bed for Keller to take her from behind. As soon as Keller entered Sarah with the strap-on, the singer moaned her pleasure into Louve's completely shorn folds. Resting on her elbows while her lover fucked her from behind, Sarah was able to insert two fingers into the French woman's tight depths. They were immediately clenched by strong muscles and she knew Louve wouldn't last long. She turned her head to look behind her. Catching blue eyes darkened with arousal, she whispered to her. "Harder, my love." Sarah's eyes nearly rolled into the back of her head with pleasure when Keller complied with her wishes. Trying to hold off her own impending release, the singer once again turned her attentions to the woman below her. She curled her fingers deep inside with each thrust and lapped the smaller woman's clit repeatedly. In a matter of seconds Louve was forced off the bed with the strength of her orgasm, muscles clenching in fluttering waves around Sarah's fingers. However, instead of relaxing into the afterglow, Louve quickly turned herself around, and took Sarah's clit into her mouth. Keller adjusted her knees to accommodate the woman below them as Sarah's moaning quickly built to a crescendo. She screamed out with a voice already hoarse from earlier and then she finally broke. Back bowed taut, her fingers dug into the bed below them while she writhed in pleasure. Still buried deep inside her lover, Keller rode her own orgasm then rolled them to the side when Sarah collapsed to avoid landing on the French woman below. Finally, Keller pulled out of the momentarily unconscious Sarah. Letting the harness drop to the floor, she curled around her lover from behind.

Louve had righted herself on the bed and reached across to run a finger down Sarah's cheek. "She is amazing." She pulled back and gazed at Keller. "You are both amazing to me. Thank you for tonight, mon ami." She glanced back to Sarah, who had still not roused. "You are more than welcome to stay and join me for breakfast in the morning. I suspect we will all be well and truly hungry by then."

Sarah's eyes were still closed when she pulled Keller's arms tighter around her. "Stay, breakfast in the morning."

Keller grinned back at Louve. "Well I guess you have your answer." There was no more to be said so the French woman simply grinned back before turning the lights off with a remote and pulling a large blanket over them all.

SARAH DIDN'T ARRIVE home until noon the next day. As promised, Louve provided breakfast. It was a traditional French affair with fresh croissants, coffee, fruit, and yogurt. She was relieved when the French woman declared the previous evening's activities nothing more than a bit of fun. And fun it was but the singer was still glad to avoid any more emotional connections being piled onto her plate. The twins were up and onsite when they finally emerged from the apartment below, so Louve asked one of them to take her two friends home. Keller's car was at Sarah's house so that's where they were dropped off. The bar manager had a few things to take care of at the club that afternoon so Sarah promised to come over later in the evening for dinner. Plans made and a million things flying through her head, Sarah watched as the little blue car turned the corner at the end of her street. She was greeted by an overly affectionate Husky when she finally walked in the house. Rounding the corner, two familiar faces met hers. Annie and Jesse were eating bowls of cereal and watching the cartoon network. She rolled her eyes at them. "Really guys, did you both regress back into childhood last night?"

Jesse smirked at her. "That would be implying that we actually left at some point."

Meanwhile, Annie's eyes narrowed when she took in her sister's rumpled outfit from the night before. "Um, Sarah, don't you keep clothes at Keller's house?"

Sarah looked at her curiously. "Yeah, I keep a few things over there just in case. Why?" She gingerly walked across the living room and sat on the loveseat and Duke jumped up practically laying in her lap.

Annie abruptly sat forward, startling Jesse. "Oh my God! Are you freaking kidding me, Sarah? Does Keller know where you were and what you were doing last night?"

Confused, Sarah startled at her sister's outburst. "What are you talking about?" She shifted on the couch, still sore from the night before.

The younger woman pointed a finger at her. "Are you telling me that you didn't hook up with someone at the club last night and bail on Keller? Why else would you be strolling in right now, without even a shower, looking like —"

Jesse looked at her girlfriend now, trying to piece together what Annie was saying. "Looking like what, babe?

The younger Colby sister leveled a gaze at her. "She's walking funny, Jesse, and that doesn't happen when you crash on a friend's couch for the night." Jesse's mouthed *Oh* with understanding, but smartly remained silent.

Sarah snickered when she caught on to what had Annie so fired up. "Um, Annie?"

"What!"

"Neither one of us went home last night, I was with Keller."

Confusion washed over the younger woman's face. "But— what, where?"

The older sibling smirked. "Louve took us to the apartment below the club. We spent the night there and had breakfast with her this morning."

"Oh, you just crashed with Louve." It was small voice that came from the chagrinned woman, immediately sorry for jumping to conclusions.

Jesse cocked her head to the side in thought after watching the exchange. "So why are you walking funny?"

Sarah chuckled and smirked at the two women. "It's not the first time." Annie threw her hands up in the air and with a rapidly reddening face she proceeded to clean up the bowls and box of cereal. When she left the room, Jesse stood to follow her. On her way by Sarah, she held out her fist for a bump. Humoring the younger woman, Sarah obliged.

Jesse smirked back at her. "Nice!" Then she walked into the kitchen to find her sheltered girlfriend.

NEARLY THREE WEEKS passed since their night at Temple du Loup. Despite their erotic encounter with Louve, the evening had only succeeded in bonding Keller and Sarah closer together. Sarah and Duke spend most nights with the bar manager and Keller was happy to have her there, but she wanted more. One afternoon when Annie and Keller were both at the bar, Keller brought up an idea she had been thinking about. "Hey Annie, can I ask you something?"

Annie set down the stack of flyers she had been perusing and looked at her boss curiously. "Sure, what's up?"

Keller took a seat at the table across from her and got right to the point. "I want to ask Sarah to move in with me. Do you think she'll —"

Annie sat forward. "She'll freak!"

The bar manager frowned. "In a good way or in a bad way?"

Annie made a face and idly scratched at her temple. "Hmm — well..."

Keller sighed. "In a bad way. But why? I mean, she's practically living with me as it is!" Frustrated, she scrubbed her hands over her face and through her hair, elbows on the table. When she sat back again, her already messy hair was even more in disarray. "I just —" She growled in frustration.

Annie understood all too well what her sister was like. She knew her older sibling was terrified of tying herself down. It was directly related to the death of their parents and having to step into a parental role for a younger sibling. She also suspected that Keller's condition played a major part in her sister's reticence. She wanted Sarah to move in with Keller for her own good but she couldn't just ask her to leave. Maybe they could come up with something if they worked together. "You want to go to sleep every night knowing she'll be in your arms when you wake the next morning. Am I right?"

Keller groaned. "Yes, that's exactly it. But no matter how much time she spends with me, I don't think she'll be willing to move in. She's so afraid of commitment, Annie! I'm not going anywhere. I would do anything for her!"

Annie smiled at her sadly. "I think that's the problem, isn't it? She's spent her whole life running and she knows if she moves in that she'll be tying herself down to one place and one person. Moving in with someone is a big deal. It's a promise to stick around."

Her boss groaned again and dropped her head to the table, hiding her face. After thumping it a few times she sat back up. "So what do I do?"

Wheels turning, Annie smirked at her. "You mean, what do *we* do? I have a plan, are you interested?"

Instantly alert, Keller looked at the younger sister of her lover. It was obvious that Annie and Sarah were related. They shared their dark hair, mouth, and nose. However, Annie was definitely the slyer of the two. She always had plans and always thought ahead. Keller had seen it many times while the younger woman was working for her. Keller grinned at her. "You've been thinking about this, haven't you? What's the matter, is your big sister cramping your style?"

Annie laughed. "I have been thinking about it but it's not because she's cramping my style. Jesse and I love having her live with us, it's just..." She trailed off, thinking about what she would say.

"It's just what?"

"Well, Jesse and I have been talking about this for a while, and we just really want to see you both happy. You two are meant to be together, any fool can see it." She laughed again. "Well, maybe not my fool of a sister."

The bar manager smiled with affection. Annie had been more than just an employee for a long time, she really was a good friend. "So what did you have in mind? I know you, you've probably got some grand plan and an even better name for it."

"Well, as a matter of fact I do. It will be a lot of work for me and Jesse but I'm calling it 'Operation PDA'." Keller raised an eyebrow at her so she went on to explain. "Okay, so I know how weird it is to see your sister sucking face with someone. That's why Jesse and I have a plan that involves hot and heavy displays affection whenever she walks into the room. We'll even hang around the house more until we really get to her. What do you think?"

"A lot of work for you, huh? Jesus! You're going to drive her nuts. Okay, why don't you try that for a few weeks and let me know how she's doing. Then when I sense she's reaching her breaking point, I'll ask her if she wants to move in with me."

Annie pumped her fist in the air. "Awesome! We'll start tonight."

AS PREDICTED, TWO weeks later found Sarah at her breaking point. Still clueless about her sister's master plan, she spent an entire evening ranting to Keller about her and Jesse. "Seriously, all they ever do anymore is grope at each other. It seems like whatever room I walk into in the house, they're going at it hot and heavy. I couldn't have friends over even if I wanted to. What the hell has gotten into them?"

Keller was sitting on her couch, drinking a glass of wine and watching her lover pace back and forth. She was doing some award winning acting to keep a straight face though. She'd heard the complaints many times over the past few weeks. "Well they haven't been living together that long, they're probably still in the honeymoon phase."

"Honeymoon phase? They've been living together for months, Keller! And I think they're worse than they ever were before. It's — uh, awkward sometimes when I walk in a room. Jesus, that's my sister! I don't want to see that!"

Sensing that now was the time for the next step, Keller purposely kept her words cool and casual. She was merely making a logical suggestion in order to solve Sarah's problem. Gazing at the dog that was sound asleep on his dog bed, she took another sip of her wine. "Well, why don't you just stay here then? It's not like you're not here most of the time anyway. Let the kids have their space for a while." She looked at Sarah, who had gone still with thought. "I mean, I have plenty of room, and we work similar hours. It would solve your issue..." She trailed off, waiting for the explosion.

Sarah stood by the couch, chewing her bottom lip in thought. While Keller made a good suggestion there was part of her that balked at moving in with someone new. Well, besides her sister. But she also had to admit, if only to herself, that she missed the bar manager on the days she slept at home. There was a comfort to waking in the embrace of a lover and Keller had been very good about not pushing her for anything more serious over the past few months. Sarah felt so much for Keller, but she kept all of it locked tightly behind those walls and excuses.

She looked down at the woman that she had grown so familiar with and her heart ached. At the exact same moment, Keller turned her gaze up to the singer. That moment when their eyes met sent a pang through Sarah's chest. She knew that she would be opening herself completely the minute she stopped running from Keller and all that her lover meant to her. In the past, she never wanted to spend more time with someone. The more they got to know each other the more Sarah wanted to escape. But, it was exactly the opposite with Keller. Continuing to stare at the woman on the couch, Sarah could feel her breathing increase with the beginnings of panic. But one thing stopped it and calmed her down. Keller smiled and that one look held many meanings. She could see fear and uncertainty, but also kindness and affection. Beneath it all was that one emotion that Sarah was afraid to name, was not ready to name.

The moment was broken when Keller spoke. "Sarah? Do you want to move in with me?"

The singer didn't like to see so much fear and uncertainty on the face that had grown to mean so much. She thought back to her sister's words all those months ago. She did want more with Keller. She wanted to fall asleep each night and wake each morning with her. She enjoyed it when the two of them took Duke for walks in the park, or even the simple evenings when neither was working and they opted to order Thai Guys and watch Netflix. Despite all the things that Sarah knew made them different, they shared a remarkable amount of similar tastes and needs from life. She wanted to move forward despite her fear and despite that secret part of her lover that Sarah found terrifying. With a smile of her own, and no small amount of trepidation, she answered honestly. "Yes."

Regardless of the hope she had been clutching for months, Keller was surprised. *"Seriously?"*

Sarah laughed at the look on her face and came around to sit on the couch next to her shocked lover. She carefully took the wine glass from Keller's hand and set it on the low coffee table. With long fingers tangling into shaggy blonde hair, Sarah pulled Keller so close they were breathing the same air. Then, with all the surety she possessed, she whispered her response again. "Yes" The kiss that followed was one of joy and relief, and also one of dawning hope. They spent a long time on the couch, touching, kissing, and connecting with each other. Keller was basking in warmth of that single word and in Sarah's touch. And Sarah's hesitance and concern were rapidly fading away in the wash of contentment she felt lying in Keller's arms. She was getting tired of running anyway, it was time to explore her new life.

They were interrupted by a cold nose and a few urgent whines. If any dog could do the pee-pee dance, it was Duke. They broke apart laughing and Sarah stood with a sigh. "Of course you decide you want to go out right now, you mangy mutt!" Duke whined one more time before running to the door. His leash was kept on a hook right next to it. Sarah just shook her head and followed the anxious dog. "I'm going to run him down to pee. I'll be back in a few minutes." She slipped on her jacket then paused and looked at Keller. "You know what, we should celebrate somehow since I've never lived with anyone but family. We could skip cooking and order a pizza or something. After we could maybe do wine and a movie, or wine and the Jacuzzi?"

Keller stood and brought her nearly empty wine glass to the kitchen island. "How about Pad Thai, followed by champagne and the Jacuzzi?"

Sarah grinned with delight. "Ooh, Pad Thai? You really know the way to a girl's heart! And champagne, so fancy!"

Keller smirked. "So I'm assuming yes to both? So Jacuzzi or a movie?"

Ignoring the dancing dog for just a few seconds longer, Sarah walked over to the other woman and grabbed her by the front of the shirt. Drawing her in slowly, Sarah leaned down and ran her tongue around the helix of Keller's ear. When she felt the shorter woman shudder against her, she whispered in her ear. "What do you think, hot stuff?"

Keller swallowed when Sarah stepped back. "I think I'll go call Thai Guys Xpress, and run some water." The sound of Sarah's laughter carried well through the apartment door.

As soon as she was sure the musician was gone, Keller grabbed her cell phone to text Annie.

```
FYI, Operation PDA was a success. She said yes!
Talk to you later!
```

She grinned like an idiot for a full minute before remembering the food. "Shit!" Sarah said yes, and there was no way she was going to screw things up. She had three promises to keep—food, champagne, and Jacuzzi. Well, she actually had four promises but the last was merely implied. She felt her face flush when she thought about where the Jacuzzi would lead them. What a perfect end to the evening.

Chapter Nine

AFTER ALL THE plotting and planning, moving Sarah was a bit anticlimactic. Because of all her time spent on the road, she really didn't own much beyond music equipment, clothes, and dog stuff. It was a pretty sad testament to her life actually. After the move, they invited Annie and Jesse over for Sarah's first official dinner living in Keller's condo. Both younger women ooh'd and ahh'd at the modern hi-tech abode. Jesse, with her always tech-oriented brain, started asking questions and making suggestions minutes after walking through the door. Annie spent her time jealously drooling over the view and the Jacuzzi. As they sat around the dining table after eating Keller's homemade lasagna and garlic bread, Annie proposed a toast. "Here is to Keller's amazing lasagna and her even sweeter condo!" They all clinked glasses and took a sip of their drinks and Annie continued. "And here is to Sarah finally moving in with a girlfriend after all these years!"

Sarah immediately choked and sputtered, surprise causing her to inhale her drink. With wide eyes, she looked back at her sister. "G—girlfriend?"

Annie's eyes were just as wide as she stared right back at her. "Um, hello? You moved in with the woman you've been banging for months. If that's not a girlfriend, what is?" Keller and Jesse sat slightly in shock and remained silent. Keller knew that Sarah hadn't quite put a label on their relationship yet but she was content to let Annie push for her.

Sarah looked at her sister and then turned startled eyes to Keller. "I, uh—" She cleared her throat and tried again. "I guess you would be my girlfriend, huh?"

Keller gave her a serious look. "Are you comfortable with that?" Annie and Jesse held their breaths waiting for the answer.

It took the mercurial singer only a second to answer. "Yes I am." She laughed self-consciously. "It's just been a long time, that's all. I'm very comfortable with it."

Keller gave her a broad grin then leaned over and followed it with a sweet kiss. "I'm very comfortable with it too."

Crisis averted, Annie caught her older sister staring at her with an unreadable look on her face so she winked at her. Sarah merely smiled and shook her head.

DESPITE SARAH'S PROGRESS in the relationship department, it took less than a month for her and Keller to have their first big fight as an official couple. It was a Saturday morning and the front page of the paper featured an article about a hit and run on the east side of town. The description of the vehicle perfectly matched the truck that the police had been looking for in connection with the murder and gay bashings that happened over the summer. While the incident didn't occur near any LGBTQ establishments, it was mere blocks from Sarah's teaching studio. To be fair, Keller probably wouldn't have panicked as much if Sarah didn't have a lesson scheduled at eight that night. "You should reschedule or let me come with you!"

Sarah sighed with frustration as she put her breakfast dishes in the washer. "I'm not going to cancel, this is a regular client. She only has one appointment a month and I have this specific time slot reserved for Sadie because it's the only one that works for her." She turned around and pointed at Keller. "And you have your own job to go to!"

Leveling worried blue eyes at her lover, Keller pleaded. "Sarah—"

"No, I'm not going to change my mind. The cops patrol our area pretty good and the hit and run happened in the early hours of morning. I'll be out of there by nine-thirty. Even the coffee shop two doors down will be open later than me. Its fine, Keller, stop worrying so much."

Keller walked over to her and took her hands. "I worry because your life is my life. I told you that already. If something happened to you, I wouldn't survive it."

Sarah jerked her hands free and stepped back. "This? You're going to bring this up again? I'm not saying it wouldn't hurt but if something happened to one of us, we'd eventually get over it just like everyone else. I will not let you pressure me into letting you turn me into—" She stopped, out of words at last. But Keller was just getting started.

"Into what, Sarah? Turn you into whatever I am? What do you think I am exactly? A monster?" Her anger was growing the more she thought about Sarah's stubborn refusal to see exactly what was going on between them.

Sarah's stomach was twisting with her lover's anger. "Keller, no! That is not what I meant at all. We've discussed this multiple times and you know how I feel about being infected. I will not be taken from Annie!"

Keller's voice was like steel when she spoke. "No, that's not it at all. Because you know that being infected wouldn't take you from anyone. You're just afraid of losing Annie, afraid of her growing old and leaving you behind. But I meant what I said, we are connected now. Your death is my death and you need to start facing some facts about the reality of our situation." With that she turned and stomped off to their bedroom, slamming the door behind her.

Sarah just stood there, heart hurting and unsure where to go. Finally, she whistled to Duke. "Come on boy, let's go see your aunt Annie." She texted Annie when she got to her RAV4.

Keller and I had a big fight. Can I come over to talk?

Annie responded less than a minute later.

Always, I'll be waiting with the cookies.

When she arrived at the house, Jesse was just leaving with her laptop case and a box of electronics. "Hey, Sarah, Annie's inside. You girls have fun!" She scampered off to her car before Sarah could say anything to her.

She found Annie in the kitchen, pouring two glasses of milk. Then she glanced at the blue and white bag on the counter. "Ooh, double stuff!"

"Well, I figured I'd call out the big guns since it sounded kind of serious. First fight since the move?"

Sarah sighed. "Yeah. And my stomach still hurts. Did Jesse have to work today?"

Annie gave her a curious smile. "No, she had some stuff to take care of at a friend's house. She said she'd be back in a few hours." She reached down to pet Duke, missing the big ball of fur since Sarah had moved out. "So, are you going to tell me what happened?" Sarah finished chewing her cookie and grabbed another. They were quiet for a few minutes, just content to dunk and chew. Annie didn't push. She knew Sarah would talk when she was ready.

"We've had an ongoing disagreement and I thought she was finally going to back off about it. But today's headline set her off on some overprotective streak and now she's bringing it up again. She wants me to cancel my lessons tonight, or have her follow me everywhere."

Annie cocked her head. "Wait a minute, first, what is this ongoing disagreement? And second, what headline? Wait, I'll be right back!" She jumped up and ran into the living room, returning a minute later with the current paper in hand. After scanning the article, she looked back up at her sister. "Isn't this right around the corner from your studio?"

Irritated, she answered. "Yes, but that happened in the middle of the night! My last lesson is from eight to nine, and there is a coffee shop that's open later two doors down. I'll be fine!"

Annie set down her half eaten cookie. "Sarah, I don't blame her for being concerned. These guys have hurt a lot of people and killed one now. It's no joke. So what is the ongoing disagreement and how does it relate to the hit and run?"

"Do you remember when I told you all about Keller's condition and how she kind of feeds on emotions so she doesn't have to feed on blood all the time?" Annie nodded and continued to dunk her cookies. "Well, from almost the beginning she's been saying we're connected, that we are soul mates. She's convinced that when I die she will as well. And she's asked me a few times if I would consider letting her infect me with the same thing she has. Now she's even more afraid for me because of the article."

The younger sister swallowed her bite of cookie and stared. "Wow. Uh, that is a lot to take in." She waved her hand through the air. "I mean, the whole vampire succubus thing is a lot too. But my question for you is why does the idea bother you so much?"

Sarah grabbed another cookie. "Which idea, her suggestion that we are soul mates and are bound together for life, or the suggestion that I should let her infect me?"

"Hmm—let's start with the easy one. Why does the idea that you're bound for life bother you?"

The singer glared at her younger sibling. "You know why, Annie. That's just a lot of metaphysical crap. No one is bound to another person for life. Please!"

Annie burst out laughing, spraying cooking crumbs onto the

floor. However, any mess that may have occurred was quickly cleaned up by a bushy-tailed dog. "Really, Sarah, Metaphysical crap? And vampires are everywhere today, am I right? I mean, it's completely normal and natural to have speed healing, be able to manipulate people's memories, feed off an entire club full of sexual energy, and—oh yeah, have pointed teeth to drink blood! Why are you quick to accept those things yet be just as quick to deny that there could be more? That's just bullshit." She leveled a gaze at her sister. "You don't want to admit that you could be connected to anyone in any way. You are so afraid of commitment that you're letting it prevent you from opening your mind and accepting something that is completely wonderful!"

Sarah scowled. "Wonderful? So it's a good thing to be told that you're bound to someone forever and oh by the way, you won't outlive the other person!"

Annie laid her hand across her sister's. "If she's your soul mate, do you really want to?"

"I...it's...hell I don't know. It's just so confusing! It's a lot to deal with right now."

"Okay, so that's a better answer. Now what about the other thing?"

Sarah gave her a surprised look. "Are you seriously asking me why the idea of being infected bothers me?"

Annie grinned. "Frankly, yeah. Let's see, increased strength, healing, and health, and you live practically forever. All in exchange for a little aversion to the sun and mentally sucking in some sexy vibes? Why in the world is that a problem?"

Sarah slapped her arm, not lightly. "Be serious! You're telling me you would want to grow old over the years and watch me stay exactly the same? That wouldn't bother you at all?"

Annie sighed and drained the last of her milk. "Honestly? It's something I have thought about ever since you told me about Keller. I think I'd be jealous more than anything else. But if it meant never having to lose you the way I lost Mom and Dad—I would take it, Sarah—in a heartbeat." She took her sister's hand in her own. The musician's fingers were long and graceful with callouses on her fingertips. "I think this is something you should really consider." When Sarah began to protest, Annie held up a hand to stop her. "No, I'm not saying right now, or even soon. But sometime in the future you should give it some consideration. And as for being careful in the meantime, I always agree with that advice."

Sarah met her sister's eyes, taking in Annie's words. At last, she nodded to the younger Colby and Annie smiled. "Now how about this? I don't work tonight, how about if Jesse and I meet you for coffee after you finish with your last lesson? We haven't really seen you since you moved out and Jesse just said something the other day about getting together to catch up."

Sarah sat there, unable to speak. Annie started cleaning up, letting her sister have a few minutes to digest what she had said. When Sarah finally spoke, her eyes were slightly damp. "I'll think about it, *all* of it. And I'd be happy to meet you two tonight after my lesson. Thanks, A." She stood and threw away the paper towel she had used to wipe her face. "I think I'm going to take Duke to the dog park down the street, want to come with us?"

Duke's ears perked up when he heard the word *park* and Annie laughed. "I'd love to. Let me grab my coat."

TWENTY MINUTES AFTER Sarah left the condo, Keller got a phone call from Jesse. "Hey Keller, I got that stuff for the new entertainment system and I've got some free time today. Are you going to be home so I can install it?"

One part of the bar manager didn't want to be disturbed. She just wanted to sit home and worry and not have to talk to anyone else. But the other part wanted to have a distraction so she didn't sit home and worry about Sarah. She sighed and gave in. "I'm home until I leave for the club at seven. Stop by any time."

Jesse laughed over the phone. "Oh, uh, well how about now?"

Keller paused and shrugged though the other woman couldn't see over the phone. "Sure, come on over."

"Okay, great! Now come down and get me, I'm right outside."

The bar manager shook her head again and grinned. "Sure, I'll be down in a sec."

Despite the day's bad start, Keller actually had a decent time hanging out with Jesse. Annie's girlfriend was mature for her years, intelligent, and could carry on a discussion about almost any topic. Keller thought of Jesse much the same way she thought of Annie — they were both friends who felt more like little sisters. Before Jesse left to go back home, she leveled a gaze at the younger woman. "So did Annie ask you to come over here and hang with me today or did you really just get the parts in and want to set up my system?"

Jesse gave her a smile that carried a hint of shyness. "Honestly? I picked up the parts yesterday but when Annie said that you guys had fought and that Sarah was on her way over — well I decided I'd rather hang with you. Keller, I think you're fun and good people, and we always have interesting conversation. And — I can never have too many friends."

Keller smiled back at her with affection. "Thanks J. That means a lot to me. I too can always use more friends, and well — you've really helped me take my mind off some stuff. And you are welcome any time, not just when Sarah and I have a disagreement."

As she was walking out the door, Jesse glanced back at Keller with a worried look. "You guys are solid, right?"

Keller gave her a sad smile. "I hope so. She means the world to me." She shook her head to clear the melancholy. "Have a good day, Jesse, I hope I see you again soon."

"Same here. Hang in there, she'll come around. Bye, Keller!"

THAT EVENING SARAH, Annie, and Jesse were sitting in lounge chairs at the coffee shop two doors down from Sarah's studio. They were laughing uproariously at Sarah's story about one of her clients and his banjo lesson. When they caught their breath, she finished the tale. "...so after all that, he says to me 'Do yah thank yah can show mah good friend Clem how tah play the washboard?' and it took every ounce of professionalism I had not to crack up. He was dead serious!"

Annie snorted. "He did not!"

"I swear he did!"

Jesse looked back and forth between the two women. "I don't get it, what's a washboard?"

Annie looked at her girlfriend. "Babe, just google hillbilly music." Jesse's mouth made an O shape then she immediately got her phone out of her pocket. Annie turned back to her sister. "So what have you got going on tonight? Any plans?"

Sarah shrugged. "Nothing really. Keller has to work so..."

"Well I'm all wound up from this mocha latte, why don't we go down to the club for a while?" Annie leaned closer and whispered in a conspiratorial manner. "I'm in real tight with the manager. I can get us in without cover."

Sarah leaned over and whispered back in the same way. "I'm frequently *in* the manager and I can confirm that she's real tight."

Annie's face turned scarlet. "Oh my God, you're such a perv!"

Jesse looked up from her hillbilly education. "Who's a perv?"

Annie jerked a thumb in her sister's direction. "Her! We were actually just talking about going to the club."

"*You* were just talking about the club, *I* was talking about my girlfriend."

Jesse's face fell. "Oh man! Of all the weekends I volunteer to help someone — don't you remember? I told Jon I'd come over and help him set up his HD system and surround sound before the big game tomorrow. I promised I'd be over first thing in the morning, and his wife is making us breakfast. I still have to sort out all the gear I'll need for his place tonight!"

Annie gave her a sweet smile when Jesse mentioned her brother's name. She knew that having Jon extend an olive branch was a big deal to Jesse when the rest of her family had disowned her for coming out. "Hon, it's okay, as long as you don't mind me going with Sarah tonight. We can do something fun tomorrow after you're finished at Jon's."

Jesse stuck out her bottom lip in a pout. "Promise?"

Annie leaned over and gave her a kiss on the cheek. "How about a trip to the comic store, Thai Guys takeout, and a movie?"

The pout immediately turned into a grin. "You have a deal!" She turned to Sarah. "I'll drive Annie's car home if you can drop her off later."

"Sure J, I'd be happy to."

It was nearly eleven by the time the Colby sisters arrived at The Merge. Big Teddy greeted both with a hug before they made their way across the packed bar. Annie waded through the crowd for drinks while Sarah went in search of her girlfriend. Not seeing her anywhere obvious, she decided to try the back office. She knocked and pushed her way in, speaking while stepping through the door. "Excuse me, I have a complaint for the manager — "

Keller looked up and delighted surprise washed over her face. "Sarah! I didn't know you were coming down tonight!" She immediately crossed the room to the singer and wrapped her in a full-body hug.

When the embrace ended, Sarah pulled back far enough to gently cup the shorter woman's cheek. She whispered "I missed you" before claiming Keller's lips with a series of sweet kisses. It didn't take long for the sweet kisses to escalate into something that had both women moaning.

When Annie pushed her way into the office carrying two beers, she found the long leg of her sister planted firmly against Keller's crotch. A quick look confirmed Keller's hands were busy as well. She tried clearing her throat to distract them. "Ahem." When that didn't work, she slammed the door shut. The loud bang immediately startled the passionate women and they jumped apart in surprise. Keller blushed at being caught losing control in her office. Sarah had a different reaction.

"You're such a brat! You nearly gave me a heart attack!"

The younger sibling chuckled and handed her the extra beer. "I think you're gonna make it." Still grinning she looked over at her boss's flushed face and couldn't resist teasing the woman. "Hey, Keller, how's it hangin'? Good crowd tonight, it's pretty hot out there, hmm?"

Keller groaned and scrubbed a hand through her hair. "Are you two just here to torment me, or what? Where's Jesse?"

Sarah smirked and took a swig of her beer while Annie explained their impromptu night out. "She has an early breakfast with her brother and sister-in-law tomorrow morning, and some work to do tonight, so it's just me and this one." She aimed a thumb toward the other Colby sibling. "Now if you two are finished making out like teenagers, let's go dance!"

Keller laughed. "I'm supposed to be working."

"Pshh! I saw Lynne on my way in and it's not like you're leaving the building. You'll be fine!" Annie turned to head back out the door and called over her shoulder. "I expect you two to be right behind me!"

The bar manager shook her head at her employee's antics. "Well, we wouldn't want to incur the wrath of Annie now, would we? Shall we go dance?" She held her hand out to Sarah, who immediately took it and moved them into another embrace.

"It's almost worth it if you keep kissing me." Keller smiled tenderly and did exactly that. The kiss was slow and deep, leaving both women reveling in the heat of their connection. When they pulled apart again, Sarah looked into her lover's blue eyes.

She loved the way they looked, loved the way they seemed to pull her in and hold her. "I'm sorry I keep running from you. I really don't know why I'm doing it."

Keller ran a finger over the taller woman's bottom lip. "It's okay. Things have been going really well with us. I love — spending time with you and waking up with you every morning. It's a very different and special feeling for me."

Sarah could read between the lines of what Keller was saying. She stared into the eyes that carried so much hope and finally acknowledged the emotion between them. It filled her with light and took away that ache that had been in her chest for so long. It took everything she had to say the words aloud and not bolt for the door, but it was time to take some of the weight off Keller's shoulders. It was time to reassure the woman that had come to mean everything to her. "Keller, you don't ever have to worry about me." She kissed her lover lightly on the lips and continued. "I love spending time with you too, I love going to sleep each night and waking in your arms in the morning. I love that we laugh at the same things, and how amazing our sex is. It's like each day is brand new. Does that make sense?"

Keller nodded and choked back the ball of emotion that was lodged in her throat and waited because Sarah's body language made it obvious that she wasn't finished.

The taller woman swallowed then looked back into those too-familiar blue eyes. "Keller, I—" She stopped awkwardly and abruptly kissed the startled blonde. Every bit of emotion and passion she felt, she shoved down that line of connection and hoped that Keller would understand. When they slowly pulled away again, Keller's eyes were swimming in tears. Their world seemed to fall away when Sarah opened to her completely. "I love you, Noble Keller." That was when the tears finally fell, running into mouths that were opening and searching. The barrier that Keller had been maintaining between them to protect her reticent lover, washed away with the force of their emotions.

"I love you too, Sarah Colby. Always." They held each other for a few minutes, just letting it sink in and getting the tears under control. Sensing that Sarah was at her limit for emotional admissions, Keller changed the subject. "So, are you guys staying until close?"

"Yeah, I think that's what Annie was planning. I just have to give her a ride home when we leave."

"Or, you could let her take your RAV4 and we can get home faster to celebrate the fact that you finally told me you loved me."

Sarah blushed and laughed self-consciously. "Or I could do that. I'll see what Annie wants to do when we catch up with her."

After giving Annie her keys, Sarah took Keller to the dance floor and didn't let her leave for an hour. The music and heat of their close movement was erotic but the throbbing sexual energy that Keller was pushing through their connection had her ready to explode. Finally, when Keller could no longer take the teasing, she led them to the bar for a break. They chatted with Annie and a few of their mutual friends for a while before heading back to the dance floor for more torture. In the middle of their sexual haze, Sarah was surprised when the ugly lights came on. She looked at Keller and her sister in shock. "Holy shit, I didn't realize it was that late! Where did the night go?"

Annie snickered. "Apparently down your pants. Jesus, Sarah, I couldn't even dance by you two, you were practically throwing off sparks!" The next words were said in a singsong voice. "Awkward for your sister."

Sarah laughed and tugged Annie's earlobe. "Come on, we're not that bad." She then turned to a smirking Keller. "Are we?"

Keller grinned. "I think we are."

Sarah groaned and covered her eyes. "Great."

The bar manager waved them to a table. "Come on, let's sit over here and finish our beers. One of the perks of being the manager is that we don't have to leave at two with everyone else." Once they were seated, she directed a smile at Annie. "I don't know about you, but it's nice not helping clean up, for once."

Annie made a face. "But I feel so guilty."

Sarah took a swig of her beer. "I don't."

Annie swatted her on the arm. "Shut up, you!"

They were still sitting at the table when Big Teddy and Lynne walked up. Keller looked at her watch, then back up at them. "Oh shit, when did it get so late?"

Big Teddy laughed, a sound like a bass rumble coming from his chest. "I don't know little K. We just came over to tell you that me and Lynne are the last two left. I can walk her out and come back for you three if you like."

Keller waved off the idea. "That's all right, Ted, you can go ahead and leave. We'll all walk out together and I'll set the alarm when we go. Have a good night you two."

The bar seemed eerily silent once Lynne and Teddy had said their goodbyes. Annie was first to finish her beer and the sound of the empty bottle hitting the table was loud to their ears. "Come on, slowpokes, I'm all warmed up now and I want to go home and have some hot sex with my hotter girlfriend."

Sarah set her own empty bottle down and promptly plugged her ears. "I don't want to hear that, la la la—"

"Oh please, spare me! You and Keller were practically scrumping like bunnies on the dance floor! What kind of example are you setting for your little sister?"

Keller snorted. "This is coming from the woman who apparently christened every room of her house with the previously mentioned hot girlfriend." Annie blushed and Sarah cracked up laughing. Keller stood and collected the three empty bottles. She put them in the recycling can before waving them toward the door. "Are you two clowns ready to go?"

Sarah jumped up. "I just have to get my messenger bag from your office. I'll be right back."

While she was gone, Keller leveled a gaze at Annie. "Are you okay to drive, A?"

"Not to worry, I'm good. I only had a couple drinks all night. I was mostly drinking water the whole time I was on the dance floor."

"Okay then, as long as you're safe. Thanks again for taking Sarah's RAV4 home. She—" She swallowed the unexpected lump of emotion. "Um, she told me that she loves me tonight."

"No shit?"

"No shit. It was—amazing."

Annie pulled her into a quick hug. "That's awesome, Keller, seriously. I've never seen her this happy before and no matter what, I'm glad you two met each other." She laughed. "Could she have picked a less romantic place though?"

Just then, Sarah reappeared with her bag slung across her body. "Hey, hands off my woman, brat!"

"Oh whatever! Keller's like a sister to me and you know it."

The three women were laughing when they walked out the front door. But as soon as they got outside, Keller swore. "Shit!"

Sarah looked at her with concern. "What's wrong?"

"I forgot that I was going to bring my laptop home to work on the budget. You guys stay here, I'll be right back!"

Sarah pointed at her RAV4 that was conveniently parked

right across the street. "I'm just going to walk her to the SUV, I promise." Keller nodded then dashed inside. There was a vehicle coming from a few blocks away, probably someone making their way home from another bar. They started across the street knowing the car would have to stop at the stop sign.

Annie got Sarah's keys out of her pocket and then promptly dropped them. The force of the snap ring hitting the pavement popped it open and half a dozen keys fell off. "Goddamnit all to hell! Why do you have so many keys anyways?" Sarah stopped with her and bent down to help pick them up. She laughed and started to defend herself when she was cut off by the squealing of tires. Both sisters looked up in time to see a rusty pickup truck speeding toward them, not at all braking for the stop sign. Time slowed and the last thing Sarah remembered was pushing Annie out of the way. The front of the truck caught Sarah at both mid-thigh and across her lower ribs. The force of the blow caused rusted metal from the fender to gouge into her inner thigh and raked across the front of her left leg. The singer was spun around, blood arching outward as she fell. Annie lay on the ground in shock for critical seconds while the truck sped away.

Keller walked out in time to see the entire thing and it only took a second for her to see the license plate number before the truck disappeared around the next corner. Her attention was pulled away by Annie's scream. "Sarah!" The younger sister looked up at Keller, her hands bloody from trying to stop the flow from Sarah's femoral artery. There was already a large puddle under the unconscious woman. "Keller, do something!"

When Keller knelt she realized the nature of Sarah's injury and immediately grieved. The blood loss already had the heartbeat she was so familiar with fluttering. She turned helpless tear-filled eyes to Annie. "There's nothing I can do, Annie, her artery is severed! She's bleeding too fast—" She looked down and added her hands to the younger woman's, hoping the extra pressure would be enough but knowing it wouldn't be.

She was surprised when Annie pulled away and slapped bloody hands against her chest. "I said help her, dammit! Don't let my sister die!" When Keller hesitated she added, "I know everything, do it!"

Aware she possibly only had seconds before Sarah's heart stopped completely from lack of blood pressure, she immediately bent down to her slashed leg. It was easiest to get blood from the wound for obvious reasons. After drinking just enough, she quickly cut her own wrist open and forced precious drops into Sarah's mouth. They both waited, hoping the fast moving virus would overwhelm Sarah's immune system and go to work. Seconds ticked by and the blood slowed to a stop. Another minute was lost with no discernable change and Annie stifled a sob. Then, when even Keller was on the verge of giving up hope, Sarah's chest rose off the ground as her back arched and she gave a great gasp. Keller immediately lifted her and ran toward the bar and through the door that she hadn't yet had the opportunity to lock. Annie grabbed the keys and stared at the large pool of blood for a few seconds, then ran after her. Back in Keller's office, Annie found her sister lying on the leather couch completely still. Keller was on the phone. "Yeah, I'd like to report a truck that tried to hit me outside Club Diversity. Yes, I did get the license plate number."

Annie sat next to her sister and stopped listening when the bar manager recited the plate number and vehicle description. She watched in equal parts awe and worry as the scrapes across the unconscious woman's cheek began to heal. When she moved the ripped pants out of the way, she could see the leg was healing as well. She looked at Keller when the smaller woman walked over to the couch. "What did they say, and why did you tell them you were outside Club Diversity?"

Keller sat down closer to Sarah's head. "They are running the plate now and are sending a couple units to the address that is registered to the truck. I didn't give them our club name because I didn't want them to come over here and ask questions." When Annie gave her a confused look, Keller elaborated in a voice gone rough with a heavy accent that the younger had never heard her use. "There is a big fucking puddle of blood on the road out there, Annie!" She waved a hand toward her battered-looking lover. "And how do we explain this? In less than a half hour she's not going to have a mark on her but it certainly looks like someone died out there. The state of her blood covered clothes certainly fit the part of a victim."

Annie nodded her head at the practical reasons. "Oh, I didn't think of that."

The bar manager sighed and ran a hand through her hair. "Unfortunately, that is the least of our problems right now."

"What do you mean? Sarah's alive and the cops are going to

get the guys that did this. It's good, Keller, we're all good now! Aren't we?"

Keller shook her head and gazed down at her only love. "No, we are definitely not good. I did the one thing she was most afraid of and now I'll never get her back. If we're apart long enough, our immunity and healing will be compromised. That means we could be killed by something as simple as a goddamn cold!" She turned distraught eyes to her friend and employee. "Don't you see? This was all for nothing! My choices were to let her die and die soon after, or save her and let her kill me anyway!" She buried her face in her hands, not caring about the nearly dry blood liberally coating them. Both women were suddenly startled to hear Sarah's voice.

"K—Keller? What's going on?" She looked up at the two women with confusion swimming in her eyes and then looked around the room. "How...how did I get here? I don't remember..."

Seeing the pain in Keller's eyes, Annie explained. "Sarah, there was an accident and you were hit."

Sarah looked up at her in alarm and then glanced down at her own clothes. "What the hell? I feel fine, what happened to my clothes?" Upon further inspection, she noticed the damp feel of blood soaked jeans then looked at the blood on Annie's and Keller's hands. But if that wasn't enough to tell her the truth of the matter, the guilt written on Keller's face was. She spoke quietly at first. "What did you do?" Keller's eyes filled with tears but she didn't answer. Sarah sat up and took hold of the front of her girlfriend's shirt. Her next words were a yell. "WHAT THE FUCK DID YOU DO, KELLER?"

Annie placed a hand on her sister's tensed arm. "She saved your life, Sarah!"

Feeling betrayed and lost, Sarah turned cold green eyes toward her. "This is between me and Keller, stay out of it, Annie!"

"No, this is between all of us! She only did what I asked her to. She was going to let you die and I couldn't lose you, Sarah, I just couldn't!"

Sarah abruptly stood and walked away from the couch. "You both knew how I felt about this, how could you?"

She turned, and Keller's heart broke at the look on her lover's face. Sarah was going to run. It was written all over her face.

"Sarah, please! Can we just talk about this?"

Sarah screamed in rage and pounded her hand down on Keller's steel top desk. Then she instantly sobered at the large dent left by her fist. "Fuck."

Annie stood and slowly walked toward her. She reached a comforting hand out as she spoke. "Sarah?" Sarah spun around and batted her hand out of the way. Annie cried out in pain and cradled her hand while backing away.

Seeing what she had just done to her own family, her breath left her in a gasping sob. Turning tormented green eyes to Keller she lashed out. "This is your fault! I hope you're happy." And with those last words, she grabbed the keys that Annie had dropped on the couch, and ran from the room.

Shock kept the remaining two women silent for a minute and then Keller quickly walked over to Annie. "Are you okay?"

The younger woman gave her a pained look. "I don't think it's broken, but it hurts like hell. What about you?"

Keller looked at her with hundreds of years of sadness. Her voice was barely loud enough to be heard. "It's definitely broken and I—I'm not sure what to do about it."

Casting one last glance at the dented desktop, Annie grabbed her boss's arm and led her toward the door. "Come on, there's no point in staying here. She'll come back when she's ready, I know she will. She's alive and we have to focus on that." As they walked out the door of the club, the storm that had been building over the city finally broke. Cold rain poured over them as they made their way to Keller's car. Neither one mentioned the blood that was rapidly washing from the street in dark rivulets.

Chapter Ten

"IT'S BEEN TWO fucking weeks, Keller, where is she!" In Keller's office with the door shut — they certainly didn't need anyone hearing this conversation — Annie was going out of her mind with worry. She sat on the edge of Keller's desk and ran her fingers over the fist-sized indention. Neither one of them having heard from Sarah since the accident. Annie ran a hand through her hair in frustration. Keller had called Sarah's clients to let them know that Sarah was ill and on a temporary leave of absence but that didn't help Annie's situation. Her relationship with Jesse was suffering because she hadn't told her about Keller and Sarah's — condition. Her girlfriend could sense that something was wrong. "I'm really struggling with Jesse because she doesn't understand why we aren't out looking for Sarah. She also knows I'm keeping something from her and its killing me to hurt her like this."

Keller sighed and looked up at her friend. The similarities between Annie and Sarah were enough to make her ache with loss every time she was in the same room with the younger woman. She certainly didn't want to cause problems in Annie and Jesse's relationship on top of everything else. "So tell her, A."

Annie snorted. "Yeah right! She's going to think I'm playing a joke on her, especially since we just watched that new vampire movie that's in the theaters right now. She's never going to believe me, Jesse is way too practical."

The bar manager stood and put a comforting hand on Annie's shoulder. "So we'll tell her together. I'm pretty sure I have a few tricks that will make her a believer." She motioned toward the door. "Come on, let's go. You're done with your paperwork for the day and I'm not going to be productive at this rate, we may as well bail. Lynne and Sal are in charge tonight, between the two of them things should be well in hand."

It was nearly dinnertime when Keller parked in front of Annie's house. Annie pulled into the driveway next to Jesse's little car. They walked inside together and heard Jesse call from the kitchen. "Hey, babe, you want our Friday night usual?" She came through the door and was startled to see Keller. "Hey, Keller, you want to stay and have dinner with us? Have you heard anything from Sarah yet?"

Keller shook her head sadly and Annie spoke up. "Actually, that's what we're here to talk to you about."

Her girlfriend walked the rest of the way into the living room while the other two took off their coats and hung them up. "What do you mean you want to talk to me about Sarah, what's wrong with her? Do you know where she is?" The confused look on her face suddenly turned to one of panic. "Oh my God, something has happened to her!"

Annie rushed over to reassure her and they all took a seat in the living room. "Something has happened but she's okay. It's—well, there is something I need to tell you about Sarah, or Keller needs to tell you because it involves both of them." She gave her boss a pleading look and Keller took over.

Keller stared straight at the younger woman, who swallowed nervously. "I want you to listen to me now and just hear me out. Please, save all your questions for the end. Okay?" When Jesse nodded back at her, she told the story of her life. Even Annie didn't know a lot of it, just some of the highlights that pertained to her vampirism. When Keller finished, Jesse sat stunned.

She laughed and spoke in a voice laced with quite a bit of skepticism. "You guys are fucking with me! Annie put you up to this, right?" Keller merely stared long enough to make the younger woman nervous, then got up and went into the kitchen. She figured it would be easiest to repeat the same demonstration she used with Sarah all those months ago. She had a large knife and a handful of paper towels when she returned. Seeing the knife, Jesse jumped up from the couch. "What the hell, Keller? Stop playing around, this isn't funny anymore!" She turned to Annie, who was looking back with the most serious expression she'd ever seen. "Annie? This is a joke, right?"

Annie shook her head. "Go ahead and show her, Keller."

Before Jesse could say another word, Keller cut into her forearm with the knife and blood immediately welled up from the wound. She caught the little bit that dripped from the small cut with the paper towel and held her arm out for Jesse to see. The wound quickly and cleanly healed within seconds. Stunned, the younger woman sat back on the couch with a thud. "Oh my God." Annie wrapped an arm around her shoulders and let her process the new information. Keller returned the knife and paper towels to the kitchen and when she came back Jesse peppered her with questions. "So what does this mean? Who else knows? What does this have to do with Sarah?"

Keller took a deep, weary breath. "It doesn't mean much other than I have to move every ten to twenty years so people don't get suspicious. Only a select few know so I ask that what I've told you doesn't leave these walls, okay?" Jesse gazed back her with wide eyes and nodded. "And Sarah has always had a problem with my disease in that she is terrified of the idea that I would infect her. She doesn't want to watch Annie grow old and die without her. She made me promise that I'd never infect her and I said I wouldn't turn her unless I was asked."

"So she finally asked you?"

Annie joined in. "No, I did." Jesse gaped at her in surprise so she explained. "Do you remember how the two guys in the pickup truck made the front page of the paper a few weeks ago?"

"Yeah, they finally caught those guys that murdered that Diversity employee and nearly killed a bunch of other people."

Even now, two weeks after the incident, Annie had a hard time thinking about that night. Her eyes welled up with tears and she held Jesse's hand tight within her grasp. "They were only caught because Keller called in an anonymous tip with the license plate number. They—they almost killed me two weeks ago when we were leaving the bar. But S—Sarah pushed me out of the way at the last second and they hit her instead." She started to cry in earnest now, unable to finish the tale.

Keller continued where Sarah off. "She was dying. She would have died if Annie hadn't begged me for her life. I didn't even know Sarah had told her about me. But we couldn't let her die—I couldn't." She swallowed hard and looked down at her white-knuckled fists. Then, without any warning, Keller covered her face with her hands and broke down. Wracking sobs shook her whole body and the younger women immediately moved to sit on either side of her. They held Keller tightly between them, understanding the amount of pain and uncertainty that was weighing her down. With their arms around her and soothing words, the tears began to slow. She turned bruised and hollowed blue eyes to Annie first, then to Jesse. Her voice was rough and cracked when she spoke. "Thank you. It's just that she's been gone since that night and I'm slowly going mad."

Jesse looked thoughtful for a minute before speaking.

"Keller, are you sure you don't know where she may have gone? Annie, are there any friends she would have stayed with?"

Keller shook her head. "No, she won't go stay with any of her old friends because she's still too new. Sarah will be feeling too much temptation right now and she won't know how to control all the emotions that are bombarding her. She'll want to be alone. She needs help and needs someone who understands but we're the only — oh."

Annie jerked her head when Keller abruptly stopped speaking. "What? Did you think of something?"

The bar manager grimaced, hating the thought that popped into her head and hating that she was most likely right about it. "Temple du Loup."

Jesse brows wrinkled. "I don't get it. Why would she go there?"

Keller responded with barely restrained emotion. "Louve would help her. She is one of the few people who knows my secret."

Remembering the way the ringmaster seemed to be drawn to her sister as well as the story of how the three women had spent the night together, the sarcastic reply left Annie's lips before she could stop it. "I'm sure she would do more than help her!" Keller shot her a pained look and Annie immediately regretted her words. "Oh shit, I'm sorry, Keller. I'm sure Louve wouldn't take advantage of the situation."

The bar manager looked at her again then pulled out her cellphone and dialed. The two younger women heard a faint voice answer and Keller began speaking in rapid-fire French. Her face showed a mix of relief and concern when she finally hung up. Annie pressed closer. "Is she there?"

Keller sat back on the couch and gripped her hair in both hands. "Yes, she's been staying in the apartment below the club. Louve says she has no control yet and is starting to feel the hunger. Twice she's had to stop her from doing something unfortunate with her or the troupe."

Annie covered her mouth, shocked at the news of her sister. "What does she mean, that Sarah's losing control? Is — is she turning into an animal like the movies? What can we do?"

The bar manager closed her eyes. "She's feeling her power and she's feeling the hunger and the call of all those voices and emotions in her head. I have to think for a minute. If I go over there and she's not ready to see me—she could disappear for good."

Jesse was silent but her face was a study of concentration. She was excellent with details and something was bothering her with Keller's explanation. She cleared her throat, and got the other two women's attention. "Keller—if Sarah has what you have, how was Louve able to stop her from doing anything? Isn't she super strong now or something?"

The question caught Keller off guard and she looked from one to the other with wide eyes. "Uh...it's complicated."

Annie narrowed her eyes at the reticent woman. "The truth, Keller. We've come this far now, a little more honesty can't hurt."

"Louve—her and her troupe are more than they seem."

Jesse gasped, her eyes got bright excitement. "Temple du Loup—*loup*, as in werewolves!" She turned to Annie. "Jesus, that is so cool!"

Annie looked at her girlfriend in surprise then back at Keller. The bar manager nodded in confirmation. "So what do we do now?"

Keller abruptly stood. "We are doing nothing. *I* am going over there and you two will stay here."

Protests immediately followed her words. "No!"

"It's my sister!"

But Keller was not going to change her mind. "No, I go alone. Because I don't want you two at risk if she gets violent again or starts an incident with Louve and her people. Stay here and I'll call as soon as I know something."

Keller's mind was in turmoil on the drive to Louve's club. It had been two weeks and all she'd felt through their connection was anger and pain. What she didn't tell Annie was that she wasn't sure how she could get Sarah back, that if Sarah went dangerously out of control and wild, harming others, it would be up to Keller to put her down for good. Just like she did with Catherine. Louve wasn't strong enough by herself. Even her whole troupe would be hard pressed to hold a crazed vampire against their will. She'd seen it before hundreds of years ago. No, she would do whatever she could to prevent Sarah from going over the edge of that abyss. She had two weapons against the singer. The first was that she was hundreds of years older therefore significantly stronger than the other woman. The second was her love. She only hoped that would be enough to bring Sarah back because she wasn't sure if she was emotionally strong enough to take her lover's life. And the only way to outlive your soul mate was to find a way to break that precious bond. The single time Keller had seen it done left the remaining person an emotional cripple, never to love again. You either died with them or you wanted to die, there seemed to be no in between. No, the price of failure was too great.

She parked in the staff parking lot behind the old church. The club wouldn't open for hours still. It was also a night the circus didn't perform, just a standard evening of dancing and debauchery for the club-goers. She knocked on the heavy back door and within seconds it opened. Louve stood there looking distraught. "Come." She turned and led her down a familiar hallway until they stood in front of the door to the apartment. Before Keller could reach for the doorknob, Louve stopped her with a hand to her chest. "*Attendez une minute*, mon ami. Just one minute please."

Keller looked at her with added worry. "What is it?"

"She is strong, very strong. And she has done much damage inside. Diffuse her anger if you can. I think that is fueling the hunger which we can ill afford to turn loose, no?" The she-wolf removed her hand and added one last thing. "I will have my people listen for you. Should you be in need of help, just call out to us." She gave Keller a wry smirk and tried for a small joke. "Just cry wolf." That was the true nature of the woman she had known for so long. Louve had always been the one to lighten a crowd. But Keller was an audience of one and her heart much too heavy to be moved. She merely nodded in response and turned the handle.

SARAH WAS TRYING to think and not feel anything. For two weeks, the crowded feeling in her head remained. Emotions, some thoughts, and white noise in general—they were all pushing their way inside and she didn't know how to stop it. And she was hungry, so very hungry. Nothing Louve kept stocked in the kitchen of the apartment would fill her. Her stomach clenched and more often than not she found sharp fangs cutting into her lower lip. Nighttime though—that was the worst part of it all. When the club was open and full of all those people—she could feel them above her. She could feel all of Louve's people tempting her, promising something that would fill that ache inside. She was drawn to them in a way that only Keller had ever surpassed but Louve would let no one near.

Sarah's brows drew down in anger. "That bitch—" She laughed, feeling crazed and out of control. "Fucking she-wolf, she really is a bitch!" It didn't help that she was locked in this apartment, this torture chamber. Sarah couldn't leave to escape the emotions pressing down on her. She couldn't run away like she always had before. At first she was happy but the past few days had been too much. When one of the wolf people came in to bring supplies, she cornered her. The woman was tall, well built, and athletic, and she gave off so much energy it was like a high. Sarah tried to get as close as possible, wanted to bathe in the other woman's aura. She wasn't going to hurt her—she just needed to be close. She was so hungry. She also reveled in the fact that she was stronger than the werewolf. The bitch yelled in panic when the singer had done no more than run a tongue along the she-wolf's neck. The Louve arrived with others and forbade everyone from coming in alone. Sarah couldn't help the blind rage that overtook her then and she lunged for Keller's longtime friend, her ex-lover. She'd been locked in the apartment ever since. She was going crazy.

Keller opened the door, wary at what she would find. At first glance, she could see that the living room looked like a tornado had gone through. Furniture was overturned, and there were holes in some of the walls showing the steel-reinforced beams behind. She raised an eyebrow, impressed. Louve clearly had this apartment remodeled with her own people in mind. Occasionally new werewolves needed a safe place for their first change. The apartment was their safe house of sorts. She didn't immediately see Sarah so she slowly made her way farther inside.

Sarah heard the door open and knew someone had come in. She could smell her, and feel her through the connection they shared. She was torn between that familiar and comforting burn of anger and that soothing balm of peace that the other woman represented in her life. When Keller cautiously made her way into the bedroom, Sarah left the bathroom and silently followed. Unseen, she reached out a shaking hand to the woman she had grown to love, the same woman who had betrayed her. Then the hunger washed over Sarah once again, cramping her stomach and blinding her mind from anything but need. With an inarticulate cry, she rushed the smaller woman.

Keller was able to turn at the last second and flip Sarah over her shoulder onto the bed. Then, before the singer could re-orient herself, Keller had her pinned down. She wrapped her legs around the thrashing woman's thighs and held her wrists in an iron grip. Keller looked in dismay at the woman under her. Sarah's hair was wild, as were her eyes. "Sarah, stop!"

The brunette continued to buck beneath her. "Let me go!" Keller just held on, riding out the storm. In a shorter than expected amount of time, Keller felt the other woman's motions begin to slow. Eventually Sarah just lay there broken. She sobbed disjointed words and phrases and the sound ripped a hole in Keller's heart. "Please – please – I'm so hungry. Voices – everyone pushing down on me. Hungry, I can't take it anymore. Please..."

She could feel Sarah's anger taper out through the bond they shared but she kept her grip firm. "Sarah, love. I'm here. I'm right here and I can help you. Let me help you –" She kept reassuring the other woman with words at the same time she pushed all the love she held down that line of connection. Eventually, those green eyes looked at her with some level of sanity.

"Ke – Keller?"

"Yes, love, I'm here. I'm going to help you. Will you let me help you?"

Those sad eyes looked up at Keller. "I'm so hungry, please – I feel so empty right now. Nothing fills me up anymore."

Keller leaned in slowly, letting the other woman get used to the smell and feel of her so near. "I'm going to kiss you now, okay? I promise it will help." Sarah nodded with tear-filled eyes. When their lips touched, Keller let down the last barrier. She sent great waves of energy and emotion in an attempt to fill the other woman. It took Sarah by surprise when Keller ran a knowing tongue along her overly-sensitive canines. She gasped at the instant flash of arousal that the small action had caused. Keller continued on, making love to Sarah's mouth in a way that only centuries of practice could match. Eventually, the singer was writhing beneath her but not in fury. It was another kind of heat that set the woman on fire.

Once again, Sarah found herself begging, but with a different kind of hunger. What she had no way of knowing was that both hungers were one and the same. She rolled her hips, trying to alleviate the throbbing between her legs. "Please.... Please just touch me!" Unfortunately her efforts were met with no satisfaction because of the way Keller held Sarah's thighs clamped together. When the brunette started to whimper, Keller took pity on her. She unlocked her legs, and used her knees to push the other woman's thighs apart. Sarah moaned softly when she felt Keller's crotch rest lightly against her own. She rolled her hips again, but the contact wasn't enough, and Keller continued to hold Sarah's wrists in place. Both women were still fully clothed, so Keller shifted her position on the bed and straddled Sarah's long thigh. In doing so, she firmly pushed her own thigh right where the singer most needed it and the woman beneath her hissed her pleasure. "Oh! Yes!"

Sensing her lover wasn't all the way returned from the brink yet, she moved up slightly, kissing her way up Sarah's neck and along her jawline to lips that were parted slightly and more than a little swollen. She whispered through the entire journey. "Come back to me love, come all the way back so I can fill your emptiness. Do you want me to fill you?" Sarah's affirmative reply was swallowed when their lips met again. Slowly, very slowly, Keller released her wrists. Sarah's response was immediate. She reached her arms around and grabbed Keller's ass in an attempt to increase the delicious pressure against her clit. Keller was matched in arousal by that point and began rubbing herself on Sarah's long thigh. With hands wrapped tight in dark locks, Keller pulled Sarah's head back and stilled her thrusting. The taller woman struggled for a second then relaxed and stared up at her with those bottomless green eyes. "Let's get undressed." Her suggestion was met with a smile.

With a speed born of intense need, their clothing was removed and forgotten. The tables were turned however when Keller found herself on her back with Sarah pinning her down. She felt a split second of concern until she saw the smirk on her lover's face. The brunette taunted her. "What are you going to do, hmm? We share the same power now."

She was surprised when Keller started laughing. "Oh my love, we do share the same blood but you're forgetting something important.

"What's that?"

With a burst of inhuman strength, Keller reared up and quickly spun them around. Tables turned, she looked down at the surprised face of her soul mate. "I will always be hundreds of years older." With a smirk of her own, she added, "Which means, I will always be stronger." With those words spoken, she clouded the other woman's mind with the pleasure she was feeling and fiercely bit into her neck. Sarah cried out at the abruptness and intensity of the lust while Keller drank deep. When her mind was buzzing with arousal and their touch felt electric, she pulled away. The wound sealed in an instant. What the singer didn't realize was that Keller was teaching her, hoping she would pick up the skills necessary to survive with their condition.

Sarah licked her lips and smiled, more turned on than she had ever been before. "My turn." Just as abruptly, she copied Keller's push of power and flooded the smaller woman with arousal. Then she pulled Keller's neck down to her waiting mouth. The first taste of blood on her tongue was sweet and tangy. It tasted of iron and all the complexities of life. Sarah swallowed and moaned at the feeling of spreading warmth through her body. Keller was very much alive and filling her in a way she'd never done before. Before she had taken more than the smallest of swallows, the bar manager shifted slightly and entered Sarah with two fingers. The singer stiffened with instant pleasure and moaned while still drinking her fill. She finally released Keller's neck when those same fingers began thrusting deeply and curling just inside. Keller leaned up and kissed away the spot of blood at the corner of Sarah's mouth while the woman below her murmured soft words. "Oh God, oh God, fuck me—" The blood was her own and Keller found it was a curious experience. She was also pleased to note that Sarah was indeed a quick study.

Never stopping her motions, Keller worked her way down Sarah's body. She slowed in time to lavish attention on the singer's hard nipples, then continued on her way. Sarah was moaning by the time Keller reached her destination. Sarah gasped when she felt sharp points drag up each side of her clit, then she moaned when the fangs were followed by a hot, wet tongue up the center. Keller could feel Sarah's inner walls tightening around her fingers and she knew she was close.

Sarah pawed weakly at Keller's arms. "Please!" That was enough to return the smaller woman's attention to the matter at hand and she lapped at Sarah's clit with practiced skill. Sarah threw her head back as her legs began to shake but still Keller kept on. Finally, when Sarah could take no more, the dam broke and she came screaming her lover's name. As soon as she tumbled over the edge, Keller broke the skin with her teeth and continued to lap at that blood-filled bundle of nerves. The clouding of her mind meant no pain for Sarah, and the double feedback only seemed to take the orgasm to greater heights. All of it served to pull Keller along with her. After riding the orgasm for an unusually long time, Keller carefully removed her teeth then her fingers. The wounds closed instantly. Their connection was pulsing with pleasure but the sharp lust of earlier had faded. Keller collapsed on the bed between Sarah's legs. Her own sex was throbbing but she had been more focused on re-establishing their bond.

Sarah held out a hand and whispered to her. "My love."

Keller was next to her in an instant. "How do you feel?"

She got a lazy smile in return. After a few minutes, Sarah roused enough to give her a more verbal response. "I never knew. All this time with you and I never knew."

Keller was confused. "Never knew what, my love?"

"I never knew how it could be between us." She started crying. "I'm so sorry, Keller. I'm sorry for leaving and for being so afraid. I'm sorry for hurting Annie—oh God, she must hate me!"

The bar manager stroked her cheek. "No, love, she doesn't hate you. We've all been so very worried but I knew you needed some time to think. But none of that matters because I'm here now. I will always be here for you." Before Sarah could respond, Keller leaned in and kissed her with supreme tenderness. The strong bond between the two women was wide open, lending the kiss an ethereal quality. She pulled back and looked seriously into her lover's eyes. "Now, let me show you how to keep your sanity." She worked with Sarah for the next half hour, showing her how to build a shield in her mind. It was one of the most important lessons she could teach because it would keep the new vampire from being overwhelmed by all the emotions and energy around her. She grinned when she was sure Sarah was proficient. "Very good! Now, how about a kiss to celebrate?"

Sarah laughed at her enthusiasm. "I've been waiting for you to say that!" She pulled Keller's head toward her own and moaned when their lips made contact. Their bond had never been stronger and Sarah's senses never more alive. Each touch of her lover's skin was like heated silk. However, they were interrupted by a commotion in the hall before it could escalate much further.

Raised voices could be heard. A familiar one, and the muffled sound of response then another familiar voice.

"Let me go, my sister is in there!" The yell was followed by a loud thumping and another exclamation.

"What the fuck?" The sound of a struggle and a desperate cry followed. "Don't touch her!"

Another loud thump and a pained cry was the last thing they heard as they finished getting dressed and bolted out the door. Keller was fastest and the first into the hall but Sarah was right behind her. They were both shocked at the scene before them. While it was one thing to have her lover tell her about werewolves and to actually feel their energy, it was quite another to see one up close and in person. They ran out in time to catch the last moments of the struggle. One large furred creature was just letting Annie go and another was staring down at a prone body on the ground. It was Jesse. Annie's scream startled them all and they pushed through the two other people who were not yet furry. Sarah rushed to her sister's side while Keller knelt down and turned Jesse over. She had an oozing cut on her scalp from where she had been thrown into the wall. Keller continued to check her over until she reached the younger woman's midsection. There were bloody tears in her shirt where claws had sliced all the way through. Her first word was low and angry. "No." She looked up at the werewolf that had thrown Jesse into the wall. In one fluid motion she rose to her feet and took a step toward the now terrified werewolf. Fury laced her every word. "You did this!" The strength of her anger pressed down on everyone in the crowded hallway. It was then that Sarah understood exactly how powerful her lover really was, how powerful she herself would become with time.

That was the moment that Louve came rushing through a door at opposite end of the hall and raced toward the group. Louve stepped in front of Keller before she could advance any farther. Taking in the scene, the French woman immediately realized the gravity of the situation. She reached out her hand to plead for calm much the same way Keller had reached for Sarah earlier. "Keller—"

Faster than even the she-wolf could react, Keller grabbed her arm and spun her around. With the arm pinned painfully behind her, the blonde forced her to look at Jesse's bleeding body. "I thought we had an understanding, Louve. I thought we had peace between us. But look what your puppy has done — look!" She shook the small brunette, as if to emphasize her point.

The Frenchwoman swallowed, her enhanced senses taking in the slow and steady heartbeat of the bleeding woman. She closed her eyes, not wanting to see the damage done to Keller's young friend, not wanting to face the damage done to their friendship. "I'm so sorry mon ami. *Je voudrais prendre tous de retour, si je pouvais.*"

Keller abruptly turned her loose and shoved her forward. Only the French woman's agility kept her from falling over the top of Jesse. Annie broke free and ran to the fallen woman when Sarah relaxed her grip. The younger Colby sister dropped to her knees next to her lover and pulled Jesse into her lap. She looked up at Keller with tear filled eyes. "What's wrong, is she going to die?"

"No, she will live." Despite the verbal reassurance, the look on Keller's face was one of mourning.

Annie stared at her in confusion. "I don't understand. Why are you so upset? We should take her to a doctor, she needs stitches." She gently brushed dark hair away from Jesse's wound. "She's probably got a concussion."

Louve knelt down and put a hand on the Annie's arm to keep her from trying to move Jesse. "She will not need a doctor, mon *jeune* ami." She glanced up at Keller's angry countenance and looked back into the young woman's fearful eyes. "She is one of us now. She will heal quickly on her own. Did the wolf who held you, Joseph — did he scratch you at all?"

The werewolf in question stepped forward and spoke with desperation. His voice was low, nearly a growl but still clear. "I swear, I did not touch her, Louve!"

The small brunette's fury lashed out at her troupe member. "Silence!" He immediately lowered his head and backed away. "Please, Annie, any scratches or punctures?"

Annie had seen enough movies that she finally caught on. Her face paled and she swallowed loudly. Jesse was lying half in her lap and she clutched her girlfriend tightly when she answered. Her words were a whisper. "No."

Sarah looked from Annie to Louve then over to her lover. "Keller? What the fuck is going on?"

Keller sighed and ran a hand through her hair. "The werewolf virus is very contagious when they are in their beast form.

Their claws can easily infect an ordinary human. The other were-wolf—" She paused, unsure of his name and Louve spoke for her.

"Marcel."

"Marcel would have known this and was not careful. There was no reason to react violently against humans who could no way match their strength. There was even less reason to use claws."

Louve interrupted. "He is new, only recently coming to us from Quebec. I did not know his control was so poor or I would have never left him down here to protect your privacy."

Annie gently moved Jesse back to the ground and stood. "So what does this mean? If Jesse is going to be a werewolf, what will happen to her? What will happen to us?" With each word that came from her lips the younger woman's voice rose higher in panic.

Keller's gaze moved from Annie to the woman on the floor. Jesse looked as if she were simply sleeping. "It means her life is going to change and yours along with it. As for what will happen to her, only time will tell." She bent down and gently picked the younger woman up in her arms. She glanced back at Louve. "We're leaving. Send me the bill for the apartment repairs."

The circus owner shook her head. "Non. There will be no bill after what has happened here. I owe you a debt now."

Keller stared at her for a few seconds, then nodded toward the unconscious woman. "No, you owe her a debt. One I fear can never be repaid." With that, she led the silent Colby sisters from the building. They had three vehicles at the club so it took a few minutes to work out the logistics of their trip back to Annie's house. Keller decided to lay Jesse out in the back of Sarah's RAV4. Annie didn't want to leave her side but Keller reassured the younger woman that Jesse would be fine so she reluctantly agreed to drive herself back to the house. After they all arrived, Keller carried Jesse inside. She instructed Annie to get some fresh clothes so they could clean her up and get rid of the bloody ones.

The younger woman gasped and covered her mouth when she saw all the wounds were healed. "She really is—"

Sarah came up and put her hands on her sister's shoulders while she answered. "Wow."

Keller let out a resigned sigh. "Come on, let's finish getting her settled then we can talk. She won't wake for a few hours yet."

Once they were all seated in the living room, Annie looked at her boss and friend. "Talk to me, Keller. Between Sarah, and now Jesse, I've about had it with all this metaphysical movie-type shit! What will happen to my girlfriend, is she going to change and eat me or something?"

Sarah snorted, despite the seriousness of the situation. "You wish!" That broke some of the tension between the three of them and they started laughing. It was a desperate kind of laughter but necessary after all they'd been through.

Once they calmed down, Keller filled them in. "Werewolves used to be very pack oriented a long time ago. But since the turn of the century they have begun doing their own thing. Society has changed a lot and it's easier to be considered a little eccentric or different. Once they've learned to control their emotions, especially anger, there is no reason a werewolf can't live a completely normal, if long, life."

Sarah looked at her with worry. "And before they learn this control?"

"Well, that's why they have safe houses like Louve's apartment below the club. The new ones usually need to be contained when they first change, at least until they learn to control themselves."

Annie looked dismayed. "But we don't have anything like that here! And when is she going to change?"

Keller looked at the two sisters. "You know how doctors and nurses are always saying that hospitals are crazy on a full moon?" They nodded. "Well, for whatever reason, emotions are always stronger and more out of control at that time. Now you're probably aware of all the old werewolf tales about how they always change on the full moon. That has some basis in truth simply because their change is tied to the emotions. The change is also more likely to occur during a female werewolf's menstrual cycle for the same reason."

Sarah snorted. "Guess your girlfriend's going to be a real bitch at that time of the month, sorry, A."

"Be serious!" Annie punched her in the arm.

Keller continued. "However, once they gain control of their emotions, they can gain control of the beast. As long as Jesse keeps things fairly calm, there shouldn't be any risk of her changing until the next full moon." She shrugged her shoulders in apology. "I don't know when that is, sorry."

Annie quickly pulled out her phone and brought up the

information. "It's in two weeks."

The bar manager nodded. "Good. That gives us plenty of time to have a crew come in and make some changes to the basement. Are the walls concrete?"

Sarah answered. "Yes, except for the bathroom."

"Okay, I've got a crew I can call. It's the same one I used on my apartment and at the club. They do a good job, they work quickly, and they won't ask any questions."

Annie quickly interrupted her. "I can't afford all that, Keller!"

Keller laid her hand on the younger woman's knee. "If a person can't get rich after a few hundred years of life, they're doing it wrong. Don't worry, A, I can more than afford it. Jesse wouldn't be in this situation right now if you'd never met me and been pulled into my world." Knowing how stubborn her friend could be, she added, "Please, let me help."

Sarah rubbed Annie's back in reassurance. "Come on, Annie, she knows what needs to be done. Let's get through this together, okay?"

"Okay."

Keller pulled out her phone and looked at the time, then unlocked it and scrolled down the contact list until she came to the right name. It was a little late but she knew he'd pick up. "Hey, Jack, sorry to bug you so late. I need a favor. Yeah, time sensitive—" She explained what she needed and gave him the address then hung up. She looked up into two sets of questioning eyes. "His crew will be here Monday. He said they can have it done between three and five days. Now that is taken care of, let's get something to eat. How about pizza?"

The sisters spoke nearly in unison. "I'm not hungry."

Keller nodded in understanding but would not be deterred. She pointed at Sarah first. "You need to eat even if you don't realize it yet. We filled your energy but you still need regular sustenance." Then she looked at Annie. "And you still need sustenance as well. You cannot let worry cloud your head because Jesse will pick up on that and be more anxious. We need to keep her calm now. And werewolves need a significant amount of food after the initial infection and every time after they change form. Between the infected change and the healing, she will be very hungry when she wakes." Keller did some calculations in her head. "She will need at least two large pizzas, to start. Meat lovers would be

best. You could order an extra one for her just in case. The protein, carbs, and sugars will be building blocks for all the changes
her body is going to go through." She stopped and grinned at
them. "Besides, you don't want to see a hangry werewolf—it's not
pretty! You remember those Snicker's commercials with Betty
White? It's like that."

Annie left the room to order pizzas and Sarah found a movie
on Netflix for them to watch while they waited. When the
younger sister came back into the living room she gave the two
older women a pained look. "Really? This is what you want to
watch right now?"

Keller shrugged. "I've never seen it and I don't really care
what we watch."

The older Colby sister was unrepentant. "What? I wanted to
see something with vampires and werewolves in it and I've never
seen this movie either. Besides, Keller can tell us what they get
wrong and right."

They settled in to watch the movie, only pausing for Keller to
pay for the pizzas and to grab plates. By the time the movie was
halfway through, Keller was openly making fun. She snorted at
one scene. "Well I sure as hell don't sparkle in the sun!" A little
while later she started laughing and pointed at the screen. "Look
at the size of those boys, are they on steroids? They definitely
don't get any bigger when they turn." Suddenly, she remembered
something and looked at Annie. She called out quietly to her.
"Annie—" The younger woman paused the film. "—the change,
when Jesse changes—it's going to hurt. A lot. And she will need
you to be strong without interfering. Okay?"

Annie swallowed. "H—how bad?"

The older woman looked at her with intense blue eyes. "She
will be in agony." After letting the information settle in for a few
seconds, she continued. "She's strong though, and the pain is the
best incentive of all to learn control." Annie nodded and Sarah
gave her hand a squeeze as Keller restarted the movie.

The film was near the end when Jesse wandered out with a
confused look on her face. "Hey guys. How did I get home? The
last thing I remember was going to the club to look for Keller and
Sarah."

Annie walked over to her girlfriend cautiously. "We did go to
the club but there was a...well, an incident with Louve's troupe.
They—one of them, he—" She hung her head, unable to go on.

Jesse looked at her with concern. "Babe? What's wrong? What happened? How did I get home and changed?"

Both Keller and Sarah could feel the younger woman's anxiety level rising quickly, so they both stood and walked over to her. With only a look from her lover, Sarah knew what she wanted. In unison, they began projecting calming thoughts to Jesse. Keller clasped the younger woman's shoulder and spoke. "Let's go sit down and we'll explain. Are you hungry?"

Jesse nodded and then looked at her in surprised. "Yeah, I'm starving, how did you know?"

"Annie will go get you some pizza from the kitchen and we'll explain everything, okay?"

"You guys are acting weird, but you can explain whatever you want as long as I can eat something." She grabbed her stomach as it gave a loud rumble.

Once the young computer programmer was seated on the overstuffed chair with a full pizza box in her lap, she waved toward Keller. "Okay, explain please."

Keller took a deep breath and ran a hand through her hair nervously. "When I arrived at the club, Louve had Sarah locked in the apartment to prevent her from harming others. She had lost control with one of the troupe members a few days ago so Louve wasn't taking any chances. Once I went inside, she left a few guards in the hallway just in case I couldn't get through to Sarah and help her. Unfortunately, one of the guards was a newly turned wolf with poor self-control. He panicked when you rushed him and lashed out. You were thrown into the wall and knocked unconscious."

Jesse looked back at her with confusion, then turned her gaze toward her girlfriend. "Babe? I feel fine. I don't even have a headache. Why do you all look like you came from a funeral?"

Annie moved over to the arm of the chair and perched on the edge. "Hon, the werewolf didn't just throw you against the wall, his claws raked across your ribs. It's just like the movies, J."

Jesse's breath came out in a rush and she sat back in the chair, pizza forgotten. She looked down at her side, even lifting the shirt and stared at the perfectly smooth skin. Her first instinct was to think they were playing a practical joke but she quickly changed her mind. Just the look on their faces and the feeling in the room convinced her otherwise. "Wow. So I'm a—a werewolf now?" She looked up at Keller, knowing the older woman would have the most real answer.

Keller nodded. "Yes. You've been infected with the werewolf virus. Some of the stuff from the movies is true but other stuff is totally incorrect. Your change is linked to your emotions, which are heightened by the full moon. You will change at the first full moon, or if your emotions get out of control before that. Once you make it through the first few full moon changes, you should have enough control that you can prevent it in the future. The important thing is to stay calm and in control until you get through the first change. Good so far?"

The look on the new werewolf's face was one of awe and trepidation. "Wow. Yeah, it's a lot to take in but I've got it so far. Keep calm and 'wolf on'." Despite the life-altering news being thrown at her, Jesse still had a sense of humor. "You wouldn't want me to 'hulk out' or anything." Hearing her words, Annie began to laugh but it quickly turned into a sob. Jessie immediately threw the pizza box on the coffee table and pulled Annie into her lap. "Hey, it's gonna be okay. We'll be all right, we just need to get through this together." She suddenly had the frightening thought that maybe Annie wouldn't want to be with her now. "W — we are together right? You still want to be with me like this?"

Annie began crying in earnest and threw her arms around the other woman's neck. "Of course I do you, big idiot! We've got this, and I'm in it until the end, I promise!"

Sarah and Keller came over and crowded the two women in the chair. Sarah summed it up for them. "We've all been through a lot of changes recently but none of us is alone. We're all a team, we're family."

Chapter Eleven

ON KELLER'S SUGGESTION, Jesse found a nearby yoga class, and she and Annie started going twice a week. She stressed that it was just as important for Annie to remain in control of her emotions because Jesse's new sensitivity would pick up on her lover's distress. The basement renovations were completed in eight days and it looked better than before. Keller had them do a full remodel with reinforced walls and windows. The stairs were replaced with steel steps, and the basement door was strengthened from the inside. Even the bathroom had been updated and Keller took the luxury of having the builder install a Jacuzzi tub for the young couple. Another new addition was at the opposite end of the basement. She instructed the contractor to build a bedroom with large steel eyebolts added to the wall and floor on the side of the room that didn't have a window.

The four women had fun shopping for new furniture and other accessories to finish out the new room. Keller purchased the chain and thick buckled leather straps separately a few days later. Sarah was at her studio with a client while the remaining three of them had been arranging things downstairs. Keller surprised the other two when she made one more trip to her car and returned with the chains. Jesse's first signs of fear didn't show until she saw Keller attaching the heavy lengths to the eyebolts. Annie took one look at her girlfriend's face and went to her side. While rubbing Jesse's back, she looked at her boss. "Keller, is that really necessary?"

"The full moon is in three days."

Annie shrugged. "Yeah, but we've been going to yoga like you said and Jesse hasn't been even close to losing control since she was infected."

Keller gave them both an inscrutable look. Then she grabbed their hands and led them over to the bed. "Listen to me. She is new, therefore she will be especially vulnerable and sensitive by the time the full moon comes. There is no stopping this first change and once the pain hits her, she'll be out of her mind. She will either draw into herself when the pain hits or she'll lash out. But no one knows what she'll do until the change hits her."

Jesse stubbornly lifted her chin. "I'm right here, Keller, don't talk like I'm not. And I can handle it. I'm not your average keyboard jockey you know!"

The bar manager had to convince the younger women of the danger of not being prepared. She wished Sarah was there, thinking they would be more likely to listen to the singer. But she wasn't, so that left Keller no other choice. In a flash of movement that was too fast to see, Keller grabbed Annie and backed across the room. She held her from behind and bared fangs to the younger woman's neck. Like a light switch being thrown, a black cloud of anger came boiling out of the new werewolf. "Leave her alone!" The last word came out as more of a growl and left her bent over. She cried out as the pain hit, emotions immediately spiraling out of control. Keller quickly released Annie and sent every bit of energy she could to Jesse to help calm her before the change fully took hold. The effect on the woman was instantaneous and she dropped to a knee as all the tension drained from her body. She panted from the few short seconds of exertion and pain, sweat dotting her upper lip. In a small voice, the strong young woman broke Annie and Keller's hearts. "You're right, I'm so sorry. I thought I was in control. I thought I could handle it—" She started to cry brokenly and Annie sank to the floor with her. She rocked her lover as she tried to calm her down.

"Shh, it's okay, J. Everything is going to be okay. Let's just get through this first time, all right? If Keller says it will get better after this then it will. I trust her. I love you, Jesse." She continued to hold her and Keller used the opportunity to back out of the room. Annie could take care of her for now.

FRIDAY WAS THE day before the full moon and Annie and Jesse were simultaneously excited and anxious to be starting a four day weekend. They spent the day together watching movies and being silly to help alleviate Jesse's worry. Keller recommended that Jesse not work the day before her change and also suggested she take a few days off to recuperate after. Everyone had their schedules cleared for the next four days. Annie was going to miss one of her Sip and Chug shows that night but it couldn't be helped. Keller put Bruce in charge of the show and made sure she had all the necessary staff covering for both of them since she would not be there the entire weekend either. The plan was for the four of them to have dinner together Saturday night and then Jesse would go down and get locked up before the full moon could rise.

But no matter how much they tried to pass the time with fun distractions, Jesse was a bundle of nerves by dinner the next night. Keller and Sarah walked into the house with bags full of Thai Guys takeout and found the younger woman sitting in the overstuffed chair. Her right leg was jiggling up and down at the pace of a rabbit on speed and she steadily chewed the remainder of her already short nails. Duke pushed his way into the room ahead of the two women, excited to come back to a familiar place. As soon as he rounded the short wall separating the living room from the entryway, he stopped in his tracks. The hair of his scruff stood on end as he stared at Jesse and he growled menacingly. The younger woman's head whipped around and an alien look shadowed across her eyes when she looked at the Husky. She was immediately up from the chair, answering the canine growl for growl. Duke backed up ever so slightly as she advanced toward the protective dog. Jesse's lip curled up and her growling intensified. After nearly a minute, the dog finally backed down. Duke gave a whimper and lowered himself to the ground in submission. Keller's expression was unreadable but her voice held curiosity. "Impressive."

Jesse looked up at her, seeming to come out of a daze. She flushed bright red when she realized what she had done. "I — uh — I don't know what that was."

Keller laughed and clapped her on the shoulder. "*That* was your new normal. There are many things that you're going to learn in the coming months, Jesse. It's just you learning to be you, let it happen." She watched the younger woman's face to make sure she was taking it all in and nodded. "Come on, go grab your girlfriend and let's eat."

Dinner went well and everyone slowly relaxed throughout the meal. Because of the hell that awaited Jesse later, Sarah had bought her an ice cream cake for dessert since it was her favorite. However, once dinner was complete, Jesse's nerves began to take control again. Sarah went to help Annie clean up and Keller glanced over at the fidgety woman. "How are you doing over there, J?"

The soon to be furry younger woman snapped at her. "How the hell do you think I'm doing over here, Keller? I'm freaking the fuck out!" Her hands started clenching where they rested on the table and Keller saw beads of sweat pop out on her forehead.

She glanced at her watch, then looked up at Jesse. "Come on, Jesse, let's go downstairs."

Jesse shot her a panicked look. "Now?"

Keller nodded. "Better too soon than too late." They rose from the table and went into the kitchen where the basement door was located.

Annie smiled when they came through the doorway. "Hey, are you two here to help with dishes—" She stopped and paled when she saw where they were headed. "Already?"

Jesse tried to reassure her. "It's just a precaution. Don't worry, babe, I'll be all right."

Keller opened the door. "I'm going to buckle her in. Come down when you're ready."

It took nearly twenty minutes before the two sisters finally made their way downstairs. Annie had a minor breakdown and Sarah was quick to reassure her. In the basement bedroom they found Jesse seated in a chair against the wall. The chains were firmly attached to the leather straps buckled at her wrists and ankles. They were long enough that she could get down on all fours or lie down, but not so long that she could reach the bed or other furniture. Keller was reclining on the bed and the two women were watching an episode of *Buffy* on the flat screen TV on the opposite wall. Sarah joined Keller on the bed and Annie immediately went over to her girlfriend. She stood next to her and ran her fingers through the nervous woman's hair. Jesse welcomed the gesture but her agitation continued to escalate. Finally, she turned to the woman she had grown to love, the woman she now considered more her family than the ones related by blood. "Annie I—I want you to leave."

Annie stopped, a hurt look washing over her face. "What?"

Jesse tried to reassure her but her movements were hampered by the chains. This only made her more frustrated. "I mean, I don't want you to see me change. I—I don't want you to think of me as a monster."

The only response to her request was a sweet smile and a not so sweet kiss. It escalated quickly before Annie broke it off. "You will never be a monster to me."

Sarah looked up sharply when she felt something change in the air. Keller remained calm, as did the tone of her voice.

"Annie, it's time to come over with us now."

The younger woman began to protest but was interrupted by a gasp from her girlfriend. She took a step back and saw that her lover was sweating profusely. Jesse looked up at her with hyperdilated pupils. The pain was starting and she was only able to speak through gritted teeth. "P—please Annie, do what she says!"

Sarah called her. "Come over here with us, A, Keller says it will be over soon." Annie found herself snuggled between the older women on the bed. All they could do was watch. Keller observed with resigned guilt while the Colby sisters felt more of a horrified fascination. Keller slid off the bed and coaxed Jesse into standing. She had to remove the chair for all their safety. Once it was out of the way, Jesse slid down the wall and wrapped her arms around her knees. Her head was down but they could tell she was in pain from the way her knuckles turned white. Keller stood off to the side just in case.

Suddenly, a wet popping sound filled the small bedroom and Jesse screamed in agony. Her head came off her knees and hit the concrete wall behind her. When the next scream was ripped from her throat, Jesse's arms jerked with the pain. She cried out the only name that mattered to her. "Annie!" Then she pulled herself into a crouch and tried to move toward the bed.

The chains rattled with the force of her desperate pulling and Annie tried to leave the safety of her sister's arms to go to her. "Jesse!" But Sarah would not let her go and there was no way Annie could break her sister's vampire strengthened grip. Sarah held tight to the younger woman and whispered loving words to her until both their eyes were full of tears. Once the change was started, it seemed to move fairly fast. Keller quickly turned up the TV to help drown out the screaming. No one wanted the cops called at this point. Though it seemed like much longer, it was less than two minutes before the last scream morphed into a choked howl.

Annie sat up, slowly moving toward the edge of the bed. Where Jesse once stood, there was a creature like the ones below the club. Jessie's wolf form was black furred and roughly the same size as her human one. But she was definitely not human any longer. The werewolf crouched with her back to the wall and stared at her clawed hands. The others in the room watched as she touched her furred arms, and eventually her own face. Her hair was longer and shaggy on her head and down her neck and back. Jesse's face was slightly elongated with pronounced canines, a flattened nose, and almost too-human eyes. Her ears had changed shape with the rest. Elongated and furred, they sat farther up and back on her head. Jesse's eyes took in all her changes with something akin to wonder. Keller turned off the TV and spoke, breaking the younger woman free from her curious exploration. "Jesse—" The black furred she-wolf whipped her head up to look at the powerful woman in front of her. The alpha. "How do you feel?"

Jesse returned her gaze to her own claws, then to her girl-friend and back to Keller. Her voice was raw when it finally came out. It was partly due to the screaming and partly because of her changed shape. "I feel—okay. Strange." She stood and the rattling of the thick chains sounded especially loud in the silent base-ment. She once again looked to her clawed hands. "Is this my only form? I thought werewolves turned into a wolf."

Keller nodded. "You can and you will eventually become the wolf. The first change is—especially hard. Your body went only as far as it had to, which is normal. When you change again, it will be your choice if you want to go all the way." She thought for a few seconds, trying to come up with a way to explain what she'd been told. "The first time, all you can think about is the pain and your body stops as soon as possible. That stop is the form you're in now. It's like forcing your body to do something new and difficult. When your body gets used to the change, it won't hurt as much and you will be able to focus on letting it go further."

Jesse nodded and looked at all of them. "So how do I look?"

She got three separate responses in return. "Fierce."

"Freaky."

"Cool!" The last one brought a smile to her face because it was spoken by Annie. Annie turned to Keller. "Can I touch her?"

Sarah gripped her arm in fear but let it go just as fast when Keller reassured her. "You can touch her but be very careful. Her claws are very sharp and she is contagious in this form."

The younger woman nodded once then got off the bed and approached her girlfriend. Reaching a tentative hand out, she lightly stroked along Jesse's arm. A delighted smile came over her face. Looking back at Sarah, she exclaimed "She's so soft!" Wary of the claws, she turned Jesse's hand over in her own and traced the length of each finger. The look on the werewolf's face could only be described as adoration. When she was finished with her hand, Annie moved fingertips up her girlfriend's arms then to her neck and face. There was a point where the hair thinned and eventually stopped part way up her chest and neck, leaving Jesse's face smooth, if strange. The shape of her face vaguely resembled something that would become a snout, and her brows were a little heavier and more pronounced. While Annie lovingly traced the lines of her lover's face, Jessie inhaled Annie's scent and committed it to memory.

Jesse made a joke that was rooted firmly in insecurity. "What do you think, am I ready to enter into the Westminster Dog show?"

Annie looked into her lover's worried brown eyes and immediately understood the meaning behind the attempted humor. She let all the wonder and love she felt color her words. "You look *beautiful.*" Then, before Jesse could respond, she leaned forward and kissed her gently on the thinned lips. This prompted the werewolf to wrap her arms around her, trapping Annie in her furred embrace. Both women ignored the heavy chains, and Annie giggled. "Wow, you're really warm and cuddly like this!" Her words made them all relax and Keller blew out a sigh of relief.

The two younger women eventually slid down the floor next to each other. Annie couldn't seem to stop petting Jesse, much to the werewolf's chagrin. Jesse finally met Keller's amused eyes. "Um, so how long do I have to stay like this?"

Keller cocked her head in thought. "Well, your body needs fuel to change, energy. You need to eat something and rest then we'll see about returning you to human form."

The other woman looked at her nervously. "Wi—will it hurt?"

She was quickly reassured. "Actually, you don't feel pain the same in this form when you're changing. So the change back to human will feel nothing like the change to wolf or beast form. It—" She stopped and the other three women in the room were surprised to see her blush.

Despite the changed facial shape and features, surprise was still easy to read on Jesse's face. "It what?"

Keller scratched at her temple and cleared her throat. "Um, all the senses and feelings that you have in this form have to be closed back up into your human body. It's like putting an air mattress back into the box, it never fits. This will cause a — sensory overload. And for many werewolves, it can be a highly erotic experience. In short, the change will leave you tired, hungry, and horny."

Annie grinned. "What she's saying is that we're gonna get some food in you, then they're going home!"

Jessie looked back at Keller. "So this is it? I don't have to do anything else and I'm good to go?"

"No, this isn't it. You will have to keep developing your self-control. You need to learn how to change to wolf form when you want, to control the change. You will have to practice changing to both wolf and half-wolf forms, and practice changing back. Your senses will be heightened as well as your strength and reactions, even when in human form. It actually might be best if you could speak with Louve or one of her people and get more information about what living as a werewolf is actually like. You both should so that you know what you'll be dealing with going forward. And as an extra precaution, you should probably keep locking yourself up on the full moon for the next few months. However, I don't think you'll need us here after this one." The two younger women nodded, understanding there was still much to learn. Keller went over to Jesse and unlocked the buckles on her restraints. Annie quickly helped her.

Once she was free, the new werewolf took a few turns around the room to get used to her new gate. It was quite different. The foursome went out the door of the bedroom and into the main part of the basement. The biggest difference was that her legs bent the wrong way, and her arms seemed longer. She addressed no one in particular when she said as much. "This feels weird."

Keller laughed. "Of course it does, you're wearing a new body. Try running from here up to the top of the stairs and back again."

Jesse looked at her with ears up and then gave a slight shrug. "Okay." Faster than either one of the Colby sisters could believe, she turned and leaped over the couch then took the steps three at a time to the top of the stairs. Unfortunately, she didn't know her own speed and quickly crashed into the steel-reinforced wood door. *Whump.* "Ow, damn!" Then a brief pause and she spoke again as she turned to look down to them from the top step. "I'm okay!" Keller snickered and Sarah swatted her arm. Jesse's return only took seconds as she discovered why her arms were longer. It was easier to run on all four limbs than for her strange half-wolf self to run on hind legs alone. She stopped in front of them with a smile. "Wow! I'm not just stronger and faster, I can feel that my stamina is better too. And when I take a deep breath it feels like I can breathe in forever!"

Keller nodded. "Yes, you have increased lung capacity, greater blood flow to your muscles, harder bones, and incredible hearing and sense of smell. I'm afraid your eyesight won't be much better though. You might want to consider installing one of those oversize treadmills down here to practice running and to burn off excess energy on those days you have a hard time changing back."

Jesse looked at her with a bit of worry. "Will I have a hard time changing back?"

Keller shrugged. "Some do. Let's get some food in you and find out, hmm?"

This statement was finally met with a smile and fervent nodding. "Oh my God yes, I'm starving!"

The two younger women began walking up the basement steps and Annie snorted. "When aren't you hungry, seriously?"

"But I'm a werewolf now! A big, bad, hungry werewolf. I need to keep my strength up to be scary and menacing."

"Uh huh, as if! I saw you run from a bee the other day."

"I bet you'd be scared of me in the woods. Then I'd be the big bad werewolf and I'd eat you like Little Red Riding Hood."

"I wish—" They broke into laughter.

Keller and Sarah watched the two women walk up the stairs, their bantering continuing long after then went through the door. And then as one, Sarah and Keller cracked up laughing. The laughter did them both some good but it was short-lived. Like water funneling down a drain, it slowly slipped away leaving Sarah with a pensive look. "Are they going to be okay?"

Keller took her hand and lightly brushed the knuckles with a kiss. "Yes. They are definitely going to be okay."

Sarah gave her a piercing look. "Where is your big fancy scientific explanation for this one? I watched her change Keller, it's like—magic."

The shorter woman shrugged. "I don't have an explanation for it, it's not something I ever studied. It just is, and I accept it."

They exited the basement and the scene in the kitchen was

enough to make them pause. Annie was doubled over in laughter and Jesse was trying her best to eat a slice of leftover pizza. Sharp claws had reduced the piece to a gooey mess of pizza-ribbons. She had sauce in her fur and a string of cheese coming off her right ear. Her mostly wolf teeth were doing their best to mash together the bites she was getting into her mouth. Jesse spoke around a mouthful of half-masticated pizza. "Babe, you're not helping at all here. Can you get me something to drink?"

Seeing that her sister was not even close to getting herself under control, Sarah offered to help. "I'll get it, J, what do you want?"

"Dr. Pepper, please." She gave the singer a smile that looked more doggy than human.

Sarah noticed the younger woman had a bushy tail sticking out the back of the chair and chuckled to herself when she saw it wagging. She grabbed a can from the fridge, opened it and set it in front of the starving wolf without thinking. Keller held up a finger and started to comment. "Uh—" But it was too late.

Jesse awkwardly grabbed the can and held it to the front of her mouth, then tipped it back. Her face was pulled forward into more of a snout shape meaning anything going in the front was bound to run out the sides. And it did. Like a car wreck, Keller knew what was coming and continued to watch anyway. But she did manage to stifle a laugh before it could escape. This was not the case with Annie. Cold, sticky liquid immediately poured from the sides of Jesse's mouth and down the front of her fur. The fact that the younger woman was only dressed in a sports bra and boxers only added to the hilarity of the situation. "Sono-fabitch!" Shocked by the sudden mess, clawed hands fumbled the smooth can and the drink went flying into the air. It landed with a wet clank and jerkily rolled across the floor to Keller's foot, dribbling brown fizzy fluid as it went. Sarah could no longer hold her own laughter in as Jesse sat there with a surprised yet disgusted look on her face. Keller just reached down to pick up the can and put it in the sink. Then she grabbed some paper towels and proceeded to clean up the floor. But the time she was finished, the sisters had stopped laughing. Jesse brushed at the liquid on her fur with a paper towel that Keller had given her. After a few swipes, she decided it was a futile effort and shrugged. "Well clearly there are some more differences to get used to." She looked back at a smiling Keller. "So how the hell am I supposed to eat or drink anything?"

"I recommend squeeze bottles for liquids, and any kind of finger food will work. You might want to switch to calzones, instead of normal pizza, if that is what you want to eat in this form. It will be less mess with the toppings. Some people even choose to go hunting in their full wolf forms to assuage the hunger."

Annie immediately made a face. "Oh, eww!"

The new werewolf looked at her in confusion. "Why is that so gross? I used to hunt with my brother and dad years ago. Venison and rabbit are really good!"

Her girlfriend laughed. "Is it just as good rare?"

Suddenly Jesse caught on to the fact that when hunting as a wolf, there would be no cooking of her meat. "Oh, eww!"

"Exactly!"

Sarah shuddered at the thought and Keller laughed at the three of them. "Again, your senses are different in your other forms. I've heard that not only is the chase exhilarating but there is nothing like the taste of a freshly brought down deer."

The younger woman seemed to think about it for a few seconds, then shook her head. "Nah, I'm good." She quickly scooped up another piece of pizza before folding it in half and cramming a large bite into her mouth. While a lot less messy that way, the chewing was still just as obnoxious. Annie rolled her eyes and searched the cupboards for a squeeze bottle. Once she found one, she quickly opened another can of soda and filled it. By the time she was finished, Jesse had downed her fourth piece of pizza and the new werewolf let out a loud belch. Unfortunately for Annie, it was right when the young woman was leaning down to give her the drink.

She covered her nose and quickly backed away. "That is foul!"

Jesse gave her another doggy grin. "Sorry, babe!" She was able to hold the bottle with one clawed hand and squeeze the cool liquid into her mouth. After quenching her thirst she set the bottle back on the table. "Hey, that works great! Thanks for the suggestion, Keller."

Out of the corner of her eye, Sarah saw the tail start to wag again and lost it. Not wanting to hurt the young werewolf's feelings, she took herself and her laughter out of the kitchen. "I'm going to go check on Duke!"

After finishing off six large slices of pizza, the werewolf gave a great jaw cracking yawn. Annie cleared off the table and Keller walked over to her. "Do you want to take a nap now or you want to see if you can change yourself back?"

Jesse looked down at her sticky, pizza smeared fur and grimaced. "What I'd really like is a shower, but I can't help thinking that I'll smell like wet dog once I'm under the spray. How do I change back?"

Keller pulled out one of the chairs and sat down and Annie followed suit. "Close your eyes and remember your yoga classes. Think about how calm and centered you feel when you go through the positions. Clear your head and look for that part inside yourself that feels like the old you. Focus on your hands and remember how they feel." Sarah re-entered the kitchen but stopped just inside the doorway, not wanting to interrupt. "Slow your breathing, and slow your heart rate."

The same wet popping sound accompanied her return to human but there was no screaming involved. Once she was fully back in her old body, Jesse groaned and fell forward out of her chair onto her knees. Annie rushed over to her thinking that her girlfriend was hurt and froze when she looked in the werewolf's eyes. Keller looked at Sarah and grinned. "Time to go! It was nice hanging out with you ladies. Call us if you need anything." She quickly ushered Sarah out of the kitchen to get their things. By the time they made it to the Sarah's old bedroom to get Duke, they could hear moaning coming from the kitchen. Sarah grew concerned.

"Wait, what's that sound? We should check on them, what if Jesse's hurt?"

With leashed dog in one hand, Keller quickly grabbed her girlfriend's arm to prevent the woman from going back toward the kitchen. "No one is hurt Sarah, open your senses the way I showed you."

The taller woman stopped abruptly and closed her eyes. Just as quickly they popped open and her face flushed crimson. "Uh, yeah, it's time to go!" There were some things a sister didn't need to know about their sibling's sex life.

A FEW MONTHS passed, as did two more successful changes for Jesse. They made it through Thanksgiving and Christmas together as a family. Jessie even got to see her brother Jon on Christmas Eve. Both she and Annie were growing steadily more comfortable with their new normal. Keller was certain that she would no longer need to be chained to the wall on the nights of the full moon but both younger women were vigilant in practicing self-control and calming techniques. They continued to go to yoga together and Jesse had even taken up meditation. Sometimes Annie joined her and sometimes she simply wanted to veg out in front of the TV. Sarah was also growing more comfortable with her change and continued to be a fast learner. She spent a few Saturday nights with Keller in the office at The Merge, while Keller taught her how to feed on the emotions of the crowd. They quickly learned that things tended to spiral out of control when they both fed off the sexual energy. Now they always remembered to lock the office door and the couch was well broken in. One of the quiet evenings at home found Sarah and Keller sitting on the soft leather sofa, watching the flames of the fireplace. There was a thick blanket of snow layering the ground outside and both were cuddled together enjoying glasses of wine and the warmth of each other. Sarah brought up something that had been on her mind for a while. "What's going to happen to Annie?"

Keller knew immediately what she meant. It had been on her own mind for a while too. "Well eventually she's going to have to make a choice."

Sarah cast a worried green-eyed glance at her. "What do you mean?"

The shorter woman sighed and ran a hand through her hair. It was a nervous habit Sarah found endearing. "I mean, the three people closest to her are all destined to live for a very long time. She won't want to be left behind. The question is which way she wants to move forward."

Sarah took a sip of her wine and stared into the fire for a few minutes, thinking deeply. Finally she turned to her lover. "Which choice is better? Do you think they're bonded like us?"

Keller nodded. "Yes I do. I can feel it when I walk into the room with them now. Jesse emotes a lot when she's not paying attention. Have you felt it?"

Sarah nodded. "Yeah."

Keller continued. "As for what's better, well I think that is really up to Annie. I can turn her but obviously it's more difficult. We would have to almost kill her to do it. Frankly, I'm not sure you're up for watching that. But as a vampire, she would be more powerful, and a perfect match for Jesse. They would be drawn to each other like a socket and plug, just as Louve and Catherine were."

Now Sarah ran a hand through her dark hair. "Let's hope she waits a few years to ask. I don't think it's something I can deal with just yet."

Ready to put the serious talk aside, Keller took Sarah's hand into her own. She began tracing the lines of the other woman's palm, eliciting a shiver. Then Keller spoke in a fake Slavic accent. "Let me look at your lines, you have such good lines!"

Sarah was willing to play along. "Ah, great seer, what do you see in my future?"

A pale head bowed toward the open palm and the warm wetness of Keller's tongue traced the taller woman's lifeline. She pulled back and grinned at the slightly parted lips of her lover. "I predict great passionate adventure with a dangerous woman. She is a beast who will devour you if you let her. Beware!"

Green smiling eyes met her prediction and before Keller could say another word, Sarah pulled the shorter woman over to straddle her lap. "Dangerous hmm? I think I can handle that." With hands tangled in Keller's hair, Sarah drew her down into a passionate kiss. Sharp teeth immediately pushed forward as tongues fought for dominance. Sarah pulled back slightly and let her tongue swirl around each sharp canine before she left the shorter woman's mouth completely barren. Keller groaned and rolled her hips, seeking deeper connection.

Not getting any relief, she leaned in close to her lover. Her whisper was punctuated by the light trace of a tongue along the helix of Sarah's ear. "I think you're forgetting the part about being devoured."

Sarah shivered again, a wicked smile spread across her face. "Oh, I didn't forget. I'm counting on it!" In one smooth motion, she stood with Keller in her arms and walked her out of the living room. Keller immediately wrapped her legs around Sarah's waist and her breath came faster in anticipation. Taking advantage of her new strength, Sarah crawled up on the bed still holding her lover and rained kissed down on her face and neck as she began to strip the clothes from Keller's body. She doled out a kiss for every inch of skin that was revealed, and two kisses for all the new places shown.

Keller let herself be carried away, enjoying being with Sarah as an equal. Suddenly, she found herself completely nude with a very clothed brunette straddling her hips. Sarah lightly held her wrists to the bed and Keller made no secret of her need to touch the singer's bare skin. "You have too many clothes on, my love. Take them off, please." She rolled her hips, once again seeking some friction for her throbbing center.

Sarah's eyes turned dark with lust and a newfound competitive spirit. She licked her lips and whispered to the other woman. "Make me."

Keller's own eyes turned a deeper shade of blue and her nostrils flared at the unexpected challenge. Then in a move born of centuries of supernatural speed, Keller broke the hold on her wrists and ripped Sarah's shirt open. The sound of buttons bouncing on the hardwood floor momentarily covered the sweet cacophony of panting bodies. Upon seeing the creamy breasts so near, Keller sat up and took one of Sarah's nipples into her mouth. It was large and hard with engorged blood. She moved her head back and forth, letting sharp teeth graze over the sensitive bud and then moved to the other side.

The minute she took the other nipple in her mouth and repeated her motions, Sarah held her in place and ground her hips down. "Yes!" Unfortunately for the singer, Keller was not to be held in place. She spun them around and grabbed the waistband of Sarah's pants and pulled them straight off. They were loose and came down easily. The pair of underwear that remained was quickly torn free. Sarah laughed, holding back her arousal with a thin wall of sanity. "You owe me another pair."

Keller could see how close Sarah was to the edge and smiled. She slowly climbed back onto the bed between Sarah's legs. She could see the singer's chest rise and fall faster as she parted the long limbs. Keller leaned down until her face was mere centimeters from the dark trimmed curls. They were shiny with wetness and she blew across the hot skin simply for the reaction she'd get. Then Keller looked into hooded green eyes and gave her lover a knowing smile. "What I owe you—is your fortune. You will be devoured—" She lowered her head that last little bit and completely dropped her walls as Sarah did the same. Both women cried out at the first touch of her tongue, as a sensual cacophony bounced back and forth between them. Sarah was writhing on the bed by the time Keller entered her with three fingers. The singer's nearly instantaneous orgasm was as swift as it was unexpected.

Sarah threw an arm over her eyes as she tried to catch her breath. "Oh God, that was almost embarrassing."

Keller laughed and removed her fingers, eliciting a little whimper from her lover. "It was kind of fast, wasn't it?" She smiled up at her girlfriend and tried to ignore the throbbing between her own legs.

Sarah looked down at her wearing the sexiest smile. "Come here."

Unable to resist even the smallest command when her lover wore that smile, Keller complied with the request. She also couldn't resist a little more teasing. "So yeah, that came out of nowhere, didn't it? You kind of went from zero to sixty in no time flat."

Sarah rolled over and kissed her into silence. Pulling back, she snapped her teeth together in front of Keller's face. "Be quiet you! It's your own fault, getting all aggressive with me like that. It's incredibly hot you know."

The centuries old vampire raised an eyebrow at her. "Oh really? I don't really see the draw of it myself. And you were the one who challenged me, remember?

Sarah looked at her with mischief. She smiled and flashed very sharp teeth at the other woman. "You don't see the draw of it, huh? You don't understand how being dominated can be that big of a turn on, how the danger of it could make you so wet—" Sarah watched as Keller's pupils dilated slightly and lowered a hand to the other woman's wet curls. The smaller woman gasped when Sarah ran slick fingers over that hard bundle of nerves. She leaned in to kiss her but pulled back at the last possible second. "Perhaps it's time you learned." Sarah had been practicing and not always when Keller was around. While she could never match the other woman for physical strength, she had been working on her mental one. She quickly removed her fingers and clouded Keller's mind. The pleasure Sarah pumped through her had the other woman gasping and her chest heaving. While Keller was unaware, Sarah quickly buckled the straps in place for the toy she retrieved from their drawer. After sending another wave of raw lust into Keller, Sarah rolled her lover onto her stomach and pinned her spread eagle to the bed. She knew as soon as the smaller woman began swimming up to normal consciousness again because Keller immediately stiffened in surprise.

Keller had no idea that Sarah was capable of that much control! She shouldn't be able to completely cloud someone of Keller's age and ability. She tried to turn herself over but Sarah fully covered her with that long lean body. "What the hell? How did you—" Her words died in her mouth when Sarah rubbed against her and she felt the hard length sliding against her ass.

Sarah released one of her arms just long enough to line up the tip where Keller most wanted it, and then held her down again. Lowering her mouth to the side of Keller's neck, Sarah traced the pale expanse with her tongue. The feel of the toy pressed so close to her hot center of need left Keller frustrated. She trembled when Sarah whispered in her ear. "This is what it's like to be dominated—" Keller cried out in pleasure when Sarah entered her with the toy at the same time she bit into that throbbing pulse at her neck. Her strokes weren't slow, they were fast and deep as she swallowed everything her lover had to offer.

Keller clawed at the bed as she fast approached the point of no return. She closed her eyes as flashes of light and color washed over her vision. Both women were lost in the simultaneous feeling of entering and being entered. Keller began to shake as her body lost control. Her voice grew rough from a litany of words that ran together until they had no meaning. "FuckmeSarahOhGodFuck—" When the cliff was right in front of them, they jumped over together. Perhaps one pushed the other or one was pulled. It was hard to say when the bond was as strong as theirs. Their orgasm washed over them like a tidal wave and the peak of its pleasure left them sweat-soaked, blind, and shaken to the core. Sarah barely managed to pull out and collapse to the side of her lover when the last of her strength left her. Both continued to twitch and shake even as the sweat cooled on their bodies and Sarah was barely able to release the clasps on the harness. Keller spoke first in a voice that was hoarse from too much use. "Shit." The one word summed it up completely. When she managed to turn her head to the side, she met the knowing smirk of her lover.

Sarah's eyes crinkled with delighted satisfaction. "Was I right?"

Keller sighed and laughed. "You were right." When their laughter calmed and breathing slowed, they simply stared into each other's eyes like they'd been doing it their entire life. There was no past and no future, just the comfort of now. Keller was aware of a building pressure in the bond between them. When she lowered her shield again, she was cast adrift by the force of Sarah's love. It was unexpected and she wanted to know why. "What are you thinking about?"

Her answer was simple. "Forever."

Keller's brows shot up in confusion. "What about forever?"

Sarah traced Keller's full lips and then ran gentle fingers over the pale brows that delicately sloped over incredible blue eyes. "It's not about forever. That's what I mean, there's no hurry."

Keller smiled into the other woman's caress and her words reverted to that familiar accent. "Lassie, yer na' makin' any sense. Speak plain ta me."

Sarah moved closer until there wasn't a bit of space between them then left a soft kiss on the other woman's lips. "Hush, Noble Keller, I'm making perfect sense. You're not listening." She kissed her again and sent another wave of emotion down that connection to her lover. She pulled back and smiled at her. "Marry me."

Keller's mouth opened but no words came out. When she finally found a voice, it was nothing more than a whisper. "*What?*"

"You heard me. So what's your answer? Keep in mind, I'm bossy and I don't like to be disappointed..." Her voice trailed off.

A broad smile grew over Keller's face, and she laughed at the joy of it. "Of course I will, you crazy, crazy, woman! When, where, how?"

Sarah smirked at her. "I believe I already answered that."

Keller looked at her lover in puzzlement and thought back of the last few minutes of confusing conversation. Suddenly the answer dawned. "There's no rush, we have all the time in the world. More than enough time to work out the details."

Sarah responded. "Plenty of time to practice for the party."

"To recite our personal vows." Keller laughed at their light-hearted banter, and then she stepped into a serious shadow. "That's a long time for you to commit."

Sarah looked placidly back at her and the world around them was lost. Sarah then bared the truth to Keller, and perhaps even for the first time to herself. "You fill places inside me that I never knew existed. Forever is not nearly enough."

Keller leaned in for a kiss. "It will have to do."

No more words were needed to describe a future that had been written since the stars were new in the sky. Their love, like so many others, was eternal.

About the Author

Born and raised in Michigan, Kelly is a latecomer to the writing scene. She works in the automotive industry coding in Visual basic and Excel. Her avid reading and writing provide a nice balance to the daily order of data, allowing her to juggle passion and responsibility. Her writing style is as varied as her reading taste and it shows as she tackles each new genre with glee. But beneath it all, no matter the subject or setting, Kelly carries a core belief that good should triumph. She's not afraid of pain or adversity, but loves a happy ending. She's been pouring words into novels since 2015 and probably won't run out of things to say any time soon.

Other K. Aten titles to look for:

The Fletcher

Kyri is a fletcher, following in the footsteps of her father, and his father before him. However, fate is a fickle mistress, and six years after the death of her mother, she's faced with the fact that her father is dying as well. Forced to leave her sheltered little homestead in the woods, Kyri discovers that there is more to life than just hunting and making master quality arrows. During her journey to find a new home and happiness, she struggles with the path that seems to take her away from the quiet life of a fletcher. She learns that sometimes the hardest part of growing up is reconciling who we were, with who we will become.

ISBN: 978-1-61929-356-4
eISBN: 978-1-61929-357-1

The Archer

Kyri was raised a fletcher but after finding a new home and family with the Telequire Amazons, she discovers a desire to take on more responsibility within the tribe. She has skills they desperately need and she is called to action to protect those around her. But Kyri's path is ever-changing even as she finds herself altered by love, loyalty, and grief. Far away from home, the new Amazon is forced to decide what to sacrifice and who to become in order to get back to all that she has left behind. And she wonders what is worse, losing everyone she's ever loved or having those people lose her?

ISBN: 978-1-61929-370-0
eISBN: 978-1-61929-371-7

The Sagittarius

Kyri has known her share of loss in the two decades that she has been alive. She never expected to find herself a slave in roman lands, nor did she think she had the heart to become a gladiatrix. But with her soul shattered she must fight to see her way back home again. Will she win her freedom and return to all that she has known, or will she become another kind of slave to the killer that has taken over her mind? The only thing that is certain through it all is her love and devotion to Queen Orianna.

ISBN: 978-1-61929-386-1
eISBN: 978-1-61929-387-8

Rules of the Road

Jamie is an engineer who keeps humor close to her heart and people at arm's length. Kelsey is a dental assistant who deals with everything from the hilarious to the disgusting on a daily basis. What happens when a driving app brings them together as friends? The nerd car and the rainbow car both know a thing or two about hazard avoidance. When a flat tire brings them together in person, Jamie immediately realizes that Kelsey isn't just another woman on her radar. Both of them have struggled to break free from stereotypes while they navigate the road of life. As their friendship deepens they realize that sometimes you have to break the rules to get where you need to go.

ISBN: 978-1-61929-366-3
eISBN: 978-1-61929-367-0

Waking the Dreamer

By the end of the 21st century, the world had become a harsh place. After decades of natural and man-made catastrophes, nations fell, populations shifted, and seventy percent of the continents became uninhabitable without protective suits. Technological advancement strode forward faster than ever and it was the only thing that kept human society steady through it all. No one could have predicted the discovery of the Dream Walkers. They were people born with the ability to leave their bodies at will, unseen by the waking world. Having the potential to become ultimate spies meant the remaining government regimes wanted to study and control them. The North American government, under the leadership of General Rennet, demanded that all Dream Walkers join the military program. For any that refused to comply, they were hunted down and either brainwashed or killed.

The very first Dream Walker discovered was a five year old girl named Julia. And when the soldiers came for her at the age of twenty, she was already hidden away. A decade later found Julia living a new life under the government's radar. As a secure tech courier in the capital city of Chicago, she does her job and the rest of her time avoids other people as much as she is able. The moment she agrees to help another fugitive Walker is when everything changes. Now the government wants them both and they'll stop at nothing to get what they want.

ISBN: 978-1-61929-382-3
eISBN: 978-1-61929-383-0

OTHER REGAL CREST PUBLICATIONS

VISIT US ONLINE AT
www.regalcrest.biz

At the Regal Crest Website You'll Find

~ The latest news about forthcoming titles and new releases

~ Our complete backlist of romance, mystery, thriller and adventure titles

~ Information about your favorite authors

Regal Crest print titles are available from all progressive booksellers including numerous sources online. Our distributors are Bella Distribution and Ingram.